BY J. KENNER

THE STARK TRILOGY

Release Me

Claim Me

Complete Me

STARK EVER AFTER NOVELLAS

Take Me

Have Me

Play My Game

STARK INTERNATIONAL NOVELS

Say My Name

On My Knees

MOST WANTED SERIES

Wanted

Heated

Ignited

on my knees

on my knees

A STARK NOVEL

J. KENNER

BANTAM BOOKS NEW YORK

A Bantam Books Trade Paperback Original

Copyright © 2015 by Julie Kenner
Excerpt from *Under My Skin* by J. Kenner copyright © 2015 by Julie Kenner

Published in the United States by Bantam Books, an imprint of Random House, a division of Penguin Random House LLC, New York.

BANTAM BOOKS and the HOUSE colophon are registered trademarks of Penguin Random House LLC.

This book contains an excerpt from the forthcoming book *Under My Skin* by J. Kenner. This excerpt has been set for this edition only and may not reflect the final content of the forthcoming edition.

Library of Congress Cataloging-in-Publication Data
Kenner, Julie.
On my knees : a Stark novel / J. Kenner.
pages cm
ISBN 978-0-553-39521-1
eBook ISBN 978-0-553-39522-8
1. Man-woman relationships—Fiction. I. Title.
PS3611.E665O53 2015
813'.6—dc23   2015007054

Printed in the United States of America on acid-free paper

www.bantamdell.com

9 8 7 6 5 4 3 2

on my knees

one

Jackson Steele tossed back the last of his scotch, slammed the glass down on the polished granite bar, and considered ordering another.

He could use it—that was damn sure—but probably better to have a clear head before he went to answer his brother's summons.

His brother.

That was something he didn't say every day. Hell, he'd spent his entire life avoiding saying it. Been told he wasn't allowed to say it.

"Sometimes families have secrets," his father had said.

Wasn't that the fucking truth?

The great and glorious Damien Stark—one of the world's wealthiest and most powerful men—had no idea that he and Jackson shared a father.

But in about fifteen minutes he'd know. Because Jackson was going to tell him. *Had* to tell him.

Fuck.

He held up his hand to get the bartender's attention because, screw it, right now he really could use another drink.

The bartender nodded, poured two fingers of Glenmorangie, neat, then slid the glass to Jackson. He hesitated, bar rag in hand, until Jackson finally looked up and met his eyes. "Something else?" Jackson asked.

"Sorry. No." It was a lie, of course, and as Jackson watched, the bartender's cheeks turned pink.

The bartender, whose name tag identified him as Phil, was in his early twenties, and with his hair slicked back and his perfectly tailored dark suit, he looked as essential to the Gallery Bar—which epitomized the glamour and excitement of the 1920s—as the polished wood, glittering chandeliers, and ornate carvings that filled and completed this space.

The historic Millennium Biltmore hotel had always been one of Jackson's favorite places in Los Angeles. As a teenager, when he'd only dreamed of becoming an architect, he would come as often as he could, usually begging a friend with a car to bring him up from San Diego and drop him downtown. He would wander the hotel, soaking up the exquisite Spanish-Italian-Renaissance-style architecture that blended so well with the California location. The architects, Schultze and Weaver, were among Jackson's idols, and he would spend hours examining the fine detail in all of the elements, from the elegant columns and doorways, to the exposed wood-framed roofs, to the intricate cast-iron railings and elaborate wooden carvings.

As with any exceptional building, each room had its own personality despite being tied together by common elements. The Gallery Bar had long been Jackson's favorite space, the live music, intimate lighting, excellent wine list, and extensive menu adding value to an already priceless space.

Now, Phil stood behind the long granite bar that served as one of the room's focal points. Behind him, a menagerie of fine whiskeys danced in the glow of the room's dim lighting. He was framed on either side by carved wooden angels, and in Jackson's mind, it seemed as if all three—angels and man—were standing in judgment over him.

Phil cleared his throat, apparently realizing that he hadn't moved. "Yeah. Sorry." He started to exuberantly wipe the bar. "I just thought you looked familiar."

"I must have one of those faces," Jackson said dryly, knowing damn well that Phil knew who he was. Jackson Steele, celebrity architect. Jackson Steele, subject of the documentary, *Stone and Steele*, which had recently screened at the Chinese theater. Jackson Steele, newest addition to the team for The Resort at Cortez, a Stark Vacation Property.

Jackson Steele, released yesterday on bail after assaulting Robert Cabot Reed, producer, director, and overall vile human being.

The latter, of course, is what would have put Jackson on Phil's radar. This was Los Angeles, after all, and in Los Angeles, anything entertainment-related passed as hard news. Forget the economy or strife overseas. In the City of Angels, Hollywood trumped everything else. And that meant that Jackson's picture had been plastered all over the newspapers, local television, and social media.

He didn't regret it. Not the fight. Not the arrest. He didn't even regret the press, although he knew that they would dig. And if they dug deep enough, they'd find a whole cornucopia of reasons why Jackson might want to destroy the pathetic Mr. Reed.

Well, let them. He wasn't the least bit repentant. Hell, if anything he wished he could do it again, because the few punches he'd managed to land on Reed had only been satisfying in the moment. But every time he thought about it—every time he pictured what the son of a bitch had done to Sylvia—he knew he hadn't gone far enough.

He should have killed the bastard.

For the way he'd hurt the woman Jackson loved, Robert Cabot Reed deserved to die.

She'd been only fourteen at the time. A child. An innocent. And Reed had used her. Raped her. Humiliated her.

He'd been a photographer then, and she his model. A position of power and of trust, and he'd twisted that around, making it vile and dirty.

He'd hurt the girl, and he'd damaged the woman.

And Jackson couldn't think of anything bad enough that could happen to the man.

He closed his eyes and thought of Sylvia. Her small, slim body that felt so right in his arms. The gold that highlighted her dark brown hair, making her face seem luminous. Christ, he wanted her beside him now. Wanted to twine his fingers with hers and hold her close. He wanted her strength, though she didn't even realize how strong she was.

But this was something he had to do alone. And he needed to do it now.

He slid off the stool, then dropped a fifty on the bar. "Keep the change," he said, as Phil's eyes went wide.

He left the bar, moving quickly through the hotel's glittering lobby to the main entrance that opened on South Grand Avenue. Stark Tower was just up the hill to the east. It was a cool October night, and the building glowed against the coal-black sky. Right now, Damien Stark was in the penthouse apartment with his wife, Nikki, probably unpacking after their long weekend in Manhattan.

Stark's second assistant, Rachel Peters, had called Jackson that morning. "He'll be back from New York this evening," she'd said. "And he wants to see you tomorrow at eight sharp before the regular Tuesday briefing."

"About the resort?" He'd asked the question casually, as if he couldn't imagine any other reason that Stark would want to see him.

"He didn't say. But I thought—I mean, I assumed—" He heard her draw a deep breath before her voice dropped to a stage whisper. "Well, don't you think it's probably about the arrest? And all the press coverage?"

He shook his head at the memory, half-irritated and half-amused. *Fucking summoned.*

If this was only about work, he would have waited until morning and gone at the appointed time. But this was personal, and he needed to do it now.

He'd already called security, and he knew that Stark's helicopter had landed over an hour ago. He also knew that Stark was staying in the Tower apartment overnight, not bothering to make the drive to his Malibu house.

It was eight o'clock on a Monday night, and it was time for Stark to know the truth.

As he trudged up the hill, Jackson thought about how quickly things had changed. A month ago, he would have rather eaten nails than worked for Damien Stark. But then Sylvia had approached him with the kind of project that is any architect's wet dream. To design a resort from the ground up. And not just any resort, but one located on its own private island. And she was handing him a blank slate.

The overture had surprised him for a number of reasons, not the least of which being that five years ago she'd ripped a hole in his heart, when she brutally and permanently ended things between them.

The loss had devastated him, and he'd eased his anger in the ring and in his work. Winning—and losing—fight after fight. Burying himself in his commissions, his reputation growing as his projects became more and more ambitious.

Work may have been his savior, but working for her—hell, working for Stark—was not something he was prepared to do. He knew damn well he couldn't bear the pain of being around Sylvia. Of working so intimately with her.

And as for Stark . . . well, Jackson had plenty of reasons not to work for or trust the man, not the least of which was that Jackson didn't want to see his work overshadowed by the Stark name and logo.

But revenge is a powerful motivator.

So he'd said yes, fully intending to take her to the edge of pleasure. To reclaim her. To bind her so close to him that she could see no one else, feel no one else, dream of no one else. And then, when she was stuck fast in his web, he would clip the strands and walk away, leaving the resort to flounder, and leaving Sylvia exactly the way that she had left him, drowning in pain and loss and misery.

Dear god, he'd been a fool.

He'd accepted the offer to design The Resort at Cortez for the worst of reasons. To hurt the woman who'd hurt him. To screw with the half-brother who had been the focal point of so much shit in his life. Who'd tugged hard and unraveled the threads of his life. Pulling his father away. Ripping his family apart.

Now the woman meant the world to him, and he would enthusiastically destroy anyone who hurt her.

Now the job was his passion, a project that was already fully formed in his imagination and sketches.

And as for the brother, nothing much had changed. Once again, it was Damien Stark who had the power. Who could, in one quick, violent motion, tear the world out from under Jackson's feet.

All because he wanted a job.

All because he loved a woman.

All because in addition to controlling so much of the known fucking universe, Damien Stark controlled Jackson's world as well.

And what Jackson feared tonight was that when Stark knew the truth that had been kept from him for over thirty years, Stark would wield his power like a blunt instrument.

But Jackson was a fighter, and if it came down to brother against brother, he'd do whatever was necessary to be the man left standing.

two

"Evening, Joe," Jackson said as he crossed the lobby toward the security desk. He glanced at his watch, then back at the security guard with the wide smile and weathered face. "Don't you ever go home?"

Joe's smile stretched even wider, and he tapped his index finger against the rim of his uniform cap. "My work is my life, Mr. Steele."

"Call me Jackson, and between you and me, I think you're full of it."

"God's honest truth," Joe said. "Of course, my wife and three little girls are also my life. And what with Christmas being just a few months away . . ." He trailed off with a shrug. "What can I say? I'm all about the overtime."

"Your secret's safe with me." He hooked a thumb in the direction of the elevator bank. "Can you clear me through to the apartment? I've got an appointment with Stark in the morning, but I don't think this should wait."

"Go on," Joe said, pressing the button on his console to call

Stark's private elevator. "I'll call up. If he says no, it'll just be a very short trip."

"Right." Jackson cleared his throat. "Fair enough."

It wasn't until Jackson entered the elevator car that he realized his hands were clenched as if he was waiting to punch someone. Hell, maybe he was. Because if Stark told him to go away and come back in the morning, Jackson would most likely put his fist through the elevator's polished wood paneling.

The fine oak planks were saved, however, when the doors closed and the button for the penthouse lit up. A moment later, Jackson's hand was clenched again, this time around the railing. He hadn't yet been in this car, and it definitely qualified as an express.

The elevator featured two sets of doors, and based on the position of the elevator in the bank, Jackson knew that the doors he was facing opened to the reception area for Stark's private penthouse office.

The Tower apartment took up the other half of the floor, and as the elevator slowed, Jackson turned and faced the second set of doors that, as he expected, opened into the apartment's foyer.

The area was bright and inviting, tasteful but not overdone. A marble table in the center of the space held a large but not ostentatious arrangement of sunflowers and Indian paintbrushes, and despite himself, Jackson smiled at the whimsy of wildflowers where a more exotic bloom would be expected.

"Jackson!" Nikki came around the wall that separated the entrance from the rest of the apartment. She wore jeans and a New York Yankees T-shirt and had her shoulder-length hair pushed away from her face by a headband. Despite her lack of makeup, she looked absolutely stunning, and Jackson recalled that she'd competed in several beauty pageants before moving to Los Angeles.

She padded to him in bare feet and gave him a friendly hug. "It's lovely to see you."

"I'm sorry to intrude. I know you must be tired from your trip."

"I am," she admitted, "but Damien's not. He's catching up on some work things, getting ready for tomorrow. So you're not interrupting at all. Come on," she said, leading the way. "Do you want coffee? Something stronger?"

He was tempted to have another scotch, just to take the edge off. But prudence won out, and he shook his head. "I'm fine, thanks."

Five seconds later, he was wishing he'd taken the drink. Because there was Stark pacing in front of the wall of windows, the city shining bright behind him.

And there was Sylvia, perched on the edge of an ottoman, a pad in her lap and a pen in her hand, taking detailed notes.

Her back was to him and she was so engrossed in her work that she hadn't seen him yet. For a moment, he could only stare. He'd left her only hours ago, naked in her bed, and he hadn't expected to see her again until this ordeal with his brother was finished. So the sight of her now was a shock to his senses, and for a moment he could only stand like an idiot, his lips pressed together so he didn't call out her name. His feet planted so he didn't go to her. His hands at his sides so he didn't reach out to touch her.

He must have made a noise, or maybe she just sensed his presence as strongly as he felt hers, because she turned her head suddenly and her mouth formed into a perfect little O even as her pen tumbled from her hand.

"Jackson! I didn't—I mean, I wondered—" She frowned as she cut off her words.

He understood her dilemma. When he'd left her condo, he'd told her where he was going. And yet she'd arrived long before he had. She'd probably assumed that he'd changed his mind, and expected to hear why when they met back up at her place.

Now here he was, and they were both surprised.

"—has something he wants to talk with you about tonight." Nikki's words filtered into Jackson's head, and he realized that he'd been so absorbed in watching Sylvia that he'd tuned out everything else around him. "You were engrossed in maxing out Syl's to-do list," Nikki said to Stark, "so I went ahead and cleared him to come up."

Stark turned from the window, smiling at Nikki as he did. But the smile faded when his eyes met Jackson's. "I thought we were meeting in the morning."

"That's when the appointment is," Jackson said. "But there are things we should talk about now."

Stark studied him a minute, then nodded. "All right." He moved across the room toward Sylvia and held out his hand for something. Her eyes cut quickly to Jackson, and he could see the tension in her shoulders, but her professionalism never slipped as she reached for an electronic tablet that sat near her on the coffee table.

He wondered if Stark noticed the way her fingers shook just slightly as she navigated over the tablet screen. But she held it together.

What she didn't do was look at Jackson.

After a moment, she passed the tablet to Stark. He glanced at it, then handed it to Jackson. "You've had an interesting few days," he said as Jackson looked down at the photo of him being led away from Reed's house in handcuffs.

Jackson swiped his finger across the surface and scrolled through the rest of the images. News coverage from all over the country. Most focused entirely on him—*Starchitect Jackson Steele arrested!*—but some tied Stark and The Resort at Cortez in to the story.

He kept his posture straight and his face impassive. If Stark thought he was going to get a rise out of Jackson by showing him the coverage that Jackson had already seen, he was going to be sorely disappointed.

"Did you come here to tell me why you spent a perfectly fine Saturday evening beating the shit out of some pissant film director?"

Jackson cocked his head at the pejorative, but in response said only, "No. I really didn't."

Stark's brow lifted almost imperceptibly, and Jackson stiffened, prepared to accept the brunt of his half-brother's famous temper. It was, he thought wryly, something they shared. But all Stark did was tilt his head, glance toward Nikki, then nod. "Fair enough." He gestured toward an armchair. "Have a seat."

"I'm fine standing. Thanks."

"Have it your way." Stark returned to the window, then stood with his back to the room. From Jackson's position, he could see Stark's face reflected in the glass, the lights of the city spread out behind him. Appropriate, Jackson supposed, since Stark owned half the fucking world, and most of Los Angeles. "This has the potential to turn into a clusterfuck," Stark said. "A public relations nightmare. I'm surprised we don't already have the damn tabloid reporters camped out in front of the building."

Jackson said nothing. Stark was right, so what was there to say?

"They've called me. Hell, they've called Sylvia," he added, and Jackson immediately turned to Syl. Her eyes flicked to his, sad and a little lost, before she looked down again at her notepad. She hadn't told him the press had contacted her, and that new reality made his stomach twist.

" 'No comment' is the official response of this office," Stark continued. He turned to face Jackson, his dual-colored eyes burning into him. "But it's only going to get worse. That's the bad news. The good news is that scandal doesn't scare me. I've lived with it my entire life. Neither does temper. I've met Reed, and I can only assume he pissed you off royally. It happens."

The corner of his mouth twitched in what might have been an effort to hold back a smile. "Arrest, scandal, uncomfortable press coverage—none of those things shake the foundation around here, and they don't put your job at risk. Not unless it affects your work. So tell me, Steele. Is this bullshit going to affect your work?"

"No."

Stark hesitated, as if waiting for Jackson to elaborate, then seemed to realize that Jackson had said all he intended to. And why not? As far as the resort was concerned, that one word said it all.

"Charles tells me they're going to plead you down. You'll do community service over the next six months and walk away with a clean record. He's talked to Reed's people and the district attorney's office and everyone agrees."

"That's right." Sylvia had retained Stark's lawyer, Charles Maynard, as soon as she'd learned about Jackson's incarceration, and Jackson had to give the attorney props for doing a hell of a job.

"Fair enough. Unless you've already made arrangements, you can serve it at the Stark Children's Foundation or at S.E.F.," he said, referring to the Stark Education Foundation. Both were charitable organizations founded by Stark. The first to provide play- and sports-based therapy to victims of child abuse. The second to provide educational opportunities to low-income or otherwise unfortunate kids with an aptitude in science.

"I—thank you." Jackson tried not to let his surprise show on his face. Neither Stark's reaction to the arrest nor the offer to help with community service had been something Jackson would have expected from Stark. Then again, Stark wanted the resort project to run smoothly and efficiently. So helping Jackson out made sense.

"Not a problem," Stark said. "I appreciate that you wanted to talk about this as soon as possible, but it really could have waited until morning. I'm sorry to say that around here unfortunate press coverage isn't as rare as I'd like it to be. But it will blow over."

Jackson glanced toward Sylvia, who was very deliberately not looking at him. But her relief was reflected in both her posture and her facial expression.

By the window, Stark glanced at his watch. "Now if you don't mind, Nikki and I've had a long day and I'd like to finish up with Syl and cut her loose." He crossed toward Jackson with his hand outstretched. "But it was good to see you, and I know that you'll weather this storm just fine."

Jackson hesitated, then shook his brother's hand. "I appreciate that," he said. "But there's something else I need to talk with you about. It's personal."

"All right. Sylvia? Could you give us a moment?"

"It's okay. She can stay. Nikki, too," he added, because Stark clearly had no intention of asking his wife to leave.

"Fair enough." Stark eyed Sylvia and nodded, probably assuming Jackson intended to officially tell him that Jackson and Sylvia were dating. "What's on your mind?"

"Jeremiah Stark."

"Well, fuck. What trouble is he stirring up now?"

"Nothing that I know of," Jackson said. "He's my father."

Nikki gasped. Sylvia looked down at her shoes.

Stark didn't move at all.

And for the first time Jackson regretted not taking Stark up on his offer to sit, because his knees were suddenly weak. Probably the result of all the oxygen being sucked from the room.

Stark's expression didn't change. His eyes didn't widen. His jaw didn't tighten. He didn't swallow. He stayed absolutely calm and entirely unreadable. And in that moment Jackson knew exactly how Stark had been able to acquire his fortune so fast. The man had nerves of steel.

"I should have told you before I came on board the project," he said. "But habits are hard to break, and this is a secret I've been told to keep for over thirty years now."

"Then why say anything at all?" Stark's voice was as tight as a wire.

Jackson glanced toward Sylvia, then quickly looked away. "Because it's time."

"I see." A moment passed. Then another. And though Jackson tried to discern what his brother was thinking, he didn't have a clue.

"Damien?" Nikki's soft voice seemed to fill the room.

Stark didn't turn to her. He kept his eyes on Jackson. And as Jackson watched, the tight, expressionless face turned human again. Stark smiled—not a genuine smile, but the kind of expression he might wear during a boardroom presentation. An expression of complete and total control—and that revealed absolutely no personal reaction whatsoever.

"I appreciate you telling me," he said. "Now if you don't mind, you should go. As I mentioned, it's been a long day for Nikki and me."

Jackson took a single step forward. "Damien—"

"No," Stark said, and this time the word was harsh, that slight hint of emotion revealing to Jackson just how much his bombshell truly had impacted the man. "And it really is time for you to leave."

three

I force myself to remain seated as Jackson turns and leaves. I catch his eyes once more, but like Damien, his expression is impenetrable.

Even so, I'm sure there's pain behind both men's masks, and I wish that it was in my power to make this whole situation better for Jackson, whose love I cherish, and for Damien, whose respect I crave.

In the silence, I hear the elevator doors snick closed, even from all the way across the apartment.

As if the sound is a cue, Damien turns to me. "Did you know?"

There is absolutely no inflection to his words, and despite the years I've worked for him—despite the power I've seen him wield and the flares of temper I have witnessed—this is the first time that I have been truly nervous around my boss.

"He told me on Saturday." What I don't say is that it is because of me that Jackson came here tonight. Once he'd told me his secret, he knew he had to tell Damien, because otherwise he'd have to burden me with the secret, too. And this isn't the kind of thing that I would feel comfortable keeping from Damien.

Damien says nothing, and even though I know that his silence is a time-honored technique to keep people talking, I fall headlong into the trap. "I saw him with your father at Michael Prado's charity event on Friday," I say, the words spilling out. "And I got pissed because he'd told me that he didn't know Jeremiah. We had a huge fight, and—" I cut myself off with a shrug. "At any rate, he told me."

Damien and Nikki both know that Jackson and I are a couple, but that isn't something I want to focus on at the moment. As far as I'm concerned, right now, this is all about me being as professional as possible. I glance toward Nikki. We've become good friends, and I can see the worry on her face. But she says nothing, and I'm grateful. At some point, this whole debacle may lead to many drinks with my friends. Right now, though, I just need to hold it together.

"You're not in trouble, Sylvia," Damien says, and the iron band that has tightened around my chest loosens just a bit. "If a week or two had gone by without me learning the truth, then we would have talked. But as far as your job is concerned, you weren't obligated to tell me about this until after Jackson had the opportunity to do so. Which he's definitely now accomplished," Damien adds, and there's just enough humor in his voice to make me think that maybe—just maybe—we have weathered the storm.

"Thanks," I say. "I appreciate that you understand how awkward the situation was." I hold up the notebook, hoping I don't look too desperate to get off this seriously uncomfortable topic. "Do you want to finish now?"

He waves a hand. "There's nothing on the agenda that can't wait."

"Fine. Great." I quickly gather my stuff and swing my leather tote over my arm. "I'm glad your trip was good."

"It really was," Nikki says, and her voice sounds as strained as mine feels. "Lots of excellent theater."

"Well, tomorrow, then." I turn to head toward the elevator, but Damien's words stop me cold.

"Fire him," Damien says, and the ground falls out from under me. "First thing tomorrow, I want you to fire him."

My back is to him, and I stand frozen for a moment, unable to move. Unable to breathe. *Me.* He wants *me* to do this? To take away this project that Jackson has come to love?

Bile rises in my throat, and I fear that I may throw up. But I force it down, then very slowly and very carefully, I turn around.

Damien's expression is hard, and there is no denying the contained fury in his eyes.

"But . . . but the resort?" I want to scream that he cannot make me do this. That I can't fire Jackson. Hell, that *he* shouldn't fire Jackson.

Instead, I force myself to stay calm. To appear businesslike. "It won't look good. There will be questions. The press will be all over it."

"I believe I already made clear that scandal and the press don't concern me overmuch. We'll handle it."

I lick my lips. "Don't you want to talk about it?" Immediately I regret my words. I've crossed into personal, and right now I think that is a very bad move.

"He was raised by Jeremiah Stark." Damien practically spits the name out. "Have you forgotten about the sabotage? All the bullshit we've dealt with getting even this far on the project?"

"No, of course not. But surely you don't think—"

"I don't know," Damien says. "And that's the point. I'm cutting my losses, Ms. Brooks. Take care of it first thing in the morning."

The words are a dismissal, but I don't leave. "So that's it?" I demand. "The resort is dead?"

"Maybe not," Damien says. "As it happens, Glau called me while we were in New York. He didn't ask outright, but he beat around the bush enough that I can tell he regrets leaving the project. Apparently Tibet isn't all it's cracked up to be."

"But—"

"We'll do everything we can to keep the project alive," he says firmly. "But Jackson Steele isn't going to be a part of it."

I nod, because I know better than to argue. I'd known this might happen, dammit. As soon as Jackson told me the truth, I knew that Damien might want to push him as far from Stark International as possible.

I just hadn't let myself believe it would really happen.

"Right," I mumble. "Okay. Tomorrow, then." I hitch the tote more firmly on my shoulder and start again toward the elevator. Nikki is standing in the doorway between the living area and the hall that leads to the bedrooms. I catch her eye as I pass, and she manages a thin smile, looking a bit like someone who has just witnessed a car crash and isn't entirely sure what to do now.

As for me, all I want is to get out of there, because I know that any second the tears are going to start flowing. Ironic, because until yesterday when Jackson held me in his arms, I hadn't cried for over a decade. Now I can barely hold it in.

I press the button for the elevator, expecting it to open immediately. When Damien is home, the elevator is usually where he is. But of course Jackson rode it down, and I have to wait for it to be recalled from the lobby.

I shift my weight from foot to foot, willing it to hurry. Needing to just be gone.

Needing to go find Jackson.

Finally, the elevator arrives. I squeeze in before the doors are even fully open, then jab my finger hard against the button to close them again. They're almost shut when Nikki skids to a halt outside and slides her hand through the gap, tripping the safety feature and making the doors spread open again.

She steps onto the elevator with me, then leans over and pushes the button for the lobby. "Do you want to talk?"

I shake my head. I'm still in full flee-mode, and while Nikki is a friend, right at the moment, I can't quite separate her from Damien.

"Talk to him again in the morning. This is all very . . . unexpected," she finally says, clearly searching for the right word. "Give him some time to digest, and he might change his mind."

"Do you really think so?"

She hesitates, then lifts one shoulder. "Honestly, I don't know."

"Do you think he should?" Right away I want to take the words back; I sound so damn needy.

"I think that's up to him," she says. "But if it were my decision, then yeah, I think he should keep Jackson on the project. Hell, I think he should try to get to know him. Reach out. If they're brothers, then maybe they should try to be brothers."

I lean back against the wall and look at her. It makes sense. Why go straight to enemies without first trying to be friends, if not family? "Are you going to tell him that? Or at least suggest he shouldn't fire Jackson?"

A soft laugh bubbles out of her. "Um, no. Not hardly."

"Why the hell not?" My words are sharper than I intended, but dammit, I thought I'd found an ally.

"You know why. This is between Damien and Jackson and Jeremiah. You and I can have our opinions, but it's not up to us."

"So share your opinion."

For a moment, she just looks sad. "Come on, Syl, you know I can't. If I asked, Damien would keep him here. We both know he'd do that for me. And I couldn't live with that hanging between us."

I know she's right. There is very little that Damien wouldn't do for Nikki, and it's a testament to the strength of their relationship that she understands just how much responsibility that puts on her shoulders.

Even so, her answer frustrates me. "What about me? What if I ask him to keep Jackson on as a favor to me?"

"You can try, but I wouldn't hold my breath. Friendship means a lot to him, but honesty and professional integrity mean more. Jackson should have told him the truth a long time ago. And he sure as hell should have told him before he came on board the project."

"I know. Hell, Jackson knows. But it was a bitch of a situation to be in."

The elevator has reached the lobby, and the doors slide open. I step out, and Nikki holds her hand against a door to keep it from closing as she stays in the car. "The truth is if their father wasn't Jeremiah Stark, this might blow over. But this way . . ." She trails off into a shrug. "Well, it's going to be stormy."

I sigh, suddenly mentally and physically exhausted. "I feel like Damien's punishing me, too," I admit. "Making me be the one who fires him."

"No," Nikki says firmly. "I don't think so. I think it's his way of making sure that you still want the job and all the shit that comes with being the project manager. He knows you two are together, and that means that he knows you might not want to stay if Jackson is gone. Do you?"

My stomach twists, because yes, I do. This resort is my baby—my project. I'd suggested it to Damien. I'd put it together. And I'm so damn grateful that he's given me a real chance to move up in the company by letting me split my time between being his assistant and being the project manager for the Cortez resort.

So yes, I want this job. I want the resort. I want Jackson.

God help me, I want it all.

And I have no idea if I can even come close to getting—or keeping—any of it.

four

Where R U?

I glance down at the text I sent to Jackson as I wait for Joe to check the computer logs that record vehicles entering and leaving the garage.

It's been well over three minutes, and still no reply.

I tap out another note—*???*—and am rewarded with only cyber-silence.

"Anything?" I ask Joe.

"Nothing," Joe says, frowning at his monitor. "He didn't use his key card to access the garage today."

"That doesn't make sense. I know he drove here." And I also know how much Jackson loves his sleek, classic black Porsche. I can't imagine him simply parking it on the street in downtown LA after dark.

"Maybe he parked at the subway station and walked down the hill?"

"Why do you think that?"

"I chatted with him before he went up to see Mr. Stark. Came in right there," Joe adds, pointing toward the glass doors that open onto the building's front plaza and South Grand Avenue beyond that.

I consider that tidbit of information. "Well, did you see him leave?"

"I'm sorry, Ms. Brooks. I haven't seen him since he arrived."

I frown, wondering if maybe Jackson didn't leave the building, after all. I'd expected him to want to get far away as quickly as possible—I know I would. But Jackson isn't me, and I draw in a breath as I debate whether I should go up to his workspace on the twenty-sixth floor. On the one hand, he didn't wait for me, and he hasn't returned my texts. All evidence suggests that he wants to be alone, and I get that.

On the other hand, what he wants may not be the most important factor. I'd been royally pissed off at him not long ago, and I'd wanted to be alone, too. But Jackson had followed me to make sure I was okay.

And right now, I'm terribly afraid that Jackson is a long, long way from okay.

I thank Joe for his help, then park myself on one of the chrome and leather benches that provide seating in the lobby. I tap out one more text, then actually cross my fingers.

It doesn't help, and after forcing myself to sit and wait for a full five minutes, I make a decision. Maybe it's selfish, but I want to see him. No, I *need* to see him. I need to know he's okay.

More than that, I need to know that we're okay. That despite all of this shit, Jackson and Sylvia are going to be just fine.

It's dark when I get off on twenty-six, the only illumination on the floor coming from the city lights streaming in through all the windows. The floor is only half built-out, so there are very few offices and cubicles. It's essentially a giant square with walls of glass, and because of that, the space is reasonably well-lit, like walking beneath the glow of a full moon.

I turn the last corner, and see the newly erected glass walls that define Jackson's workspace. He is standing by the window, and I'm struck by the similarity between his stance and Damien's earlier position as he'd looked out over the city.

I see Jackson only in silhouette. His shoulders squared, his body rigid. I cannot see the reflection of his face from where I stand, but I can imagine it with perfect clarity. His black hair gleaming in the reflected light. His sculptured jaw tight with anger. And his blue eyes as cold as ice.

I start to walk toward him and then change my mind. Instead, I pull out my phone one more time.

If you need me, I'm right outside your office.

I hesitate, not entirely certain I'm doing the right thing. And then, once more, I press send.

I hear his phone chirp almost immediately. I watch as he pulls out the phone. As he reads the text. As he slides the phone back into his pocket.

But he doesn't come, and as the seconds tick by, that iron band is tightening around my chest again, and I am afraid—so terribly afraid—that we are not going to survive this. Because if he can't come to me now, how much worse will it be when I have to render the deathblow?

I stay for a heartbeat, then two, but then I cannot take it anymore, and I turn away, trying hard not to cry and not to run. Just to walk slowly and carefully, as if his silence hasn't pierced a hole through my heart.

I've gone two steps when I hear him, his voice so low that it is almost lost in the hum of the air conditioner. "*If* I need you?"

I freeze, my shoulders stiff, my eyes squeezed tight to fight back the flood. And then, when I'm certain that I can manage it without completely falling apart, I turn to face him.

He fills the doorway, this larger-than-life man who right now is vibrating with so many wild emotions it is a wonder that he doesn't combust under the strain of it all. But despite all of that—despite the anger and frustration that rolls off of him in waves—it is the heat I see in his eyes that seems to propel him forward. A familiar, wild heat—and it is directed entirely at me.

"*If* I need you?" he repeats as he strides to me, all force and power and intent. "Christ, Sylvia, don't you know by now that I always need you?"

He is only inches from me, but he doesn't touch me, and that small omission suddenly seems like the most important and most horrible thing in the world.

I want to reach for him, but instead I slide my hands into the pockets of my skirt. I'm afraid he will flinch away, and I am absolutely certain that I couldn't survive that, too. "You didn't answer my texts."

"I did," he says. "I answered each one, and then I fucking deleted it. I'm a goddamn mess, sweetheart, and I didn't think you'd want to be with me like this."

"Jackson," I whisper as I step closer, thrust into motion by the force of my relief. "Don't you know by now that I will always want to be with you?"

My skin tingles, as if the emotions arcing between us are generating power, electrifying the air like a lightning storm. For a moment, he says nothing, but I watch as his chest rises and falls with each breath.

"Goddamn him," Jackson finally says, and my stomach clenches. He is cursing the man who pushed him away. Who turned cold and impassive when faced with the news that he had a brother. But how much worse will it be when he hears the rest of it? And will the fact that I must be the messenger make it easier or harder to bear?

I reach for him, as if to soothe a wound I have not yet inflicted.

The touch seems to ignite something inside him, and he pulls me close. "Syl—oh, Christ, Syl."

My name is muffled as he crushes his mouth over mine. I melt immediately, surprise giving way to the pure, sweet relief of being claimed by this man. Of being used by him. Wanted by him.

Of simply being his.

The kiss is brutal. Hard. Teeth clash. Tongues battle. And, yes, I taste blood. It is as if he needs to consume me, to prove to himself that I am real and that I am here and that no matter what, I am not going anywhere.

From somewhere in the back of my mind I know that I need to tell him the rest—that I must deliver that final, horrible blow—but I cannot find the words yet. I cannot risk that he will let me go. That he will back away from me, his eyes full of revulsion instead of desire.

And so I push reality away and lose myself in the fantasy that we are fine. That we are good.

That nothing can separate us again. Not even the iron will of a man like Damien Stark.

He breaks the kiss, pulling back and breathing hard. Our bodies are pressed tight together and my chest throbs with the violent pounding of my heart. "I need you," he says, and I can only nod and whisper yes, my body limp with both relief and desire.

His mouth claims me again, but this time his hands grasp my hips and he lifts me. I hook my legs around his waist as he carries me back into his office. I feel weightless and wild, and god help me I want to be used. I want to be the bridge—the thing that pulls him from anger and back to me.

I gasp as he slams us against the drafting table. My rear is on the surface, but it is angled, and I keep my legs around him to keep from sliding off. I lean forward and attack his shirt, tugging each button free, forcing myself to not just rip the damn thing off him. I want to feel his skin beneath my hand, the heat building inside him, growing toward a violent explosion.

He is not so gentle. He yanks my shirt open, sending buttons flying and exposing my pale pink bra. I draw in a sharp breath, the ferocity of his action making my sex clench with raw, feral need. I'm wet, so desperately wet, and I clench my legs tighter around his hips, wanting nothing more in that moment than the feel of him against my cunt and the pressure of his mouth upon my breast.

"Please," I say as he tugs my bra down to free my breasts. He bends over, trapping me between his muscled frame and the hard, wooden drafting table. He drags his teeth lightly over my nipples. I whimper, my hips gyrating in a sensual dance that becomes more frenzied as he licks and sucks, my nipples tightening painfully in response to his ministrations.

Every part of my body seems to be connected by criss-crossing strands of red-hot wire. From my breasts to my lips, to my belly, to the soft skin of my inner thighs, and to my wet and needy cunt. "Jackson." His name is a moan, forced out past my gasps of pleasure as I arch against his mouth, my breasts so wild for his touch they hurt.

He lifts his head, leaving me feeling bereft. The sensual caress of cool air against my now damp breasts is like a tease, and dammit, I want more. I want to beg, but can only manage a whimper, and I clutch the desk to give me leverage as I shamelessly grind against him, wanting to increase the pressure against my clit even as I silently beg him to just please fuck me.

We're both wild. Crazed. This isn't about sex or love or even passion. It's about need. It's about release.

It's about taking what we need from each other. Hard and fast and very, very thoroughly.

His hands are on my skirt and he is shoving it up until it is nothing more than a linen ring around my waist. He rips my shirt the rest of the way open, and the muscles of my stomach tighten as cool air brushes my overly heated flesh. His mouth settles again between my breasts, and I writhe beneath him as he kisses his way down my abdomen, my skin tightening and tingling with each erotic touch.

When he reaches my navel, his tongue dips into the indentation, and I suck in air through my teeth even as my body clenches in response to this unexpected erogenous zone. He continues down, breaking contact only to slide over the bundle of material that was once my favorite skirt but is now a hated barrier between my flesh and his mouth.

For a moment I feel nothing except the gentle press of his hands on my hips to hold me in place. I start to lift my head, but his simple "No" halts me.

"Please," I beg.

"Please what?" I hear the tease in his voice and can't help my answering smile.

"Fuck me." Just saying the words makes me even more wet. I'm certain my panties are drenched—more than that, I am certain that he can see just how aroused I am. Rather than embarrass me, though, the thought only makes me more excited, and I spread my legs just a bit more in a silent admission. *I want you, Jackson. And oh, dear god, I need you.*

He exhales, and the noise he makes is both a confession and a seduction. I melt in response, mind and body relenting fully to his touch. He kneels between my legs, his mouth even with the lowered edge of the table—and with my cunt. His soft breath teases me, like the most sensual of promises. And when his lips tease the soft flesh of my inner thigh, I have to turn my head and bite my lower lip to hold back the wild current of desire that threatens to shake me to the core.

While his mouth is busy on my leg, one hand has slipped to my panties. He teases aside the thin, damp patch of material that forms a negligible crotch, then glides the pad of his thumb over me. He doesn't penetrate, and my body clenches in protest against that denial of sensation.

His mouth moves closer to my core, and without any warning, he takes my legs and lifts me so that I slide down a bit on the table even as he hooks my knees over his shoulders so that his mouth is right there, and I am spread out on his work table, my skirt hiked up and my hands clenching the side of the desk in a futile defense against this assault on my senses.

I am still wearing my shoes—an expensive pair of heels that I bought on a recent shopping spree—and somehow that one detail drives home to me what it is we're doing. And where exactly we're doing it.

"Jackson—oh, god, Jackson, stop." His tongue teases me along the band of my panties. "The walls—the glass. Anyone can see."

"Let them." His words are little more than a growl, and as soon as he's spoken them his mouth is back on me. He uses his finger to pull the crotch aside and attack me with his tongue. I shiver with excitement—both from the way he is so wickedly teasing me and from the possibility of getting caught. Slim, I know, considering this floor is Jackson's domain alone and isn't even fully built out yet. But even had the floor been bustling, I don't know that I could have moved away. Or that I would have wanted to. I'm too far gone. Too lost.

I don't care about anything but having him. Submitting to him. To giving myself entirely to Jackson, this man who has always been able to take me where I never even knew I wanted to go . . . but never so far that I can't find my way back to the familiar.

And now I am so sensitive and close that I hook my ankles together and pull him in, wanting him harder. Deeper.

He takes me right up to the edge—my mind swirling, my body writhing—and then he pulls gently away.

"Jackson—what—no. Don't stop. Please don't stop."

He chuckles, the sound very knowing and very sexy. "Don't worry, sweetheart. I have no intention of stopping."

Gently, he moves my legs off his shoulders as he stands, then gestures for me to hook them again around his hips. I do, and am rewarded by the erotic sound of his zipper lowering.

"I have to be inside you."

"Yes. Oh, yes." I spread my legs, welcoming him. Needing him to fill me up. To complete me.

He is hard and thick, but I'm so damn wet he enters me easily. His hands are on my waist, and I push against him, then hook my arms around his neck so that my ass is against the edge of the table and my breasts rub provocatively against his chest as we move together in a wild and primitive rhythm.

He opens his mouth as if to say my name, but I don't want words. I only want him, and I claim his mouth in a violent kiss, filling him with my tongue as he fills me with his cock.

I need this, and I know that he does too. This connection. This union. It's power and strength and solidarity. It's proof that we can get through everything that has and will happen. That we can weather the gathering storm.

It's torment and treasure.

And I dread when this interlude will end and I must unleash another kind of tempest.

He is deep inside me, gravity working with his every thrust, and his thumb teasing my clit in time with his movements. I am lost—I am melting. Aware only of the way he makes me feel—wild and lost and so goddamned insatiable.

But even as he pounds into me—even as euphoria spins me higher and higher and I know that this is a coming together that we so desperately need—there's something counterbalancing it all. Drawing me down. "Jackson." I gasp out his name. "Jackson, stop. I have to—oh, god."

He has shifted, and now he pushes me back onto the table. As he does, he lifts one of my knees up toward my waist so that I am even more open to him and he is even deeper inside me. He bends over me, shifting the angle from which he is entering me, so that his pelvis rubs my clit with each thrust, leaving his hand free to cup my ass and hold me steady as he drives into me over and over, so hard and so fast that whatever foolish notion I'd had of making him stop is very soundly knocked out of my head.

"Come with me," he growls. "Dammit, Sylvia, I want you to come with me."

I arch up, one hand clawing his shoulder as I clutch the edge of the drafting table with the other. He pounds into me, his body going rigid with release. But it is his face, open and savage with undisguised need, that pushes me over the edge, and I cry out as the orgasm crashes over me again and again like a battering sea in a storm.

I am still breathing hard, still trembling from the aftershocks of passion, when he falls on top of me, his face buried against my breasts. I hook my legs more tightly around his waist so that I don't slide down, but the truth is that I want to move. I am antsy now. Guilty.

I've taken this moment—this pleasure—under false pretenses, and I don't know what to do now or how to make it right. All I know is that I have to move. That I have to get him off me, because our position is too intimate and far too fragile to support the weight of my guilt.

"Jackson." I lift his head. "I need to get up. My back." The lie comes easily, and I feel another twinge of guilt when his brow furrows with concern and he helps me off the table, and even tugs my tattered shirt closed for me as I yank my skirt back down.

"I'm glad you didn't give up," he says. "I'm glad you came looking for me."

"I—" The words seem to catch in my throat, but I have to go on. I have to get this out. "There's something I should have told you before. I should have told you the moment I found you. But I didn't," I say as I look down at the floor. "I didn't, and I'm sorry."

I'm rambling. And as I rattle off these meaningless words, I realize that Jackson and I are in the same predicament. I should have delivered the blow at the first opportunity. And he should have done the same with his revelation about Damien.

"What?" He takes my chin and gently tilts my face to his so that I must either look at him or deliberately avoid his eyes. "What's going on?"

"It's Damien," I say, then watch as his expression hardens in front of me. "And it's the resort."

He says nothing, and for some reason that makes it harder. But I have to do this and so I press on, taking a deep breath for courage, and then just blurting it out. "You're fired, Jackson. Damien said I have to fire you from the project."

The bastard.

The goddamn, fucking, holier-than-thou *bastard*.

"Fired?" Jackson repeated, even though he knew damn good and well that he'd heard her exactly right. "And, what? The great Damien Stark didn't have the balls to do it himself? He has to put that on you?"

She took a step toward him, her hand outstretched. "Jackson, he—"

"*No.*" He shook his head. "I don't even want to hear it."

For Jackson's whole life, everything that Damien wanted, Damien got. And more often than not, he got it at Jackson's expense.

Damien wanted a father? Fine, he took Jackson's.

He wanted time? No problem there, either. Because Jeremiah sure as hell couldn't stick around when little Damien needed him.

Opportunity? Why not just play grab-ass with whatever came along, just like he did in Atlanta, and why the hell should he give a flying fuck if his underhanded manipulations screwed over anyone else?

And now Damien wanted him gone, because god forbid Jackson's revelation caused him even the slightest bit of inconvenience.

"*Fuck.*"

He grabbed the first thing he saw—a plastic cup full of pencils—and hurled it across the room. It slammed into the window and the pencils went flying, bouncing off the glass like tiny spears.

Beside him, Sylvia pressed up against the drafting table where he'd buried himself in her just moments before. Her eyes were wide and he could see her chest rising and falling as she watched him warily, as if fearing that he might suddenly explode.

Then again, hadn't he already done that?

He sucked in a breath, then dragged his fingers through his hair. Christ, he was an asshole.

"Syl," he said, then felt his gut twist into knots when he saw the single tear snake down her cheek.

Oh hell. Oh fuck.

He'd done that. He'd scared her. He'd hurt her. And before that, he'd fucking used her.

And he was standing there and cursing Damien for being an asshole?

What the fuck was wrong with him?

"I'm sorry," he said. "Christ, I'm so damn sorry."

Her mouth moved, as if to say his name, but no sound came out. Just as well, because right now his name on Sylvia's lips had the power to shatter him. And he was already too shattered by half.

For a moment, he just looked at her. She stood there, her mouth slightly open as if she was searching for a single magic word that could put everything back to right. Her lips were swollen, her hair mussed. She held her shirt together with one hand, because of course he'd been asshole enough to rip the garment to shreds.

Goddamn it. Goddamn it all to hell.

He still wore his suit jacket, and now he shrugged it off and dropped it over the back of a nearby chair.

"I'm sorry about your shirt," he said. "I'm sorry about everything."

And then, without looking back, he turned and left the room.

five

I grab hold of the drafting table and suck in air, trying to gather myself as Jackson disappears down the hall.

Part of me thinks that I should follow him—that I should go after him and enfold him in my arms, then hold him like a child, kissing him and murmuring soft words until the pain goes away.

But we have just been down this road, and I know that when he ran from Damien, I brought him comfort.

Now, things have changed. And this time it is me that he is running from.

Dammit, dammit, dammit.

I pace the office, my emotions too riled to allow me to stand still. Back and forth, again and again, not seeing the room. Not seeing anything. Just moving. Just feeling the blood in my veins and the contempt that now flows as well.

Because right now, I hate myself. I hate myself for what I did to this man I care so deeply for. For that matter, I hate Damien, too, for forcing me to be the hatchet man.

I understand why he did it—I'm the project manager and that means that hiring and firing are part of my job. But it wasn't my decision to fire, and now the two best things in my world—Jackson and my job—have been tainted.

And, yes, I hate myself because despite what has happened—despite knowing that Jackson is in pain—I don't want to quit this job that I love.

"*Goddammit.*" I grab an eraser off the table and hurl it across the room. It hits the window just inches away from where Jackson's pencils had struck. It makes no sound, then drops to the ground.

All in all, pretty damn unsatisfying, and I fall back into Jackson's chair, close my eyes, and lower my head to his desk.

I'm lost and I'm angry and I'm confused.

Most of all, I'm impotent. Because I don't know what to do. I don't even know where to begin.

Don't you know by now that I always need you?

His words echo in my mind, and I can't help but wonder if he really meant them. Does he need me?

More important, does he need me now?

As it turns out, the question is moot, because Jackson is nowhere to be found, and by midnight I really don't care what he wants or needs anymore. Now it's all about me. Because I'm terrified that something horrible has happened to him, and all that matters is what *I* want and what *I* need.

What I need is to find him.

He's not answering his phone. He's not answering his texts.

I drive all the way to Marina del Rey only to discover that he's not on his boat.

And when I call the Redbury, a boutique hotel that I know he's stayed at before, I am assured that he is not registered there either.

I end up at my Santa Monica condo, and though I know perfectly well that I haven't yet given him a key, I say a little prayer that he's inside. That he's fallen asleep on the back patio, and that by the time morning rolls around, we'll be laughing about my antics to find him when he was at my place all along.

But he's not here, either, and my options are dwindling even as my fears are rising. This is no longer about soothing his anger or hurt feelings. This is about being really and truly scared that Jackson is beat up and bloody somewhere. He has one hell of a temper, after all.

Hadn't he gone after Reed?

Didn't he have a scar on his forehead, a souvenir from when I had left him in Atlanta five long years ago?

"I turned anger into fights," he'd once told me. *"And I channeled control into sex."*

We'd certainly covered the sex part already. But now I am terribly afraid that he's moved on to the fighting portion of the program.

I snatch up my phone and start to hit the speed dial for my best friend, Cass. But then I glance at the clock and see that it is after two in the morning. I hesitate, because she must be dead asleep by now. Then I say fuck it and dial. As far as I'm concerned, this is the kind of situation that is squarely covered by the best friend emergency pact.

"Who the *fuck* is this?"

The female who answers the phone is not Cass, and it takes a moment for my addled brain to regroup. "Zee, it's Sylvia. I'm sorry I woke you, but it's an emergency. Can you put Cass on?"

She sighs deeply before saying, "Sure. Whatever. Hold on." At least, those are the words that filter across the cellular connection. But I hear what she's really saying, and it sounds a hell of a lot more like, "You fucking bitch, it's the middle of the night."

Of course, I might be projecting. Cass and Zee—which is short for Zelda—have been dating for all of about five minutes, but already I'm seeing angst and insecurity all over my best friend. And I'm sorry, but Cass is on the upside of awesome, and if Zee doesn't see that, then she is seriously warped.

"What's wrong?" Cass barks out the question without preamble, and with no hint of sleep in her voice. She's good in a crisis, and always has been, and it's times like this when I'm even more grateful that she's on my team.

"Jackson," I say, then give her the quick and dirty rundown of what's transpired. I don't have to tell her that Jackson is Damien's half-brother because Jackson already did that himself. He'd been desperate to find me, and he'd gone to Cass, then laid it all out for her, knowing that if anyone could help him find his way back to me, it was my best friend.

"I know he goes to gyms to blow off steam," I say. "The kind with rings and boxing clubs. But no gym is gonna be open at this hour. What if he's gotten in with one of those underground fight club groups? You know, the bare knuckles thing where the guys beat the shit out of each other and other people bet on it."

I don't know what the hell I'm talking about, of course. I'm stringing together tidbits from fiction, movies, television, and short pieces I've caught on the evening news. But the idea that secret fight clubs exist makes perfect sense to me. And if they do exist, then I have no doubt that a man as capable and determined as Jackson would know how to find one.

"Okay, you need to seriously chill. Do you want me to come over?"

"Yes. No." I take a deep breath. "No, of course not. But I'm really worried."

"Yeah, I get that. I'm thinking." There's a pause, and I clutch my phone so hard I'm at risk of breaking it. "Wait. Oh my god, we're both idiots."

Since I'm completely willing to believe that at this point I don't bother debating. "Go on."

"When you went running off into the hills that time in his Porsche, how did he find you?"

"OnStar," I say.

"So use that."

I replay her words in my head, sure I missed something. But nope, that's all she said. So I ask the most basic question in the history of the universe: "How the hell am I supposed to do that? I'm not on the account. I don't even know the license plate number."

"Oh, please. You work for one of the original masters of the universe. Surely someone in Starkworld knows how to do that kind of shit."

I am seriously doubtful. At the same time, I have no better idea and, if nothing else, this will give me something to do other than tossing and turning and pretending to sleep. "Okay. Great. I'm on it."

"Yeah?"

"Unless you're holding back on me and have a better idea hidden in your sleeve."

"Sorry," she says. "No."

"Then go back to sleep. And tell Zee I'm sorry."

I hear a rustling as she adjusts the phone. "She's already conked out." I hear her draw in a breath, and when she speaks again, her voice is soft, but firm and full of concern. "Listen, I know everything's been pretty weird for you lately. If you need the ink, I'll open the shop right now."

I close my eyes, overcome with emotion. Of all the people in the world, Cass and Jackson are the only two who not only see me, but understand me.

I shake my head, though I know she can't see me. "I'm okay," I say, even as my hand slips to my lower back where his initials are tattooed. "I honestly hadn't thought of it."

"Really?"

I understand the surprise in her voice. My tattoos are a map of both pain and triumph. A record of the things in my life that have rocked me—and a reminder that I can and will survive.

"I don't need it," I say firmly. "This is just a bump. A blip. We've gotten through so much more, I know we can get through this, too." Just saying the words aloud gives me confidence, and I'm glad that Cass brought up the tattoo. Because it gave me the chance to say no.

"Damn straight," she says. "But call if you get weird. And call me once you find him so I know everything's okay."

"Will do. I have an idea, actually. Your OnStar spiel totally got me thinking."

"Yeah? Well, good on me."

"I love you, you know."

"Then why the hell aren't you in my bed?"

I laugh, then hang up, shaking my head with amusement. Despite waking Zee, I'm glad I called, because if nothing else I feel infinitesimally better.

I pull up my contacts and dial the home number for Ryan Hunter, Stark International's security chief. He's just the guy for a little late-night private eye work.

This time, the voice that answers is completely awake, and I can hear the stereo blaring in the background.

The voice, however, doesn't belong to Ryan.

"Hello?" the voice says. "Hey! Yo! Turn that down, will you?"

I grin as the background music fades to a sane level and Jamie Archer, Ryan's girlfriend, comes back on the line. "Okay, I can hear now. What's up?"

"Hey, Jamie," I say. "It's Syl."

"Yeah, I know. Caller ID. Welcome to the twenty-first century."

"Listen, I need a favor."

"No prob," Jamie says. "What do you need?"

"Actually, I need it from Ryan. Is he there?"

"Sure. Hang on."

I hear the clatter of the phone being passed, along with laughter in the background. I know that he's taken Monday and Tuesday off to spend time with some college friends who came into town, and I feel a twinge of guilt for interrupting. Not enough guilt to make me hang up, though.

"Sylvia?" Ryan's voice is smooth with a hint of concern. "Is everything okay?"

"No. Yes. I don't know." The words tumble out of me, and I give him the rundown of everything that has happened. Not the brother thing, but the firing. The explosion. The fact that Jackson is gone.

"I'm really worried. I thought maybe you could track his Porsche. It's got OnStar."

"Do you have his account information?"

"No."

"How about the VIN number for the Porsche? Or the license plate?"

"No."

"Then I don't know how—actually, give me five minutes. Do you want to hang on, or shall I call you back?"

"I'll hang."

"I'm putting the phone down," he says, and I'm left alone in my apartment, the worry that twines through me contrasting with the hum of music, drinking, and general revelry filtering back to me through the phone line.

Finally, he comes back on the line. "The license plate was easy—he has a card key for the garage, so we have his vehicle information."

"That's great."

"Tracking the car's another story." He sighs. "Look, Syl. I've got a friend in intelligence who owes me a favor, and I think he could manage it. But it would put his ass on the line. But if you really think Jackson's in trouble, then I'll do it. You just have to say the word."

I open my mouth to tell him to yes, yes, please find Jackson.

But the words don't come. Because the truth is that it's not Jackson I'm afraid is in trouble, it's the two of us as a couple that I'm worried about.

And until I find him—until he holds me in his arms again—then I'm the one who really isn't okay.

six

By the time four a.m. rolls around, I am seriously considering calling Ryan back and telling him to yes, please call his friend in intelligence. Hire a hacker. Contact the fucking CIA. Just do something to find Jackson before I go completely out of my mind.

I don't, though.

I do, however, send an email to Damien telling him that I've terminated Jackson. Since he's not an employee but a contractor, I don't have to deal with human resources, thank goodness. Then I shoot an email to Aiden, my immediate supervisor in the real estate division, telling him that I'll be working from home today. Fortunately, I've already asked Rachel to cover Damien's desk for the rest of the week. Not because I expected to stay up all night, but because I'd planned to spend a good part of the week with Jackson, working on the details of the resort.

Now, of course, I still need the time, because the entire project is a mess and I need to get all my architectural ducks in order.

My eyes are scratchy, and despite my worry, I cannot stop myself from yawning. I've been sitting at my kitchen table, a pad of paper in front of me so that, ostensibly, I can make notes about the resort. The pad is entirely covered with doodles.

I get up, use my Keurig to make a cup of coffee, and then go to my sofa. I wedge myself into the corner, pull a blanket up to my shoulders, and hold the mug in both hands. It's the warmth I want the most, because I feel cold. A bone-deep chill that I haven't been able to shake since Jackson walked away, leaving me alone in his office.

I know that I should sleep, but I can't bring myself to move to the bedroom. Everything around me is spinning wildly out of control, and I know that if I sleep, my nightmares will come.

But it's more than that. Somehow, letting sleep take me feels like giving up. He has to call soon. He has to, because I need to know that we're okay. I need to see his face and know that, despite the guilt that seems to cling to me like glue, he doesn't blame me for firing him.

That's what this is about, of course. That's why I have to find him. Have to see him. That's why I can't sleep. Why I am a wreck.

Because I'm afraid.

I'm so terribly, terribly afraid that despite the passion that twines us together and despite having already overcome so much, the foundation of our relationship has shifted, and nothing is ever going to be the same.

"Just as well he stays away. He's not the only one with secrets."

I blink, confused, and push myself up on the couch. The garage-style door to my patio is rolled up, and Bob stands on the threshold looking at me, one hand pressed casually against his crotch, and his camera hanging from a strap around his neck. His silky black hair is pulled back with a leather band, and he's smiling at me. "We've got a lot in common, you and I. We both want Jackson Steele."

He reaches up and slides his hand over the top of his head, and my stomach tightens with revulsion as his hair slides off. It's a wig, and he drops it negligently on the ground. "That's not me any-more. I'm a long way from that man. I'm Robert Cabot Reed, and I have all the power now. But you don't, do you, little Elle?"

I want to yell at him. To tell him my name is Sylvia. And that he's nobody. Just some slimy photographer from the Valley who's playing at making movies. But the words won't come.

"You don't have anything at all," he continues in that singsong voice. "Not even Jackson."

"No," I say. "That's not true."

"Do you think he'll still want you when he knows your secrets? My little Elle said she told him the truth, but you didn't tell him all of it, did you? Still got your secrets, don't you?"

I pull the blanket up all the way to my chin. I am so cold, and I'm scared. I don't want him to touch me. I don't want him to look at me. And I don't want to be here.

"But you have to stay," my father says. He is standing right in front of me, and he reaches down and takes the mug from me. It is full of hot chocolate topped with marshmallows. My favorite. I didn't realize I was holding it. I haven't even had one sip.

He lifts it to his lips and drinks it all up, then sets the empty cup on my coffee table. "You know why you have to stay. And you're a good girl, Elle. You're my good girl. You need to stand up now. It's time for Bob to take your picture. He has a lot of things to take."

"No," I say, but it doesn't matter. Because I see another me across the room. I'm leaning against the door frame, my back arched to accentuate my breasts, small and firm beneath a thin cotton T-shirt.

"Perfect," Bob says. He picks up the camera and starts to click. "Just needs a little bit more. Gotta look like you're enjoying it. Gotta look like you want it."

"No," I whisper, but I'm all the way on the couch and he doesn't hear me. The other me—the one he's touching, the one whose nipples he's squeezing and stroking—she just stands still, her eyes closed tight as if she wants to cry.

She doesn't. She can't.

"That's my girl," my father says.

"Your slut, you mean," Bob says. "Your whore."

"No." My father's voice is sharp, and he picks the mug back up, then slams it down against the table. Bam! *"No!" he repeats, then slams again.* Bam!

Then again and again and again until my head is full of nothing but the sound of the ceramic against the wood and I am certain that any minute the mug is going to shatter and I will—

"Sylvia!"

Jackson's voice.

I bolt upright, my heart pounding, unsure if I am still trapped in a dream.

"Sylvia!" he repeats, and the word is underscored with pounding.

My door! He is at my door.

I toss the blanket off, then hurry to my front door. I tear through the locks, then yank the door open.

He stands there, his slacks wrinkled and his shirt untucked. The wound on his cheek that had been healing so nicely is open again, red and angry and swollen. And though it doesn't look broken, his nose is caked with dried blood.

"In," I say, and hold out my hand.

He takes it, and as soon as he is inside my condo, he pulls me into his arms, his head bent so that his face is pressed against my hair. I cling to him, so overcome with relief that I'm afraid I'll fall if I let go of him, and I loosen my grip only when I hear him draw in a sharp breath of air.

I release him, then step back, finally taking the time to truly inspect him. "You're hurt."

"Trust me," he says. "I hurt a lot less now."

I wince, but don't say anything. I know what he means—how can I not? He's pounded it away—the pain of dealing with Damien. The wounds inflicted by me.

I force the thoughts from my head. He's here now, and that is all that matters. "Let me see," I say as my fingers reach for the buttons on his shirt. I undress him slowly, then carefully peel the white cotton away from his tanned body. His chest is lean and muscled, with broad shoulders and just enough chest hair to give a woman something to tease with her fingers. He is perfection, but right now, his skin is marred by bruises rising in various shades of purple and yellow.

My stomach twists, but I don't look away. Instead, I hold tight to his hand and pull him farther into the apartment. "Come on," I say. "We're going to fix you up."

"Sylvia, wait. I shouldn't have—"

I press a finger gently to his lips. "No. Please. We can talk later. Right now I just—" I draw a breath. "Right now I just need to take care of you."

Tears well in my eyes, because this is my fault. What he's done to himself. And even though it won't change anything, I need to try to fix it. Even if only a little. "Please," I say as I pull our joined hands to my lips. "Let me do this."

He nods, then follows me to the bedroom. I peel the covers back, then return to Jackson. I've left the shirt in the living room, but he's still wearing his slacks and shoes. I bend down, then untie the laces on his shoes and hold his foot while he slips each off in turn. Then I rise up, my head tilted back slightly so that I can face him as my fingers work his button and fly.

Gently, I tug his pants down, and then his briefs. His cock is semi-erect, and I press my hand lightly over him, cupping the tender skin in my palm. "Not now," I say gently.

"I know," he replies. "But I should point out that might be the only part of me that didn't get the shit kicked out of it last night."

"I'm glad you know how to protect what's important," I deadpan, and am rewarded with a twitch of his lips. "Now sit."

He does, moving to sit on the edge of the bed. I pull his slacks and briefs the rest of the way off, and then his socks. When he's naked, I silently indicate that he should lay down.

He doesn't, though. He stays upright, looking right at me. "You didn't tell me," he says. "The press. Calling you about me. You should have told me."

I lick my lips, then lift a shoulder in a small shrug. "Just a couple of calls when I went in to work yesterday morning. The resort is their angle, so of course they'd want a comment from the project manager, especially since Damien was away."

"You didn't give them one." His mouth curves up, almost into a smile.

"Not one damn word." Now it's my turn to grin. "You heard Damien. The official response is 'no comment.' "

"And if there was no official response?"

I step forward to take his hand. "I'd never say a word to them about you. About anything."

He leans forward, resting his forehead against my chest as he breathes. Just breathes. His skin is hot to the touch, and I have to resist the urge to tilt his head back and check for fever. I already know what is wrong with him. He's exhausted, mentally and physically. He needs to sleep. But I can also see that he needs to get out whatever is on his mind.

So I stand there, perfectly still. And I wait.

"I don't like my demons pushing up against you." He sits up straight so that he can look at me. "I don't like you having to carry my shit."

"I don't mind."

A muscle twitches in his cheek. "I do."

"Yeah? Well then you're an idiot, Jackson Steele."

He lifts a brow in surprise. Frankly, I'm a little surprised myself. But I forge on. "Everything you said to me—about helping me. About being there for me to work through all the baggage that comes with what Reed did to me. All of that is important. And just knowing that you've got my back makes me feel good. No, it's more than that. It makes me stronger."

I kneel on the floor in front of him. I'm still holding his hand, but I put my other one on his knee. "Don't you get it? I want to be there for you, too. I want to be the one who helps make you stronger. Who helps you carry it all."

As I speak, I realize I'm not even talking about the damn calls from the press anymore. Those were nuisances, nothing more. No, I'm talking about the bruises. The fighting.

I'm talking about the fact that he ran *from* me instead of *to* me.

And, yes, I know that I was the one who fired him. Intellectually, I get that. Emotionally, I want this man in my arms.

Very gently, I reach up and brush his cheek, just beneath where the wound has split open again. "When I told you what Bob did to me—when you learned about the nightmares and why I pushed you away in Atlanta and the stories behind all of my tattoos—you asked me if I'd ever seen a therapist."

"You said no."

"And you said that if I wouldn't talk to someone professional, that you'd be my therapy." I take the pad of my thumb and brush it gently over his lower lip, enjoying this soft intimacy. "I want to be your therapy, too."

He makes a scoffing sound. "Baby, I needed to bust something. You can look at me and see the shit I had to get out of my system. Do you really think I'm going to go there with you?"

I let my gaze drift over him, taking in his perfect body that has been so abused. Lingering on each mark, each scrape, each bruise. I can claim them all, because it was my words that had him lashing out. My words that triggered the explosion.

"Yes," I say. And then I lift my eyes to his. "Yes," I repeat.

His expression hardens, and he shakes his head. He starts to speak, but I cut him off.

"I will give you whatever you need, Jackson, that's a promise." My chest feels full, and I'm having to push the words out. I want him to comprehend this. To truly get it. "Do you think I don't understand going wild? Pushing hard? Have you forgotten about Louis? About all the initials I have inked on my thigh?"

Slowly—gently—I brush my fingertip over the bruises on his chest. I watch the way his skin shifts and tightens in response to my touch. "These should be mine, Jackson," I whisper. "Whatever relief you get from pounding away on another man, I should have been the one giving it to you."

His body stiffens beneath my touch. "I won't hurt you, Sylvia. Not like that."

"I'm not asking you to. Not exactly." I slide my hand down until I'm cupping his cock. I hear his sharp intake of breath. "But I am saying that I'll give you what you need. Whatever you need."

His cock stiffens beneath my hand, and I bite back a smile of satisfaction.

"You have no idea what you're offering."

"I think I do," I say, though in truth, he may be right. I've witnessed his need to fight. For raw violence. To lose himself in complete, primal physicality.

Translate that to sex, and can I handle it? Do I want to handle it?

Hell, yes. A tremor of nervous excitement runs through me, culminating between my legs, and I squirm a bit from the simple knowledge that I am wet. Because so long as it is with Jackson, the idea of being taken wildly, brutally, is undeniably exciting.

"You told me that I get off on submitting, so long as I'm doing it willingly. So long as I'm handing over control. You told me that I like being used so long as I'm the one who sets the ball rolling."

I release his hand, then rise to my feet. "That's all I'm offering, Jackson, but I'm offering it without reservation or conditions. Use me, Jackson. Use me whenever or however you need. I know you won't take it too far. I trust you. And I don't want you to run from me. Not again. Not ever."

I can see that he wants to answer me, but I don't want to hear it. Not anything. Not yet. So I shake my head and press my fingertips over his mouth. "No. Not now. We've said everything that needs to be said for the time being. And right now, I'm going to take care of you another way. Lay back."

He does, and I brush a kiss over his lips, then smooth his hair. "Close your eyes," I say. "I'm going to go get an ice pack."

"Yes, doctor."

"Role-playing?" I tease. "Well, we can certainly add that to our repertoire."

He chuckles, but his eyes are closed now, and the sound fades as he starts to drift.

I hurry to the kitchen, then return with a gel pack I use on days when I take yogurt and fruit to work. He flinches a bit when I hold it over the worst of the bruises, but he doesn't open his eyes.

I minister to each bruise, holding the cold against them for five minutes each. I don't know how much help it will be, but my brother, Ethan, got into a lot of fights in school trying to prove he wasn't weak and sick, and my mom always treated his bruises with ice to keep the swelling down.

Finally, I decide that there are no more bruises to treat, and that I've exhausted my limited first aid skills. I strip off my own clothes, then climb into the other side of the bed. Jackson is dead to the world, and I don't want to wake him, so I very carefully pull the covers up, then slide in next to him. Since I'm afraid of accidentally prodding one of his injured spots, I don't spoon against him. Instead, I lay a few inches away, then rest my hand lightly on his hip.

I don't like it, though. Even this small space of air between us seems like a barrier that is forcing us apart. And though I close my eyes and will exhaustion to sweep me away, sleep doesn't come.

But then Jackson rolls over, his arm going automatically around my waist. He pulls me to him so that my rear is nestled against his crotch and my back is pressed tight against his battered chest. His breath is soft and even near my ear, and as soothing as a lullaby.

And as slumber finally sweeps me away, my last thought is that I was a fool. Because I should know better than to think that even the most potent pain would keep me out of Jackson's arms.

seven

Jackson woke to realize that every part of his body ached.

His ribs screamed when he breathed.

His skin felt too tight and too damned sensitive.

Muscles burned, abrasions stung.

All in all, he was a fucking mess. And he had no one to blame but himself.

Himself—and Damien Stark.

Goddamn the arrogant prick. He'd *fired* Jackson? What kind of bullshit was that?

Even now, the memory made him want to put his fist through the wall, and he really should have worked that shit out by now. Lord knows the fifteen large he'd won in the ring last night should have been therapy enough. He'd beaten the crap out of every challenger Sutter had tossed at him, and still the rage bubbled under the surface.

And not just because of what Damien had done, but because of how he'd done it. Putting it on Sylvia. Making her lay down the gauntlet to Jackson, when Damien knew damn good and well that she wanted Jackson on the project, not to mention that they were dating.

Dating.

The word sounded too thin to hold the depth and power of the emotions he felt for Sylvia. He'd left because he couldn't stand the thought of losing it in front of her. And he'd returned because, goddammit, he needed her touch to find his way back to himself after the rage had passed. After he was aching and exhausted.

Christ, she was perfect, and all the more so because of the way she'd given herself so fully to him. Did she even realize what she'd done to him? The way his heart had flipped over when she'd looked at him with those wide, whiskey-colored eyes and told him that she'd submit to whatever he needed? That he could use her however he wanted?

Now her back was pressed to his chest and he held his arm loose around her waist. The steadiness of her breathing was like a gift, as if she was silently telling him that so long as she was in his arms, all was right with the world. She trusted him, fully and completely. He felt it now, and he'd seen it when she'd so boldly offered herself to him. In her eyes, on her face.

That trust had both humbled and excited him. Hell, even now his cock—about the only part of him that wasn't battered and bruised—was as hard as a rock and nestled sweetly against the curve of her ass.

He knew how much she craved control. He remembered with painful clarity the night when she'd finally told him why. When she'd shared not only the truth about what that fucking asshole Reed had done to her when she was a teen, but also about how she'd reacted.

How she'd wanted to run but hadn't been able.

How she'd wanted to get lost in her head, but had been denied that, too.

How her body had heated, responded. How Reed had touched her. Teased her. How he'd stroked and played with her.

He'd taken her to climax—and when she'd gone over, that loss of control had humiliated and mortified her. More than that, it had scarred her. Changed her.

In the end, it had infused her with a bone-deep need to keep control. Jackson understood that—and so he understood as well just how much of herself she'd offered him tonight.

And, yes, they had already gone part of the way down this road. Early on, he'd glimpsed the shadows lurking in her past, and had recognized that it wasn't control she needed, but submission. A safe place where she could surrender to pleasure and not feel ashamed. Where she could give control rather than have it ripped from her.

He had offered that to her, and she had agreed. So far, though, they'd taken only baby steps.

But this . . .

She'd trusted him openly and completely even though her core makeup was to not trust at all.

She'd surrendered control even though she didn't understand how far he might want or need to go.

But what had really twisted Jackson up was the realization that just saying the words had aroused her. He'd seen that clearly enough in the way her pupils had dilated and in the flush that rose in her cheeks.

And her excitement had made him hard.

Hell, just thinking about it now made him harder, though how that was physically possible he really didn't know. He was so stiff right now he felt like he'd been sculpted from a goddamn slab of marble.

If he'd had any doubts that Sylvia would go with him as far as he—or she—needed to go, she had soundly erased them. Christ, she'd put herself out there as a proxy for the ring.

That would never happen, of course; she wasn't a punching bag, and he would never, ever use her like that. But her offer, made with such sincerity and love, had stolen his breath.

He'd told her once that he'd taken all the shit from his childhood and turned it around. His anger to fighting and his need for control to sex. All true, yes. But the deeper truth was that the anger stemmed from control as well. From the lack of control, to be specific. From the feeling of being tossed aside by his father who'd had a whole hell of a lot of better shit to do with a hell of a lot better son.

Sometimes it really was about getting out there and getting bloody. Getting lost in the ring and the rage.

But more often, all that he truly needed was to release some of the pressure inside him. To fight back against whatever cosmic joke the universe was pulling at that moment and grab control where he could.

Before Sylvia, that would have been cause to call a few friends like Sutter who were uniquely hooked in. Find out what warehouse was hosting the action that night, and see if he could get a piece of it.

Now, though, they could fight their demons together. Yin and yang. Control and submission. Pleasure and pain. And on and on and on until they sent each other spiraling over that invisible line where it all became the same. Where pain gave way to pleasure, and control revealed itself to be nothing more than surrender.

That was the heart of the truth, wasn't it? Because no matter what games they might play in bed—no matter how much he professed to be the one in control—in life, Sylvia held Jackson's heart in her hands, and he was utterly hers.

Right now, though, she was his. And he was too hard and too eager to decline the pleasure she had offered. Use her? Hell, yes he would. Deeply, intimately, and very, very thoroughly.

Slowly, he moved his arm from around her waist, trailing his fingers up so that he could gently stroke her perfect skin. So that he could glide over her curves—her hip, her waist, her breast.

He pressed his palm over her breast, cupping it, feeling his cock twitch as her softness filled his palm. Then he flattened his hand and very lightly stroked her nipple with his palm. She whimpered in sleep, but didn't wake. Her body, however, was beginning to rouse in response to his ministration, and the nipple he'd been teasing was now taut and tight. He took it between two fingers, rolling it gently but firmly as her areola puckered.

As he teased her breast, he pressed his lips to the back of her neck, brushing a kiss over the tattoo there. She had so many, all marking her battles and triumphs over her demons. *Too many,* he thought. And two of them, he knew, were because of him. The flame on her breast, and his initials on her lower back.

His chest squeezed tight as he pulled down the sheet so that he could see her ink in the afternoon light now streaming through the window. He slid down, pressing his lips to her skin, dancing his tongue along the line of his initials. He heard her soft moan, and stopped briefly, but she hadn't awakened.

Good.

He knew now what he wanted to take. How he needed to use her, accepting the gift of herself that she'd given him, and returning it with pleasure and with a silent promise that they belonged together.

Not a hard, pounding fuck. For now, at least, he'd exorcised his demons. But dear god, he did need to be inside her—to claim her fully and control her pleasure completely. To see her face as she awakened with his cock deep within her and her body primed and wet and soft with need.

He wanted her to realize that he understood the depth of what she had offered him and that he welcomed it. Hell, he craved it.

Gently, he eased her onto her back and then straddled her. His cock brushed her stomach as he leaned over, and he had to pause to take a breath so that he didn't come right then.

He closed his mouth over her breast, teasing her already tight nipple, then slowly stroking his hand down her abdomen as he eased his way down her body. He saw the way her skin tightened in the wake of his touch, and he felt the quickening of her pulse. She writhed a bit, then reached out, her hands fisting in the sheets as her lips parted on a soft sigh.

He paused, unsure if he'd awakened her. But she was still asleep—she'd stayed up throughout the night worrying about him, and he knew that exhaustion had swept her away.

Slowly, he trailed his fingers down between her legs and used two fingers to stroke her cunt, already slick and wet for him. Slowly he eased those fingers inside her, and when she tightened around him in welcome, a fresh wave of desire, so strong it seemed as though it could destroy him, washed over him. He craved her, dammit, as painfully and potently as a drug. And the glory of it was that she was his. Truly his.

And he didn't have a clue what he'd done to deserve her.

Rhythmically, he thrust his fingers inside her, keeping his eyes on her face as the pressure built, watching her eyes move behind her closed lids. She was dreaming, he realized, and he couldn't help but wonder what those dreams entailed.

Then her lips parted, and he heard a soft "yes" drift from her lips.

Right then, that single word was the most erotic—and most powerful—sound he had ever heard. And just in time, too. Because he couldn't wait any longer. He had to be inside her. Had to have her before the need destroyed him.

He lowered himself over her, his cock pressing against her slick cunt. She was so wet that he slid into her easily, gratified by the way her hips rose in silent welcome. He thrust in deep, filling her so completely that his balls rubbed against her, and his cock tightened even more inside her. Again and again, and with each thrust he watched her face, bathed in passion even though she was still lost in sleep.

And then, oh Christ, she murmured his name. Still lost in slumber, but so desperately aroused.

And so very, very his.

eight

I am not Sylvia—I am simply pleasure, surging forward like a wave. Pushing up with such force and perfection I am surprised that I can bear it, and at any moment I expect to explode, rendered to ash by the heat and power of these decadent sensations that flow through me.

It is the thought of such an explosion that brings me back to myself. That settles awareness over me. My limbs. My breasts.

The desperate, heated ache between my legs.

I am motion.

I am wild.

I am lost, scattered to the wind by the glorious sensations bursting through me. The pressure filling me. The rhythmic motion of my body. The heat above me, and the musky scent of him that fills my senses and rocks me to my core.

"Jackson."

It is his name on my lips that wakes me. Not the fact that he is inside me, because that feels right and glorious and real.

Instinctively, I spread my knees, giving him deeper access even before my conscious brain acknowledges this delicious reality.

"Harder," I murmur, and as the mist of sleep starts to dissipate, I arch up, wanting more. I am so close. So alive. So sweetly, wonderfully his. "Please," I beg as he thrusts harder into me. As I reach for him, my hands on his back pulling him against me, wanting everything that he has to give.

I've gone from floating to attacking. From peaceful to feral. I want this—oh, dear god, I need this, and hear myself calling to him. His name. My moans. My cries of "Oh, god, yes, fuck me, please, Jackson, please fuck me harder."

He is above me, his body undulating over mine, his stormy eyes wild with passion. He is filling me up and sending waves of pleasure coursing through me. I am so close—so ready—and I feel more alive and more awake than I have ever been in my life.

"You offered," he growls. "I took."

"Yes." I suck in air as ripples of electricity zing over my body, the precursors to an orgasm that just might kill me. "Jackson—oh, god, Jackson."

"That's it, baby. Come for me."

His hands are on either side of me, but now he lifts one, taking his weight only on the other as he closes his now free palm over my breast. I rise up, my body craving more, and he takes my nipple between two fingers, pinching me to the point of pain.

I gasp—in surprise, yes, but even more from the sweet sting that spreads through me, fiery hot like an electrical storm that seems to connect my breast to my core.

I hear him moan and know that he has felt this new sensation as deeply as I have. "Again," I beg. "Harder."

He doesn't disappoint, and I bite my lower lip as he torments my nipple, making me writhe on the bed in the throes of a sweet pain that sends riots of pleasure through me, making my clit throb and my cunt tighten and convulse around him, silently demanding that he fuck me harder and deeper until finally the entire world seems to explode around us.

I think that I call his name, but I am not sure. I'm not sure of anything, actually, until the world re-forms around us, and I am limp beneath his weight as he collapses on top of me. His cock is still inside me and his face is buried in my hair. His hand remains on my breast, and even now, even sated, I want more.

"Jackson," I murmur, then move my shoulder so that my still-erect nipple brushes against his hand.

He makes a soft noise against my hair, and though he is otherwise still and spent, his fingers tease my breast, his fingertip stroking the areola, making the skin tighten and pucker.

I am breathing harder, wanting more, and I drag my teeth over my lower lip in dire need of his touch. He doesn't disappoint, but at the same time the touch is only a tease, a soft stroke of his fingers on my nipple, when I want that heat. That shock. That sting that shoots all the way through me.

"You want more?" he whispers.

"Yes."

"Touch yourself."

I open my eyes, only then realizing that I'd closed them in the first place. His face is right there, his jaw firm. His eyes hard and full of passion and heat.

"Touch yourself," he repeats, and because he has told me to, I comply. I slide my hand down my belly and find my clit. I'm wet and slick, and my fingers slide over my sensitive flesh.

I buck a little, my body once again reaching for release, and as I do, I am rewarded by his fingers tightening upon my nipple, giving me what I had so desperately craved. And now that heat—that connection—seems to shoot through me, making my breasts heavy and my skin sensitive. Filling and teasing me.

And as I stroke myself in small circles, I slide my fingers down to brush against his cock, feeling that place where we are connected. I feel him harden inside me, and I gasp at the power that seems to arc between us, firing both our bodies with such wild electricity.

"Now, baby," he whispers, tweaking my nipple even as a second, explosive orgasm rocks through me, making my muscles tighten around him, making him harder and wilder and oh, dear god, I still want more. I want everything. I want Jackson.

And he, thank god, wants me.

Still inside me, he rolls onto his back so that I am straddling him, impaled on his cock, my body still sensitive from the last climax. "My turn, sweetheart," he says, as he takes my hips and guides me up and down as he pumps into me, using his control over my rise and fall to thrust deeper and deeper, until he finally explodes inside me, and I watch as he goes over the edge, and am humbled by the pleasure and wonder I see on the face of this man I love.

When the last tremors subside and his body relaxes, I lean forward so that my breasts press against his abdomen and my cheek rests against his chest. He is warm, like a furnace, and his scent is intoxicating. I am tired, sated, but I can't resist the urge to tease his nipple with my tongue.

When I do, he laughs, then quickly flips me so that we change positions and he is over me. "Someone's energetic," I tease.

"Someone had a nice long nap." He lifts his eyebrows. "Care to go again?"

"Always," I say, meaning it. "But I think we should probably eat. What time is it?"

"Late. Early. I don't know." He props himself up on an elbow and grabs his phone off my bedside table. "Late. We slept all day."

"Makes sense. We were up all night."

He pulls himself up to a sitting position, then leans his back against my headboard as he uses his phone to order pizza. He doesn't bother to cover himself with a sheet, and he isn't the least bit self-conscious. Nor does he seem to be aware of the fact that—as the most incredible hunk of maleness that I have ever seen—he is entirely distracting me. His hard abs, his muscled arms. That tight V of muscle that some men have that traces the way from waist to groin, and his still quite impressive, though no longer fully erect, penis.

In my current state of arousal, even the bruises that mar his body are sexy, and I can't help but wonder if this isn't some sort of anthropological thing. The young woman attracted to the male in the tribe with the visible marks that prove he is capable of protecting her.

He clears his throat.

I realize that not only is he no longer on the phone, but that I have been staring at his waist—okay, at his cock—and lift my head sheepishly.

"Like what you see?"

"Just checking out what belongs to me," I say boldly.

"Good answer. Come here."

I've been wrapped in the sheet, but he pulls me free of it so that I am tucked in naked beside him. It seems decadent, somehow. Spending the day naked in bed. Or it does until he bends over to kiss my forehead and says, "I'm sorry to have kept you up all night. I didn't intend to worry you. Honestly, I didn't intend anything at all."

I sit up, then grab for the sheet and wrap it around me again. If he asks, I'll say that I am cold. But the truth is that I just feel a little bit exposed.

I don't plan to say anything, but then I hear the words and realize that they've come out of my mouth. "I thought you were mad at me. I thought that's why you left."

"Mad?" He looks so confused that I immediately relax, because no verbal denial could be more reassuring. "Oh, baby, no. I probably could have ripped the great Damien Stark to shreds for making you do that—and it was his face I saw on every man I went up against in the ring—so I was mad, yes. But not at you."

He reaches for me, sheet and all, and once again pulls me close. I curl against him, and the world seems to right itself again.

"Not at you," he repeats. "At Damien."

"I know. I'm mad at him, too," I admit. I don't say that I understand why Damien did it. Right now, what Jackson needs is solidarity.

"For that matter, I'm mad at my father, too. And we might as well add my mother to the equation." He grimaces. "Although you'd think I'd know by now that getting mad isn't even worth the effort. My whole life has been run by Damien's needs and whims. I don't know why now would be any different."

"You've never really told me about your family," I say softly. "Not much more than the big picture, anyway."

"It's hardly a story worthy of Disney," he says wryly. "But I suppose it has dramatic potential." He tilts his head back. "I told you I'm a bastard, and not just of the asshole variety?"

I make a face. "Very funny. You told me that your dad was married."

"To Damien's mother. But they didn't have any kids when Jeremiah met my mom, about a year before I was born. Her name's Penny, by the way."

"They had an affair. And he didn't just walk away when he learned Penny was pregnant?"

"No. And she has always given him too much credit for that. I think she's the one who should have run. Far and fast. But she had no education. No skills. She was a waitress in a bar when Jeremiah met her. And I don't know how much you know about Jeremiah, but he was blue collar all the way. At least until he met Damien's mother. She had money."

"Really?" I hadn't heard that. From the stories about Damien's start in tennis, I had the impression that they were relatively poor, with the family's hope resting on Damien.

"That's not altogether wrong," Jackson says when I tell him as much. "It's just later in the story."

"Okay. Go on."

"So Damien's mother, Carol, had family money that she inherited. They were married. Happy. Why wouldn't they be? All Jeremiah wanted was money and a beautiful wife and he had it."

"He burned through the money," I guess.

Jackson touches his nose. "Right you are. Although to be fair, Carol got sick. So it was really the medical bills that eventually burned through it."

I nod, because I understand that only too well.

"Meanwhile, before she became ill, Damien was born. I was two at the time, and don't even remember the blessed event. But I know that Carol and Jeremiah had been trying for years, and now suddenly he had what he wanted—a legitimate son."

"And you started to see less and less of your dad."

His smile is thin. "Are you sure you haven't heard this story?"

"Sadly, it's not too hard to guess the plot. But go on."

"That's really the way it shook down. It started with my father simply shifting his attention to Damien. To his happy little perfect family. And I had to keep it a secret, because our money was Carol's money, though I didn't realize that at the time, either."

He gets out of bed, gesturing for me to stay put, then pads out of the room. "Things coasted along for a while. I saw my dad, knew he had another family, tried to pretend I wasn't jealous of my smelly, stupid little half-brother, and got on with my life."

He returns with two bottles of sparkling water and hands me one. "Then Carol got sick."

"Damien was about eight," I say, remembering details from the various biographies I've not only read but edited over the years.

Jackson nods. "I was ten. Old enough to understand things I overheard, but not to really comprehend them. And what I came to realize was that she'd been declining for a while, but it really got bad that year. Their money was dwindling, and there was no more to be had. Jeremiah had actually started working on an assembly line and had moved the family to Inglewood."

I nod, because I happen to know those are some of Damien's earliest memories.

"But what I found really interesting was that Jeremiah told my mother that Carol wasn't going to make it. And that when she passed away, he was going to be with her—my mother, I mean. Move me and her into the house he shared with Damien. And we were all going to be one big family."

"Did you want that?"

His smile is so sad it almost breaks my heart. "I did. Because I saw how much my mother wanted it. And because I thought my father would want to be around me more if I was part of an actual family and didn't feel so much like a side note."

I reach out to hold his hand, the gesture seeming feeble against the weight of the pain I hear in his voice. And my heart is so tight that I'm afraid it's going to break for the little boy he used to be. "Why didn't it happen?" I whisper the question, somehow afraid that by speaking too loudly I'll shatter the boy and the man.

"Because Damien turned out to be a goddamn tennis prodigy."

The words seem to crack in the air like a bullwhip, and I can't help but flinch from the force of them.

"But why—" I begin, then stop myself. I get it. Because Damien's career took off. The golden boy. The young celebrity athlete. And even after Carol passed away, Jeremiah wasn't about to risk that cash cow by tossing scandal into the ring. Another family. Another child.

And so instead he went the other direction. Told Jackson that if he breathed a word of the family secret, then Jackson and his mother would starve. And he justified his absences by his need to keep the meal ticket performing.

He drew upon and honed his skills as a con man, a player, and left his blue-collar days behind for good.

And in the end, both Jackson and Damien suffered.

The intercom buzzes, and Jackson goes to let the pizza guy up, pulling on a pair of sweatpants that he's left as a permanent fixture in my apartment. I slip into a robe and follow him into the living room, feeling a little bit shell-shocked.

I want fresh air, and so I open the big, garage-style door to my patio.

Jackson joins me out there, and we sit on the oversized lounge chair and balance the pizza box on the smaller chair that is the only other place to sit out here.

"I'm so sorry," I say as I grab a slice of pepperoni pizza. "I get why you hated him growing up. I really do. But don't paint Damien with his father's brush."

"The day after he fired me probably isn't the best time for you to make that case," Jackson says, and I have to admit I see his point.

"Can I ask you something else?"

"Of course."

I brush my fingers lightly over his bruises, leaving a streak of oil from the pizza. "Where did you go? You said you belong to a gym, but it was the middle of the night."

"A fight club," he says. "Bare knuckle. It's gambling and it's illegal, but it takes the edge off."

My stomach twists. "Jackson."

"Hey, I won the purse."

I shoot him a scowl. "To the best of my knowledge, you're not hurting for money. How'd you find the place, anyway?"

"A friend from my rough-and-tumble high school years. Name's Sutter. He owns the gym I belong to. And as for the fights, well, he's hooked in."

"I don't like it," I say, voicing the understatement of the century. "I mean, it's dangerous, right?"

"Compared to what? To boxing with gloves? Gloves add weight. More risk of head injuries."

I put my pizza down. "Jesus, Jackson, why compare it to anything? It's just dangerous."

He says nothing, and I sigh. "Look, I'm not going to sit here and debate the right way for you to get the shit beat out of you. I just don't want you to get the shit beat out of you at all."

I shift on the lounger so that I'm looking at him straight on. "I meant what I said earlier. You want to pound something, then I think you should just pound yourself inside of me."

His smile is slow and deliciously sexy. "All right."

I blink, surprised by his quick acquiescence. "All right?"

"What? Didn't you think I'd take you up on your kind offer? Did you not mean it?"

"No," I assure him. "I meant it. I just thought that you—"

He cuts me off by taking my hand. "Listen, Syl. I can't promise I won't ever want to beat the crap out of something again. But I was thinking about your offer while I was watching you sleep."

"Watching me?"

"Oh, yes. You're beautiful, baby. I could watch you for hours. And so I watched you, and I thought."

"And?" My palms are suddenly sweaty, and I wipe them on my robe.

"And the thing is that sometimes my fights are about temper, and I really do want—like you say—to just beat the shit out of something. And maybe I can rein that in a bit. I don't know. But the truth is that most of the time, it's not temper that sends me into the ring but frustration. The need to wrap control around an uncontrollable situation."

"And I'm controllable?" Even as I say the words, I realize that my voice sounds breathy, and that my nipples are tight with excitement and anticipation. Hadn't he said that I got off on submitting, so long as it was my choice?

Well, he was damn sure right about that.

"So you'll use me?" I ask, my voice husky.

"Baby," he says, pulling me close, "it will be my pleasure."

nine

I stretch in the shower, then press my hands against the tile as the water pounds down on me, soothing my body. I feel sore and achy and very well-fucked, and I smile with satisfaction. If I felt this sore after a gym workout, I'd vow to not go again for a week. As it is, I want nothing more than to crawl back into bed, wake Jackson, and spend the day riding him hard.

Sadly, that's not going to happen.

Instead, I'm going to go to work, and Jackson's going to sleep in and then head to his boat. The thought is bittersweet, and I push it away, not wanting to think about the implications of Jackson not working on the Cortez resort. Not wanting to worry about the fact that his main office is in Manhattan, not Los Angeles.

Not interested in fretting over the reality that Jackson will soon be looking for another commission, and god only knows where on the planet that might take him.

Frustrated, I tilt my face up and let the spray wash over me.

Then I step out of the shower, dry off, and wrap the towel around me as I head back into the bedroom.

I get dressed quietly, careful not to wake Jackson. I know he must still be exhausted—god knows, I am—but I also don't want to say goodbye. Not when I'm heading off to a job we should be going to together. And yes, I realize that's stupid because this is reality now, and we are going to have to deal with it, but I'm not ready to face that reality yet. And if I don't say goodbye, then maybe I can pretend that I'm at my desk on twenty-seven and he's in his area on twenty-six, and everything is chugging along just fine.

God, I'm pathetic.

I push aside a pile of clean laundry so that I can sit in the blue upholstered chair by the window to put on my shoes. I bend over and tackle the tiny buckle on the tiny straps, and when I sit back up, I see Jackson watching me.

"Hey," I say.

"Hey yourself." He pats the spot next to him. "Come here."

I do, perching on the edge of the bed beside him as he props himself up on an elbow. I bend over and brush a kiss over his lips. "You should sleep." I trace my fingers lightly over the bruises on his chest. "The rest will do you good."

"*You* did me good," he says, the words so heavy with meaning that they seem to fill me up.

"I'm glad."

"And now you were going to sneak out without even saying goodbye."

"No," I say, but then blush when his brows rise with obvious disbelief. "Only because you were dead to the world, and I figured you needed the sleep."

"Bullshit," he says.

I lift a shoulder, looking not at him but at the bed. "Fine. It's weird going without you."

He's silent a moment, then he tilts my chin up and looks at me.

"Go," he says. "And when you get home tonight, I'll take you out for dinner. Deal?"

"Deal," I agree, then laugh when he kisses my knuckles.

My mood stays light all the way to the office, but shifts toward gray when I meet with Damien to go over some of the pending details for the resort, including replacing Jackson. It's the longest forty-seven minutes of my life, and I'm not sure how I manage to keep my mouth shut and not tell Damien that he is making a huge, huge, huge mistake.

"Under the circumstances, I think Glau is our best bet for a replacement," Damien says. "I'm willing to consider other candidates, if you have them, but it's going to have to be a perfect storm of availability, skill, and reputation to make it work."

Other candidates.

As in, not Jackson.

As in, another architect that I will be working with. Because as much as I want Jackson Steele on this project, I don't want it enough to walk away from the project manager position.

And that is the real elephant in the room. The monkey in my wrench. The worm in my candy bar—I haven't told Jackson I feel guilty as shit for not quitting the resort. And he hasn't told me that he doesn't blame me for doing so.

But I know that he must, because how on earth can he not be pissed? Maybe not that I'm the one who fired him, because that really is on Damien's shoulders. But that I stayed when I could have walked.

The gray cloud that had settled over me turns stormy, and it's not even soothed by a double latte and chocolate croissant from Java B's, the coffee shop in the Stark Tower lobby.

Nor does being at my desk on twenty-seven improve my mood, and for the first time in a long time I wish that I was sitting at the desk outside Damien's office on thirty-five, and not here in the real estate department. Because every piece of paper I put my finger on reminds me of Jackson.

That's especially true when I pull Glau's preliminary sketches from the file and start to study them.

And goddammit, there is no comparison.

Everything about Jackson's work is better. The presentation. The layout. The flow.

Where the resort that Glau had envisioned is undeniably dramatic, what Jackson has put on paper enhances the beauty of the island. Instead of using Santa Cortez as the equivalent of a concrete slab upon which to plunk an architectural masterpiece, Jackson has incorporated the island into his design. He used the tide pools, the inlets, the hills, and the valleys to define the layout, making the structures seem organic, as if they were part of the land and the sea.

Glau's resort could be built as easily in Idaho as on Santa Cortez. But Jackson's vision is inextricably intertwined with the island, so much so that I can imagine no other architect coming close to creating such a sweetly perfect design.

And yet somehow I have to find just such an architect.

Well, damn.

What I should do is march back up to Damien's office and argue on Jackson's behalf. But I can't seem to make myself push back from the desk. I don't want Damien to think that I'm simply arguing for the man I'm sleeping with, and that frustrates me even more. Because, dammit, the man I'm sleeping with really is the best man for the job.

"Fuck."

"Trouble?" The voice is cultured East Coast with just enough of a British flair to be inherently sexy. All of which means that it belongs to Aiden Ward, the vice-president of Stark Real Estate Development, and my immediate superior for The Resort at Cortez project.

I twist around in my chair to find him leaning against the entrance to my cubicle, which constitutes my temporary office in the real estate department. When and if I leave Damien's desk to be a full-time worker bee on this floor, I'll get an office with a door and windows. Until then, I'm in cubicle land.

"Usually you're so bloody cheerful," Aiden says amiably. He has dark blond hair and green eyes that flash when he's amused. Like now. "Whatever could be the matter?"

I make a face. "Don't even pretend you haven't heard."

"I have, and I'm sorry. For what it's worth, I think Damien's making a mistake. In this day and age, Jackson's arrest is hardly a blip. Hell, the PR department could probably have a field day leaking stories to the press. We'd end up selling out opening day so fast we'd have to arrange for a month-long opening extravaganza. What?" he adds, frowning at me.

I shake my head and adjust my expression. "It's just that I agree with you. Did you talk to Damien?"

"Haven't seen him. I was in New York yesterday and I've been at the Century City site all morning. Why?"

"No reason," I say, and I have to wonder if Damien's going to tell Aiden the whole truth. I suppose there's no reason to, especially now that Jackson's off the project. But at the same time, the truth about Jackson and Damien's relationship is out there, and I've never known Damien Stark to let other people be in control of key information.

"So was it your general malaise at the situation that had you muttering curses when I walked up? Or has something more specific got you riled up?"

"This," I say, passing him the folder of Glau's work. "It's trite and mundane and downright dull compared to the work Jackson was doing."

He sits down on the corner of my desk and flips through the folder. Then he looks over at my bulletin board where I've tacked up Jackson's sketches. One beat, then another. Then he tosses the folder with Glau's work in my recycling bin. "So we ask him for a fresh approach or we find another architect."

"Time's an issue," I admit. "Quality and experience are another. We've been down this road already, remember? When Glau quit, Jackson was our only legitimate option. Who else had the kind of reputation that would keep the investors happy?"

"Agreed," Aiden says. "But we're further down the road now."

"Not by much." Although it feels like Jackson and I have been working together for ages, the truth is it's barely even been a week since he officially signed onto the project.

"No, but sometimes it's more about psychology. They've turned the ignition key twice now. That means that they think it's a viable project. And no one likes to second-guess themselves."

I consider his words and have to agree that he has a point. "The investors are invested?"

He chuckles. "Something like that."

"Even if you're right, I still have to find someone that I can live with." I lean back in my chair and focus on the ceiling. "What about Nathan Dean?"

"Really?"

I sit back up again, the chair creaking slightly with my movement. "You'd veto him?"

"I might," Aiden admits. "More importantly, I think Damien would."

"Yeah?" I'm surprised. Dean recently told me that he and Aiden have been friends for years. But more than that, Dean designed Damien's extremely awesome Malibu house, so I happen to know Damien is pleased with his work. And since I was the point person for Damien on that job, I know that Dean is easy to get along with and doesn't freak out at last-minute changes. I also happen to know that although his experience is primarily residential, he wants to branch out into commercial projects. And considering how much Damien enjoys finding and nurturing talent, I'm surprised by Aiden's reaction.

"I think the only reason Damien is willing to let Glau back on

the project after he quit is because the man has a worldwide reputation. Dean doesn't have that going for him."

Aiden has completely lost me. "But Dean didn't quit," I say stupidly. I mean, I should know. I was the one who brought Damien
the final check to sign once the house was complete.

"The bungalow," Aiden says, and I shake my head, still clueless.
"Apparently Damien wants to build a small bungalow on the property, but closer to the beach. A few months ago, last February, he
and Dean talked about it, and Dean put together some rough
sketches that Damien loved, but a few months later when Damien
said they should go to contract and get started, Dean pulled out.
Said he couldn't do the project, after all."

"Why the hell didn't I know about this?"

"No need to hook the assistant in until there's a contract. I only
know about it because I had a lunch meeting with Damien the day
Dean pulled the plug, so I got the full story. Let's just say that
Damien wasn't pleased. He doesn't like having his time wasted."

"No, he doesn't." I lean back in my chair again. "So it was
Damien who told you? Not Dean?"

Aiden's brow creases a bit. "Actually, Dean hasn't mentioned it
at all. Maybe he figures it's a sore point around the office."

"I guess it's not too bad between them. I didn't notice any tension when we had cocktails at his house the other day."

"Who knows? Damien is more than capable of keeping his personal feelings to himself. Besides, I believe Nikki pulled together
the guest list. And since the bungalow was going to be a surprise,
it's quite likely that she's not even aware that Dean shot himself in
the ass."

I have to laugh at the somewhat vulgar expression pronounced
by someone with such a hoity-toity accent. "Trent must not have
known, either," I say, referring to Trent Leiter. He's under Aiden in
the overall company hierarchy, and is directly in charge of all the
projects in the Southern California area. All, that is, with the ex-

ception of The Resort at Cortez. I'd brought that idea to Damien personally, and he'd put me on as project manager, reporting directly to Aiden.

"Trent? What does he have to do with it?"

"He's the one who suggested Dean as a replacement for Jackson." At the time, I'd thought he was just being helpful. But if he did know about the bungalow, I can't help but wonder if maybe his suggestion was a passive-aggressive way to make me suggest someone to Damien that would piss off the boss.

I hope not. Trent's not on my favorite person list, but I don't actively dislike him. I do know that he was irritated when I got Cortez, but I can't imagine that he'd go out of his way to screw with me. And the idea of interoffice backstabbing just really turns my stomach.

Aiden promises to think some more about possible replacement architects, then heads off to an afternoon meeting with one of the construction managers for a Stark Real Estate project. I decide that it's time for another caffeine boost, and head down to the lobby and Java B's. Since it's a typically gorgeous Los Angeles day, I take a minute outside, and am sitting by the small reflecting pond sipping my latte when my phone pings, signaling a text from Cass.

> Sorry about the shitstorm
> Call if you need me
> {{{{{{{HUGS}}}}}}}

I stare at the text, completely baffled, but with a very bad feeling growing in the pit of my stomach. And then, since I do need her to tell me what the hell she's talking about, I hit the button to speed dial her cell phone.

It rings once, then rolls to voice mail. "Dammit, Cass. What the hell? You said to call. Call me."

I end the call, then scowl at the phone, my mind whirling. Did

Jackson go to the press with news of his firing? Did he tell them the real reason why?

Because Damien Stark with a secret half-brother definitely qualifies as TMZ material.

I stand up and toss my half-finished latte in the trash, then hurry back toward the building, dialing Damien's office as I do.

Rachel answers on the first ring. "Mr. Stark's office."

"It's me," I say as I enter the lobby. I wave at the security desk as I head for the elevator. "Is he there?"

"In a meeting," she says. "Do you need him?"

The elevator doors open and I step on, then hit the button for thirty-five and the reception area for Stark International. "I just wanted to check on something," I say, but of course she hears none of that because the elevator is already moving and I lose the signal.

I tap my foot until the elevator comes to a halt, and then hurry to Rachel's desk. She doesn't look the least bit ruffled, and I frown, confused. "Who's he meeting with?"

"Preston. Why?"

I shake my head, but I'm secretly relieved. Preston Rhodes is the head of acquisition for Stark Applied Technology. If there was any sort of a shitstorm surrounding Damien right now, he would have rescheduled.

But then what the hell is Cass talking about?

"Syl?" Rachel is peering at me, clearly baffled. "Do you want me to tell Damien you need to see him?"

"No. It's okay. I just—" I take a deep breath and start over. "I had a thought about the resort," I lie. "But I'll run it past Aiden and we'll pull Damien in if we hit a snag."

She gives me a quick nod, then taps her headset to answer an incoming call. I wave as I head back to the elevator, relieved, but confused.

As soon as I'm back in the real estate division, I open a web browser so I can see if there's anything popping on the social media sites. I'm distracted from that task, though, when my phone buzzes on the desk beside me, surprising me and making me jump.

According to the caller ID, it's Jamie. I consider letting it roll to voice mail, but I've never been good at blowing off my friends. So I answer the call, but start the conversation with, "I've only got a second."

"You didn't tell me you were a teen model," she says without preamble. "That is seriously awesome."

I freeze. Literally, I just sit there, unable to move. And I'm cold, so cold I'm trembling. *That must be why they say you're frozen,* I think stupidly. And that thought is immediately followed by, *You're in shock. This is shock.*

"You there?" Jamie is as chipper as always. She hasn't picked up on my distress. Just the opposite. From the trill in her voice, I'm the new celebrity *du jour.*

"I'm here." My voice sounds a million miles away. Surely she will notice. Surely she will ask me what's wrong.

"Did you do any acting? Or just the print stuff?"

I try to make a sound, but don't quite manage.

"Syl?" For the first time, Jamie's voice holds a hint of concern. "You okay?"

"How did you know I modeled?" Somehow, my voice sounds reasonably normal. But I'm clutching my phone so tight my hand has gone numb.

"I saw it on the internet. Why? What's wrong?"

"Where?"

"Everywhere," she says, though now she's sounding like she's wishing she hadn't called. "Syl, what's up?"

"Why? Why is anyone talking about what I did when I was a teenager?"

"Come on, Syl. You're weirding me out here."

"Dammit, Jamie, just tell me." I spit the words out, then immediately wince.

"Okay. Sorry." I hear her draw a breath. "It's really not that big a deal. And the pictures are great, so it's not like they're releasing crappy unairbrushed pics, if that's what you're worried about."

"Why are they posting pictures of me at all?"

"The Jackson story, of course. He beat the shit out of Reed, and this is Hollywood so you know they're going to plow that story to death. Today's exposé is on you. Because, you know, you have a connection to both of them."

I close my eyes as if to block out the truth as she continues.

"You're working with Steele on the resort and back in the day, Reed photographed you. Right?"

"Right." I'm not sure how I manage to say the word, because I'm pretty sure I'm about to hyperventilate.

"They'll be even more on top of you when they realize you guys are dating, but I don't think the press has clued in to that yet."

"Gee. I can hardly wait." I try to keep my voice light, but I can't help but fear that if the press realizes I'm starchitect Jackson Steele's girlfriend, they'll start digging even deeper. And then they really might manage to unearth my secrets.

"Listen, don't worry," Jamie says. "I get that it's weird that old pictures have resurfaced, but it'll blow over. You're just today's flavor while they dig around for the real story."

"The real story." My words don't sound like my own.

"Yeah, you know. Why Jackson beat up Reed in the first place."

The numbness has spread to my entire body. Because the real story is that Jackson beat the shit out of Reed because of what he'd done to me. How he'd molested me when I was a teenager. But that's not a story I ever want to see go public.

"Everyone has a theory," Jamie continues. "Most folks are speculating that it's about the movie, though no one knows what the big deal is. I mean—"

She stops talking, as if suddenly realizing something. "Hey, you found him, right? Because you didn't call back, and so I just assumed that everything was okay."

"Yes." My word is short. Curt. "I have to go," I add, then hang up before she can respond.

I close my hands around the edge of the desk and sit very still, willing myself to be calm. To just be calm.

When I'm pretty sure that I won't throw up, I stand. I need to get out of here. I need to get home. I can feel the nightmares—the memories—pressing up against me, and I want Jackson. His arms. His strength.

But he's miles away in Marina del Rey, and I have to hold it together. Because I will not, will not, will not lose it in the office.

Slowly, carefully, I make my way toward the elevator. I pass the reception desk for Stark Real Estate Development and give Karen, the receptionist, a wave.

"Heading out?"

I only nod; I don't trust myself to speak.

I jam my finger hard against the elevator call button, then again and again when the doors do not immediately open. Finally, it arrives, and I step inside. It's crowded, and I clench my fists at my sides, willing it to go faster, because I can feel both panic and tears rising inside me, and I need to be clear by the time the explosion hits.

It stops three more times, and each time more people get on than get off. I am trapped behind a wall of bodies and I will not scream, I will not scream, and when the doors finally open to my floor in the parking garage, I push out past the three men who still stand in front of me, broad shoulders and tailored suits blocking me from freedom.

"Hey!" one calls, but they are not getting out here, and as the doors close on their startled faces, I bend over and press my hands to my knees and breathe and breathe and breathe.

Okay, I think. *You can do this. Car. Home. Jackson.*

Go.

I have an assigned spot near the elevator vestibule, and I hurry in that direction, thankful that despite my complete and total freak-out I didn't forget my tote. I shove my hand inside, find my car keys in the small interior pocket, and pound frantically on the button to unlock the door.

As soon as I'm inside, I yank the door closed and clutch tight to the steering wheel.

Good. I'm good. I just need to get home.

But my hand is shaking when I try to put the key in the ignition. I try again, but still I can't quite make it. I curse and toss my keys across the car, which is stupid, because now they have bounced off the window and fallen between the passenger seat and door. And I'm trapped here, and I'm panicking, because I just need to get home.

I just need Jackson.

I fumble in my tote until I find my phone, but there's no signal down here. And that's it. The last straw. The end of the line. The final curtain.

I can't fight anymore. I can't hold it in.

And just as the tears start to flow, I hear the squeal of tires and then the slam of a car door.

I don't lift my head. I no longer care who sees me. I just have to let go. I just have to cry. I just have to survive this, even though I'm not at all sure how to do that.

But then my door is jerked open, and I feel his hand on my arm.

And he's pulling me out, and his hands are on my face, and he's saying to me, "Open your eyes. Dammit, Sylvia, open your eyes."

Jackson.

His eyes are wild. His brow furrowed with concern.

"You came," I say stupidly. "You're here."

"Of course I am," he says, as he pulls me close and holds me tight. "You need me. Where else would I be?"

ten

"How did you know?" I am still in shock that he is here. Still so desperately grateful that his arms are tight around me.

"Cass," he says. "She saw the pictures, and when she called and you didn't answer, she called me."

"But you were all the way at the Marina."

"I was in Beverly Hills," he says. "I had errands."

I start to ask what errands, but it doesn't matter. I'm just rambling. My head trying to adjust to this new reality. A reality where photos taken of me by Reed are back in circulation. "Have you seen them?" I ask, and Jackson, thankfully, doesn't ask what I mean.

"Yes." He steers me back to my car, but opens the back door. "Come sit with me."

I slide into the backseat, and he gets in beside me.

"They're not bad. From what I've seen, they're ads that were used years ago, then pulled from circulation. Local retail mostly."

"I want to see."

I remember every ad that was published, and Jackson is right.

As far as images go, there is nothing risqué about them. But I know the backstory. To me, each and every one is vile. And just the idea that they are out in the world again is tearing me up inside.

But that's not the only reason I want to see the photos. I believe Jackson, of course, and yet I need to see for myself. Because I remember the *click click* of Reed's camera. I remember everything he had me wear. Every pose he had me strike. Every button on every piece of clothing.

I recall with unerring, horrible clarity where he had me put my hands. The way he told me to touch myself.

I know what other photos he took. Ones that were never intended for retail ads.

And the thought that those horrific images might now be circulating, too, makes me cold with terror.

Jackson hands me his phone, his web browser already open to the proper page. I glance at the photos, then sag with relief when I see that, yes, they really are just the ads.

When I pass the phone back to Jackson, I see that he is watching me intently. "There are others, aren't there?"

I nod. "I've never seen them," I admit. "But I know he took them."

He closes his eyes, his entire body tense. I understand why— he's fighting for control the same way that I am.

The knowledge soothes me, because I know that I'm not alone.

"I hate it," I admit. "Not knowing what's coming next. Even having these bland ads out there bothers me. I mean, I know that the public doesn't know the backstory, but I still hate it. I don't like the reminder of what happened to me. I don't like anything about it at all."

I kick off my shoes and put my feet up on the seat so that I can hug my knees. I'm wearing a skirt, but it's loose, and it drapes over my legs like a blanket.

I feel foolish, like a little girl needing comfort. Because nothing bad has actually happened today. Everything that is bothering me is in the past or a vague possibility of something that might happen in the future.

But I am bothered nonetheless.

Jackson's arm is already around me, but now he pulls me closer. "Tell me," he says. "Tell me what you're thinking."

I hesitate, but I comply. "The reality of the moment isn't terrible at all," I say. "But look at me. I'm a mess. I mean, how much of a wreck am I going to be if the worst really does happen?"

"It won't," he says.

I almost laugh. "You're a lot of things, Jackson Steele, and I know that you're a man who likes to be in control. But I'm pretty sure this one is out of your hands."

For a moment I think he's going to argue, but instead he just looks at me with eyes filled with pain. "I'm so sorry I brought this on you."

"You didn't. Reed did."

"I'll grant you that," Jackson says. "But I think the fact that I beat the crap out of him brought it to the press's more immediate attention."

He puts a hand on my knees and eases my legs down, turning me a bit as he does so that I'm sitting sideways in the backseat with my legs over his thighs. I'm not wearing hose, and as he strokes my calf, I close my eyes, enjoying the sensation of his fingers upon my skin.

"They're just poking into me, you know," he says. "They found this connection, and it's interesting because of the resort. Because we're working on the resort together, and because you work for Damien. That's where the photos came from." His hand stops moving, cupping my leg. "But the truth about what Reed did to you isn't going to come out. They won't even get close to it."

I nod.

"Everyone assumes I assaulted Reed because of the movie, and you just watch. That's where the next round of idiotic tabloid coverage is going to focus. My shit, not yours." He cups my chin so that he can look me in the eyes; his are warm and tender and concerned. "Okay?"

"Okay." I draw in a breath. He still hasn't told me why he doesn't want the movie made. All I know is that Reed is producing a feature film that is based on the events surrounding a residential property in Santa Fe that Jackson designed and built. It's an exceptional house that sealed his reputation as one of the world's most talented contemporary architects.

I'd read all about it at the time, both because I was following Jackson's career, despite the fact that we weren't together then, and because architecture is a passion of mine. And because I'd followed it, I knew what came after—a murder-suicide that tainted the spectacular property, forever burying the exquisite architecture under a layer of scandal.

Though I haven't read the script, I've been told that it focuses on the family, but that Jackson plays a role, too, supposedly as the reason the young woman took her own life and that of one of her sisters.

And though I know that Jackson was long gone by the time the murder took place, I also know that it's true he doesn't want the movie made. Not only has he told me so, but I also know that he punched out the screenwriter.

Reed, however, isn't the kind to back down. And although the real reason Jackson assaulted him was in retribution over what Reed did to me so many years ago, as far as the public knows, that assault was Jackson's way to, once again, express his displeasure about the in-development project.

One day, I want Jackson to tell me the full story behind the house and the secret he is so determined to protect. Right now, though, I'm interested only in my own secret.

"I know you'll do whatever you can," I tell him. "But that doesn't erase my fear that it's all going to come out. And I know that's unreasonable, but I can't shake it. I feel like I'm losing my grip, and I know that's ridiculous because it's those stupid ad photos, and no one even cares about those."

"You do." His voice is gentle, and his hand is stroking my leg again. "And it's not the pictures that are bothering you. It's what happened when he took them. It's how you felt—and now you're remembering it all over again. It's about what he stole from you."

"Control," I whisper. "And choice. He took them both away."

I'd been so young. And I'd wanted so badly to run. To hide. To shut off my emotions, my feelings. But he'd touched me, and he'd aroused me. He'd made me feel sexual pleasure along with horrible shame. And he'd made me come.

I'd hated him for that, but I think I hated myself more.

"Yes," Jackson says. "He took that from you. Ripped it away. Stole it. Baby, you need to steal it back."

I close my eyes. "I don't know how," I say, and I hear my voice tremble.

"Yes, you do." His words are firm. Commanding. "You steal it back. You take back control, and you give it to me. Not because I'm demanding, but because you're giving."

As he speaks, he continues to stroke my leg. Only now his touches are going higher, skimming under my skirt above my knee. Grazing along my inner thigh.

The movements are casual, almost innocent. As if he's not even aware that he is doing it. But I know that he is, of course. Jackson does nothing unintentionally. And right now, he is very slowly and very methodically teasing my senses. Getting me very wet, and very, very turned on.

"You think you hate not being in control?" he asks, without missing a beat. "Let me prove to you that you like it. Because when you've given it away, sweetheart, I know that you do." His fingers are only inches from my panties, and I am tense with longing.

"Say it." Though his voice is soft, his words are firm. Deliberate. And I know that he will not touch me until I concede. Or, rather, until I cede control to him. Until I submit to whatever sweet pleasure he intends for me.

"Yes." My word is a whisper, and even as I speak, I shiver in anticipation.

"Good girl," he says, and then he very gently strokes the edge of my panties between my thigh and my crotch before cruelly pulling his hand away.

I actually whimper.

"Oh, yes," he says. "You like it."

I feel my cheeks heat, but I can hardly deny the truth. Not when my body tingles with anticipation. Not when I know that right now I would do anything he asked of me if the prize was Jackson's touch.

"Take off your panties."

I lick my lips. "Why?"

His eyes flick to me. "Because I told you to," he says, and I immediately melt, my cunt going wet and my nipples straining against my bra. *Yes,* I think. *This is what I need.* I want to lose myself. To abandon control. To let him take me as far as I can go, and then safely bring me home again.

I meet his eyes and nod. And then, because I'm both aroused and inspired, I whisper, "Yes, sir," and am rewarded with his low, sensual growl of approval.

"Now," he says, and I don't hesitate. I reach under my skirt and wiggle out of my panties, then drop them on the floorboard.

"Good girl. Now take out my cock."

I glance down and see his erection straining against jeans that are so tight now it must be painful.

"Jackson . . ."

"Hesitation?" I hear the tease in his voice. "Sounds to me like the lady wants to be punished."

Frankly, the lady might enjoy that. But since the most keen punishment would be to not touch me at all, I shake my head.

"Then do as I said. Take out my cock, and then fuck me. Slide that sweet cunt onto my cock, and ride me."

His raw words are like a sensual tease, and my body clenches in response, so sensitive now that even the brush of clothing over my skin seems like an erotic exploration.

I want this—oh, dear god, I just want to do as he says, losing myself in the knowledge that surrendering to his demands will make the pleasure that much sweeter.

But even so, I continue to hesitate. "We're in the garage."

"And no one's around. And we're in the backseat of a car with tinted windows." He lifts a shoulder. "But you're still in control, baby. You want to stop, we stop. Anytime, no questions asked."

My mouth has gone suddenly dry, and I lick my lips.

"Do you trust me?" he asks, as if in response to my hesitation.

"You know I do."

I can see on his face that my answer pleases him. "Then trust me to take you far and keep you safe."

I swallow, but I nod. "I don't want to stop."

The corner of his mouth curves up. But all he says is "Then fuck me."

I maneuver my position in the backseat so that I am straddling his legs, most of my weight at his knees. I lean forward and stroke his erection through his jeans, then revel in a surge of feminine satisfaction when he tilts his head back and moans with pleasure.

I unfasten his jeans. They have a button fly, and I maneuver my fingers over each button slowly and methodically, enjoying this moment of power. He's wearing boxer briefs, and I reach into the fly and ease him free. And then, because I just can't resist, I slide off him and onto the floorboards, spreading his knees as I do.

I glance at his face just once and then bend forward and run my tongue along the length of his cock. He tastes earthy and male, and I'm tempted to suck him off, but I'm selfish, too, and my cunt is throbbing with need, practically begging to be filled.

I circle his cock with one hand as I tease the crown with my tongue. But I slip the other between my own legs, unsurprised to find that I'm so wet my thighs are creamy.

"Now," he demands. "I want to be inside you now."

Since I want exactly the same thing, I don't hesitate. I rise up and straddle him again, this time easing forward so that I am over his hips. I hold his cock steady, my eyes on his as I gyrate my hips, teasing him before lowering myself so hard and so fast that the tip of his cock hits my cervix and I feel the denim of his jeans rub against my ass.

One of his hands is on my lower back to balance me, but the other is between our bodies, and he's touching me, stroking and teasing my clit as I hold on to his shoulders and lift and lower myself, the sensation building and building, and all the more exciting because we're in a car and we're clothed and there's something that just feels so wicked about that.

He leans forward and closes his mouth over my breast, teasing me through the cotton of my shirt and the lace of my bra, and that extra sensation tips the scales. Suddenly, it's all too much, and everything that has been building inside of me begins to spiral, wild and out of control.

"Please," I beg as the climax rises up, ready to sweep me away. "Jackson, please come with me."

And then I'm reaching up, my hands pressed against the roof of the car, because the explosion is too strong, and I have to hold on to something to keep from shooting off into space as every atom in my body goes absolutely nuclear.

"Oh my god," I murmur when I finally collapse back onto him, my head bent down to tuck against his shoulder. "I'm completely shattered."

"Completely?"

There is humor in his question, and I gather enough strength to pull back so that I can face him. "That's just a figure of speech." I lean forward so that my lips brush his ear, and as I do I slip my hand down to where our bodies are still joined and tease the base of his penis with the edge of my finger. "I want more," I whisper. "Lots more."

"Then that works out exceptionally well. Because more is exactly what you're going to get."

He shifts me off him, then nods toward the front seat. "Get your things. We're taking my car. Except your panties," he adds. "Leave those here."

"Jackson!" My protest, however, is only for form, and I eagerly grab my tote. Then remember that I'd thrown my keys across the car, and they'd disappeared into some crevice or other. It takes a moment to find them, but as soon as I do, I lock my car and join him in the Porsche.

"I bought you something," he says as soon as I'm settled in the seat beside him.

"Really?" The thought of a present makes me glow a bit.

"I told you I had errands to run today. One of them was for you." He leans across me to open the glove box, then pulls out a small, pink gift bag. He dangles it from his index finger. "For you," he says, then grins. "Or, more accurately, for both of us."

My brows rise. "Oh, really?" Now I'm even more intrigued, and I peek into the bag, then pull out a white rectangular box that's about four inches long with the word CRAVE embossed on it. It weighs next to nothing, and when I shake it, it makes no sound.

"I'm completely clueless," I admit.

"There's no prize for the best guess," he says. "Go ahead. Open it."

Since I love presents, I eagerly comply. The lid lifts off the box, and inside I find a small velvet bag, like the kind that holds jewelry. Sure enough, there is a necklace in the bag, gold with a long, thin pendant that looks a bit like the pen that Joan, the character from *Mad Men,* wears around her neck.

"A pen?" I don't see a nib, though, and I look more closely, figuring there must be a cap that pulls off or unscrews.

"Not exactly," Jackson says at the same moment that I discover the tiny button on the side.

I press it, expecting a retractable ballpoint to appear. Instead, the pendant starts to vibrate.

Oh. My. God.

I whip my head around to look at him, not sure if I'm aghast or excited or just completely befuddled.

"You didn't—I mean, it's not—"

"Oh, yes," he says. "It is. High end and very classy. But, yes, a sex toy."

"Wow." I cycle through the speeds and vibes, and I have to admit it's pretty darn cool. And definitely one of the most unique gifts I've ever received. "Um, thank you."

He laughs. "Don't sound so unsure. I promise you'll enjoy it. In fact, I'm thinking we should take it for a test run very, very soon. But until then," he says, taking it from my hand and looping the long chain over my head, "I want you to wear it. In fact, sweetheart, I want you to wear it all day, every day. For at least one entire week."

"I—what?"

"You heard me."

"But—"

"No buts." He reaches over and follows the chain down to my cleavage, his fingers stroking my skin. "You can tuck it under your shirt," he says, "but you will wear it—except when you're not wearing it at my command. Are we clear?"

"Yes, sir," I say. Then I draw in a breath, a little bit nervous, a little bit more aroused. And very, very curious about where this week will lead.

eleven

Leather cuffs surround my wrists, my ankles. Each has a small metal loop through which Jackson has threaded nautical rope. My arms are spread wide across the mattress, lashed into place by the rope, which is knotted firmly somewhere near the ground, outside my range of vision.

My legs are spread wide, too, and bound similarly.

But for the small vibrator that I still wear on a chain, I am naked. And I am alone.

We're on Jackson's boat in Marina del Rey, the *Veronica,* a small yacht that serves as both home and office.

We'd come here straight from the parking garage, and Jackson had wordlessly led me to his bedroom below deck. He'd gestured for me to sit on the edge of the bed while he opened a small trunk that he keeps in the bottom of his closet. I've seen it before, though I have never gotten a look at the contents. Only what he's removed.

This time, he removed the cuffs and the rope.

I wanted to slide off the bed and peek over his shoulder. Even more, I wanted to ask with whom he has shared those toys. But I kept quiet; that is a conversation for another time.

And now I am alone, naked and wanting. "Anticipation," he'd said. "And imagination. And, yes, something with a little bit of a tease."

The tease is the vibrator, which he turned on before brushing a soft kiss over my lips and then pulling back. When he left, I had moaned in protest, but he had only looked back at me from the doorway, his heated gaze sweeping over me and affecting me as potently as a caress.

He'd put his finger to his lips for silence. And I, who have agreed to submit to his demands, pressed my lips together.

"Soon," he said, and then he was gone.

According to the clock mounted on the opposite wall, it has been thirteen minutes since he left.

Thirteen minutes I have been alone, aware of the gentle rocking of the boat. Aroused by the sensation of the vibrator buzzing between my breasts.

At first, the pulses had been localized. A slight tickle over my breastbone that seemed odd, but not uncomfortable. Intriguing, but not arousing.

But then I closed my eyes and let myself drift, and the sensation began to spread. To my breasts. Down to my belly. To the soft skin between thigh and torso where Cass has inked a red ribbon, a reminder of the mistakes I've made.

In fact, it is almost as if the vibrations are following my ink, following the path of my triumphs and tribulations, only to culminate now between my thighs as I think of where all those trials have led. *To Jackson.*

Deep, rhythmic vibrations fill me, along with soft, gentle teases that skitter along the surface of my skin like an electric current connecting each tiny hair along my body.

The pendant hasn't moved at all, and yet I feel the sensations racing through me. And they are growing. Building.

Before he left me, Jackson told me that I'm not allowed to come, and I had scoffed when he'd said so. Come? How could I possibly when I couldn't move? Couldn't touch myself? When his erotic toy was between my breasts and not between my legs.

How wrong I'd been.

Now, as my body tightens and my arousal grows and my sex feels heavy with need, I can't help but fear that I will break his rule and explode. Right here, right now, I'll shoot up into the heavens with nothing but my imagination and these wild, trembling sensations to bolster me.

Frustrated, I writhe on the bed, but I can only manage the smallest of motions with my hips, and though I want to stroke myself, my hands are a long way from my clit, which is so damn sensitive that even the still air in this small room is tantalizing.

I glance at the clock. Fourteen minutes now. Just one measly minute has passed since I last glanced that way, and I can't help but wonder when Jackson will return—and how I will survive until he does.

I close my eyes and try to focus on something other than my current state of arousal. But that's really not possible. I'm nothing but sensation now, and even when I try to think about something other than the way I am feeling, all I can do is imagine him. Beside me. Touching me. Teasing me.

A tremor cuts through me, and I bite my lip. Hard. So much for trying to keep my thoughts under control. Right now, I am incapable of thinking about anything but him.

And then—as if the universe has decided that I've suffered enough—he is there. He stands in the doorway, his hands thrust casually into his pockets. And even from this distance, I can see that he is fully erect, his cock straining to burst out of the tight denim of his jeans.

I think I whimper. Because oh, dear god, I want him inside me.

"This is a truly spectacular sight."

"Jackson, please."

His brows lift, and I can tell that he is enjoying this game. This torment. "Please what?"

"You know."

"Say it."

"I want you inside me."

"Not like that. Tell me." He takes a step toward me. "Tell me exactly what you want. Because right now, what I want is to pleasure you. I want to see your skin ripple under my touch. I want to hear your breath stutter as you try to keep control. I want to see your cunt glisten as I make you more and more wet. And I want to watch your breasts pucker and tighten, your nipples as hard as nails and so very ready for my touch."

Oh my.

"But I need you to tell me, baby. How should I touch you to get you there? Tell me what you want. Tell me what turns you on."

My cheeks burn, which is ridiculous considering how open I am to him at this moment. But I can't help it.

"Tell me," he says, stepping closer. "Or have none of it."

My eyes cut to him. "Cruel, Mr. Steele?"

"I can be. Or I can be very, very kind." As he speaks, he moves his fingertip over my body. Literally over it, by about two inches. So that while I can imagine his touch, I do not get to experience it. Even so, it seems to me like he is leaving a trail of heat in his wake.

All that does, though, is drive home how much I will be missing if he doesn't touch me for real. And though I am not sure what I intend to say, I start talking. "I—I want your hands on my breasts. Tight on my nipples. And then gentle touches, light and teasing, all the way down my body. And—"

I stop myself, because he is smiling, and the expression is both aroused and victorious.

"This is as much for you as for me, isn't it?"

His brows lift. "I certainly hope so."

"I mean—" I cut myself off. "I mean that everything that happened today. With me. With me freaking out and you, well, having me surrender control and—" I draw a breath. "It's just that you hate it, too, don't you?"

"Hate it? Hate what?"

"Not this," I say quickly. "Not us. The situation. The not knowing. And the fear that they might find out that your run-in with Reed wasn't about the movie at all, but about me. And the fear that you can't protect me."

His posture has stiffened as I've spoken. And now he says only one word. He says, "Yes."

I nod, because that is what I expected he would say. So I continue. "You were right about me, you know. I do like to submit so long as I've willingly relinquished control."

"I know," he says. "I can tell."

Since I'm certain that he can, I don't argue.

"But what about you? I want to be there for you when you need to keep control. Like the other night, with the fighting. But what about now? Is it as satisfying for you to take control when I'm already giving it?"

He looks at me for a long moment, his eyes traveling up and down my body. "Sweetheart, nothing could be more satisfying than you giving yourself to me."

It's the perfect answer, even better because I can see the truth in his eyes.

After a moment, though, his smile turns wicked. "It occurs to me, though, that you've changed the subject. I believe you were telling me how you want me to touch you."

"Oh. Right."

"I suggest you continue."

"Or?" I ask, feeling playful.

He crosses his arms and looks stern.

"Or what?" I press. "Or you'll spank me?"

"Careful, Ms. Brooks. You're walking a line."

"Am I? After all, I already told you I wanted more. In fact, I believe that more is just what you promised me."

"Definitely naughty," he says, making my smile grow even wider.

"You want details, Jackson? You sure you want to know what I really want?"

"Very much."

I meet his eyes. "All right. I want it rough." It's not until I say the words that I realize how very true they are. "I want it wild. I want you to fuck me hard. And I want to forget everything that's going on out there. I want to be lost in you, Jackson. Lost in us."

He remains perfectly still, only the tightening of his jaw revealing that my words have affected him.

"Those are dangerous things for a woman to say when she's all tied up."

"Maybe I like danger."

I watch as the storm builds in his eyes. "Do you?"

Gently, he presses a fingertip to my lips. Then he starts to trail it lightly down my chin, my neck. "Oh, baby. What you do to me. I want to give you everything you want. See pleasure bloom in your eyes." The finger dips lower, and he takes one nipple between two fingers, then rolls it, tightening his grip as he does.

I bite my lower lip as the pressure increases, tighter and tighter, bringing more and more pleasure-like pain to the surface, until I feel it not just in my breast, but in my clit as well.

"I want to take you to the edge and bring you back in my arms. And then I want to hold you close, calm you down, and take you right back out again."

He releases my nipple, and I gasp, unprepared for the amazing sensation that accompanies the return of blood flow.

"Is that a promise?" I have to concentrate to force out my whispered question.

"Sweetheart, it's a bond."

He makes a crooking motion with his finger and tells me to lift my head. I do, and he removes the vibrator from around my neck.

"Jackson . . ."

I'm not sure why I've said his name. A warning not to go too far? A plea that he take me as far as I can go, and then some?

It doesn't matter. Because Jackson will do what he wants. And in doing it, I know that he will do what I need.

He presses the tiny button to rotate through the settings. And though the vibrator is very small and very quiet, I hear the whisper-soft hum of the pulses, then the increase in frequency as he sets it at maximum.

He slants a look at my face, and then he very slowly trails the tip of the pendant over the swell of my breast. The sensation is delicious, and I close my eyes, giving myself permission to simply float as he ministers to me.

The touch cuts through me, rousing me, but it is also relaxing, and I drift a bit, letting myself simply feel.

And then he ramps it up.

He moves the pendant in a spiral, as if drawing a series of decreasing circles on my breast. Getting closer and closer to my nipple, until finally the pendant edges up against my now-tight areola.

I am no longer drifting. Now I am on the verge of begging. Because the sensation has started to grow, and I am not sure that I can keep it all inside, and I am moving back and forth as much as I can with my arms and legs bound, as if by writhing and swaying I can somehow regain control over the riot of sensations inside me.

Of course I cannot. I have ceded that control, after all. I am in Jackson's hands, and he is relentless, and I am wondering now about the wisdom of telling him to take me far. To take me hard.

Because so far, I am barely managing even this relatively mild touch. How will I survive a full-blown onslaught of sensuality?

He lifts the pendant now and then touches the tip ever so softly to my nipple, which is already so sensitive and tight that even this butterfly-kiss contact rockets to my cunt and—oh, dear god—I feel the tremors of a building orgasm rise through me, set off by nothing more than Jackson's teasing of my breasts.

"Oh, yes," he says, then very gently strokes his fingers over my sex. "I think someone likes this."

I say nothing. But I do whimper a bit.

I hear him chuckle, and then he moves on, teasing my other breast similarly before easing the vibrator down my belly. I arch up, wanting both to escape the relentless sensation and to silently beg for it to continue.

When he reaches my pubis, he pauses, then lifts his head to look at me. It's a challenge, I think, and I stay silent. Neither protesting nor begging, despite wanting to do both.

His small, smug grin suggests he knows exactly what I am thinking. My pubic hair is waxed into a thin landing strip, and he teases me by tracing the edge before finally trailing the tip of the vibrator around my clit. Close, but not on the most sensitive part.

I writhe, testing my bonds, needing to escape or control this growing, wild sensation. But I am bound and there is no escape. There is only submission. And excitement. And pleasure so keen it is disguised as pain.

"Please." It is the only word that means anything. "Please."

But he doesn't listen. He torments me for another minute, an hour, a year. Until finally—*finally*—he brushes the tip of the vibrator over the sensitive tip of my clit and I explode as a knife edge of pleasure slices through me, cutting me to ribbons and then sending those shards up into the sky, higher and higher until I finally, blissfully, fall back to earth, my body still tingling. Still hyperaware.

"Oh, god, oh, Jackson."

I am still trapped, and I struggle against the bonds, wanting to touch him, but he is having none of that.

He strips quickly, and he's so hard that I think his erection must be painful. "Hard, you said? You want to be fucked hard?"

"Yes." I buck my hips. "God yes, please."

He doesn't disappoint. He slams into me, and I am so wet and aroused that he enters me fully in one deep, amazing thrust. Over and over, his body pounds into mine, and the friction on my still sensitive clit sends me spiraling up over and over—one, two, twelve, a million—I have no idea how many times I come, but I seem to be nothing more than an explosion of light and sparks. No longer myself, but simply pure pleasure.

And when I finally do drift back to earth—when he unties me and pulls me close—I realize that he did exactly what he promised. He took me somewhere I have never been. And in doing it, gave me the most profound sexual experience of my life.

"That was wonderful," I say, though the word sounds weak. "Profound. Life-changing. A religious experience."

He laughs. "That is very good to know." The vibrator necklace is on the mattress beside us and now he picks it up and puts it back over my head. "And I have to say, I very much like you wearing this."

I raise a brow as I trail my finger over the delicate chain and down to the pendant. "Like a slave collar."

His eyes widen just a bit. "And what would you know about that?"

"I read. I watch movies. I surf the internet."

"Do you?"

"And what do *you* know?" I counter, thinking about his trunk, the contents of which I still haven't inspected. But leather cuffs are rather telling, as far as I'm concerned. And, yes, I am intrigued.

"I think there are some very interesting things that can be adopted from the BDSM repertoire," he says as his finger strokes my collarbone, then my breasts. He flicks his thumb over my nipple, and I can almost see him thinking about the possibilities.

After a moment, he looks up at me again. "As for the collar, that's a symbol of ownership. Do I need to mark you as mine?"

I lean forward to kiss him. "You already have."

His expression hardens. "Your tattoo. On your back."

I cringe and shake my head. "No. God, no." My words are vehement, and he relaxes. "I was lost when I had Cass do that tat. It was a way to keep you without keeping you. And that wouldn't satisfy me now. Not even close.

"No," I continue, taking his hand and pressing it to my chest. "You've marked me here. You've marked my heart, Jackson. And we both know that I belong to you."

He is not beside me when I wake in the middle of the night, and though I try to drift back to sleep, I can't seem to manage it without Jackson beside me.

I find his T-shirt on the floor and put it on, wanting the scent of him more than I want the warmth of a robe. Of course, as I climb topside, I begin to regret that. California is mild, but in October by the ocean, there is a definite chill.

Fortunately, he is not outside, so I am not too cold when I find him in his office, which is made from the converted entertainment and living area on this exceptional floating home.

He is sitting at his desk, facing the blackness of the ocean and a few sparkling lights from Catalina Island in the distance. He is flipping through a folder, and from where I stand at the top of the stairs, I can see that the documents inside are photographs and sketches.

"Fucking ridiculous," he mutters, and I take a step toward him, curious.

"Jackson?"

He looks up, and I'm grateful that he looks happy to see me and not irritated that I'm intruding. "Hey. Couldn't sleep?"

"Not without you beside me."

He holds out his hand for me, his smile tender. "Then I apologize for leaving. Come here."

I do, and he slides his arm around my waist as I look down at the documents he's studying. They are his sketches. And I can see that his reaction is identical to mine—no matter who follows him, the resort will suffer for it.

"It's not going to be as good," he says, though I'm not sure if he's talking to himself, to me, or to the universe at large.

I sigh. "No, it's not." I lick my lips, and then voice the thing that has been troubling me. "I'm sorry."

"We've had this discussion. Stark is the asshole who fired me. You were just the messenger."

"Not for that. For staying."

"What?" He looks genuinely baffled.

"I could have walked out, too. I probably should have."

"No." He shakes his head vehemently. "Good god, Sylvia, did you think that I would want you to?"

"I don't know," I say honestly. "Didn't you?"

"This is your project. Your concept. Your baby. Of course I don't want you to toss it away for me. I'm the best—I'm not going to argue that point—but no matter who you end up with, it will still be an excellent resort, and you are the reason why." He pulls me close and kisses my forehead. "I would never ask you to walk away from something you love, and you shouldn't ever do that. Not without a reason that makes sense. And misplaced loyalty isn't a good reason."

"My loyalty isn't misplaced," I say.

"No, you're right. But the urge to quit because of me is."

I think about it. "Maybe," I say. I'm honestly not sure. But I do know that I am relieved that he isn't angry that I stayed. And, more than that, that he doesn't even want me to go.

"So who will you pick to fill my very large shoes?"

"Damien wants Glau back on the project. Did I tell you he was less than enthusiastic about Tibet?"

"Good god."

"I know." I drag my fingers through my hair. "Even if you're gone—which sucks—but even if you are, surely I can find someone better than him. Someone with more enthusiasm, at least. I mean, Glau actually walked off. I don't want him back."

"Say so. It's your project, after all."

I consider that. And he's right. "It is my project," I say firmly. "And if Damien can veto you, then I can veto Glau."

Jackson grins at me. "That's my girl. Can you hold on to that attitude in the face of my brother?"

I make a face. "I guess we'll see."

"Well, good for you." He puts his hand over mine. "Apparently I'm just going to sit back and say fuck it." He pushes away from the table and rises from his stool. "Dammit, that's just not me. I don't take shit lying down. I never have."

"Then why now?"

"Because apparently I'm one of Pavlov's fucking dogs."

I have no idea what he's talking about and say so.

"All my life, moving to the whim of Damien. He said jump, and my family asked how high." He makes a derisive noise in his throat. "Bastard has his finger on the control button and he is constantly pressing."

"So take it back. Take control back from him. You're good at that."

He's been facing opposite me, but now he turns, and I can see that he's considering something. "You're right," he says as his expression clears and a wide grin spreads across his face. "I absolutely am."

He pulls me to a kiss. "Come on. It's late, and you have work tomorrow."

"I do," I say. I gently trace my finger over his fading bruises. He's shirtless, wearing only sweatpants that are loosely tied at his waist. "How are they?"

"Better."

I press my palm against the largest one and feel his muscles quiver under my touch. I bite back a satisfied smile, delighted to see such tangible evidence that he desires me as much as I do him. "I hope so. They still look painful."

"Better now with you," he amends.

I slowly slide down to my knees, my fingers plucking at the drawstring of his sweats as I descend.

"Something on your mind, Ms. Brooks?" He sounds both amused and aroused. And his erection—now growing beneath the thin material—is certainly proof of the latter.

"I believe we discussed playing doctor?"

"Did we?"

"Mmm-hmm." I tug loose the drawstring, and then let the sweats fall off him, though I do have to rearrange the material a bit to free his growing erection.

His sweats pool around his ankles, and as they do I lean forward and lick the tip of his cock.

"Oh, dear god," he says, and twines his fingers in my hair. "What the hell are you doing?"

I laugh. "Sweetheart, if you don't know—" And then, because I'm inspired, I grin up at him. "I'm taking your temperature," I say, and then take him into my mouth as deep as I can.

He tastes wonderful. So male. So *Jackson*.

And as I stroke and lick and tease, his cock tightens, and he groans in a way that makes me go completely wet. And though I don't want to stop—though I am loving this jolt of feminine power—right at this moment, I desperately want him inside me.

As if he can read my mind, he slowly pulls back, freeing his cock and then easing me up.

"What's wrong?"

"Not a thing," he says as he scoops me up and cradles me next to his bare chest. "Except that I think I might just die if I can't lay you out on the bed and have my way with you right now."

"Oh." A wonderfully sensual tremor rolls through me. "Well, in that case, who am I to stop a man with a plan?"

twelve

"I have to be honest, Damien. I'm not thrilled with any of them. But I'm definitely vetoing Glau."

"Are you?" He lifts a single brow, obviously amused.

We're in the sitting area of his office, with me on the small sofa and Damien in a chair across a low coffee table from me. I've put together files of every possible architect for the Cortez project, and I'm holding them in my lap, ready to run through each candidate's pros and cons. Now I lean forward and put the stack on the table, then sit back and cross my legs, hoping I look more confident and in control than I feel.

"Yes, Mr. Stark," I say firmly. "I am."

"Mr. Stark," he repeats. He stands up and moves to the bar across the room. "I was wondering how pissed off you were. I guess now I know."

I don't try to deny it. I routinely call him Mr. Stark when I'm working his desk or when we're with other people. But I've gotten so close to Nikki that formality feels awkward when I'm not in the role of his assistant. So yes, the fact that I called him Mr. Stark just now is my passive-aggressive way of telling him that as far as I'm concerned he's making a huge mistake by cutting Jackson from the project.

He pours himself a shot of scotch, neat. "Care for one?"

I glance at my watch. It's a quarter to five, and I figure that's good enough. "Hell, yes."

He chuckles, then returns with a glass for each of us. "I take it we're not drinking to Martin Glau?"

"I mean it, Damien. I've spent days staring at his concept sketches and they're just not up to snuff. You vetoed my choice without asking for my input despite the fact that I'm the project manager—"

"I just thought what with me owning the company and all . . ."

"No," I say, the words spilling out before I can censor myself. "That's not what you were thinking and we both know it. *Shit.*" I lift the glass and take a long drink. "Sorry. Apparently I'm in the mood today to commit career suicide. All I'm saying is that you don't want Jackson and I don't want Glau. So there you go."

I take another sip of the drink and try to look as calm and composed as possible despite the fact that inside my head I am running a steady stream of *fuck fuck fuck fuck fuck.*

For a moment, Damien says nothing, and I wonder who in town might be hiring and whether or not Aiden will write me a good letter of recommendation. Over the years I've learned to read Damien pretty well. Right now, I don't have a clue what he's thinking.

And that's really not a good sign.

"Listen, I'm sorry. This whole thing is a sore spot and I know that, and I shouldn't have said anything." I stand and start to gather the files. "I'll ask Rachel to squeeze me onto your calendar tomorrow. Or I can come by the house over the weekend. I just think that now's not the right time and—"

"Sit."

I hesitate, then comply. But I keep the files in my lap in case a quick escape is called for.

"So if Glau is out, who does that leave us with?"

I tilt my head a bit. "Really?"

"You say he's not up to snuff, then I believe you. So who should we consider?"

I'm tempted to tell him that no one even comes close to Jackson, but I don't want to upset this shaky detente. "Phillip Traynor's work is quite interesting." I open the top folder and pull out a photograph of a hotel in Prague that put Traynor on the map three years ago.

I've loved and studied architecture my whole life, and next to Jackson, I think Traynor is one of the most talented architects working today. Even so, as far as I'm concerned, he's sloppy seconds.

Still, I'm in cooperation-mode, and so I pass the picture and the folder to Damien, who studies my notes as I continue speaking. "He's done a number of hotels, so he understands the travel and entertainment aspects. But he's never worked on an all-out resort, so I think the project would intrigue him."

"Looks promising. What's the downside?"

"He has a reputation for being difficult," I admit. "But despite that he's very in demand. Which raises the second mark against him—his schedule is incredibly tight. I talked to his people, and he's finishing up a project right now, but he was planning on taking three months off. If we bring him in, he's going to up his fee to cover the inconvenience of canceling his R&R."

Damien nods, taking it all in. "Who else?"

I open the next folder. "Allison Monro."

"She did the Petri Museum in Seattle. I've met her."

"She's also done some really interesting residential work that I think might translate to the island bungalows." I'm passing a photograph of one of Monro's houses to Damien when his intercom buzzes.

"I know you said no interruptions," Rachel says, "but Mr. Steele is here. And since you're already meeting with Ms. Brooks, I thought I should let you know that he'd like a moment of your time."

I realize that I have frozen in place, my arm outstretched, my body tense. I've been that way since Rachel said his name.

Damien looks at me, then takes the photograph, and the movement seems to break the spell. I sit back, hoping desperately that Damien cannot tell how violently my heart now beats against my rib cage.

"All right," Damien says as he puts the Monro photograph on the coffee table, right on top of the Phillip Traynor file. "Send him in."

A moment passes, then another. Then the door opens and Jackson strides in.

That morning, he'd told me that he intended to spend the day on his boat, working out of his office there on some minor projects that his New York staff is handling. So when Rachel announced him, I expected to see him in casual attire. Not swim trunks, but nothing more tailored than nice jeans and a starched button-down. Probably even with canvas shoes and windswept hair.

But that is not the man who enters.

Jackson strides into Damien's office as if he owns it, and he's certainly dressed for the role. He wears a charcoal gray Armani suit with a crisp white shirt and an arctic blue tie that almost perfectly matches the color of his eyes. It's the uniform of a corporate warrior, and Jackson has come to do battle.

He moves toward us without hesitating, apparently unperturbed that Damien has not risen in greeting. He stops at the edge of the oriental rug that defines this area of Damien's huge office, then inclines his head. "Stark," he says, then turns to me without waiting for a reply. He takes two steps toward me, then takes my hand and very gently kisses my fingertips. "Sylvia. I'm very glad you're here."

His eyes linger on mine for a moment, but though I search his face for a hint of what is to come, I see nothing. He is cool and confident and holding his cards very, very close to the vest.

Damien indicates an empty chair. "Please. Have a seat."

"I prefer to stand."

"Suit yourself." He leans back in his own chair, his control just as intact, his expression just as unreadable. And in that moment, it finally strikes me that, yes, these two men really are brothers. "What can I do for you, Steele?"

"You can let me back on the resort."

Damien steeples his fingers beneath his chin. "And why would I do that?"

"Because you made a mistake when you fired me."

"Did I? Or are you just hoping to coast on a misplaced belief that I'm going to be swayed by familial loyalty?"

"Not hardly," Jackson says, taking a step forward. "As far as my work is concerned, family doesn't mean shit. I'm here because I'm the best. You came to me because I'm the best. You wanted me on this project because of my vision and my talent, and yet you tossed me off for reasons that have nothing to do with my work. Honestly, Stark. You surprise me."

"And yet you were the one who raised the issue of family. And not when you were brought on board—when it would have made rational sense to mention it. No, you waited, timing the revelation to suit your own purpose."

"No purpose," Jackson says. "No agenda. I told Sylvia because I didn't want that secret between the two of us, but I've told nobody else, and I don't intend to. And I told you because I couldn't in good conscience expect her to keep that large a secret from the man who employs her. *That* was my purpose, Stark. Not because I want to start exchanging Christmas cards, and certainly not because I want any special consideration on this project or any other. My work stands on its own, or it doesn't stand at all."

For a moment Damien says nothing, but I think it is respect that

I see on his face. Then he nods—just one simple incline of his head. "Go on."

"This is a unique, innovative project. I'll admit I didn't want to be a part of it at first, but I'm invested now. I lost out on the deal in Atlanta because of you, Stark. I'm not losing Cortez, too. Not without a fight."

I press my lips tight together. I know that Jackson blames Damien for the Brighton Consortium deal in Atlanta falling apart because Damien swept in and bought up key parcels of land. But Damien has told me that Jackson doesn't have all the information, and that the deal was badly run. According to Damien, if he hadn't stepped in, then Jackson and everyone else involved, including my old boss Reggie Gale, would have found themselves embroiled in a huge mess.

I'm not entirely sure what "a huge mess" means, but my fear is that there was some sort of criminal real estate scheme going on, and I intend to ask Reggie the next time we meet for lunch. But I've told none of this to Jackson. I didn't see the point until I knew what to tell him. Now, of course, I'm wishing I'd said something. And, honestly, I expect Damien to clear the air.

Damien, however, says nothing, and during his silence, Jackson glances at me. His gaze lingers for less than a second, and yet even in that brief span of time I see the heat on his face. The need in his eyes.

"I walked away once before from something that was important to me." He doesn't look at me again, and yet I know without the slightest doubt that he is talking about me. "That was a mistake. I should have stayed. I should have fought." He cocks his head. "I've learned my lesson, Stark. You want me gone, I'll go. But I'm not leaving until I've done my damnedest to convince you to let me stay."

I realize I am holding my breath, and I try to fill my lungs without gasping. So far I've managed to fade into the seat cushion, but now Damien turns to face me, his expression entirely unreadable. I expect him to ask me to leave. Instead, he levers himself out of his chair and crosses to his window. He stands there for a moment, looking out at the world like a monarch surveying his kingdom.

I want to look at Jackson, but I also don't want to move. Right now, I am cautiously optimistic, and I'm afraid that even breathing wrong will shift the balance. It's not a risk I'm willing to take. And so I stay as I am, looking forward, several files still clutched in my lap.

After what feels like hours but is in fact less than a minute, Damien returns. He takes the Traynor and Monro materials from the coffee table, then hands them to Jackson. "We've identified possible replacements. All exceptional architects. All without baggage."

"No one is without baggage," Jackson says, and I am relieved to see the corner of Damien's mouth twitch just slightly.

"I'll concede that point to you, Steele," Damien says. "But I still want an answer. Why you and not them?"

"I'm better." Jackson is looking directly at Damien, and his gaze never wavers.

"You're very confident."

"I am," Jackson agrees. "I'm also very capable."

Once again, Damien looks at me. "Ms. Brooks seems to think you're the choice for the job, too."

"She's a very smart woman."

"Yes," Damien agrees. "She is."

He goes to the bar, and returns with a single glass of scotch. He hands it to Jackson, then takes his own from the coffee table and raises it in a toast. "All right, Steele," he says. "You're in. Don't make me regret it."

Damien keeps me in his office after Jackson departs. We discuss resort management and the need to start recruiting and training top-level staff. We bounce ideas about advertising and promotion. We talk about recreation and whether we should keep dive instructors and a tennis pro on the full-time staff.

All stuff that has to be addressed, of course, but none of it is time sensitive, and I honestly can't decide if he's keeping me in his office out of spite or in order to maintain a sense of normalcy.

Or, possibly, he simply wants to clear stuff off his to-do list.

"All right," he says after the longest forty-five minutes of my life. "I guess that's it for the day. Who's on my desk tomorrow?"

"Rachel." I stand and gather my things. "But I'll be covering it on Monday."

"Good." He meets my eyes. "She's doing a fine job, Syl, but she's not you. Then again, I suppose I'll have to get used to that. I imagine I'll be losing you to twenty-seven soon enough."

"Will you?" I can't keep the spark of interest out of my voice.

He leans casually against his desk. "I'll be honest. I wouldn't have given you the project manager position if I didn't believe that you could handle it. But handling and excelling aren't the same thing."

"Oh." I start to say thank you, but hold my tongue. Just to make certain I know where he's going with this.

"If you want to excel at something, you can't let anything or anyone stand in your way." He nods toward the files I now hold in my hands. "You stood up for what you wanted today. That showed balls."

"With all due respect, if you'd wanted to block me, there's not a lot I could have done about it." I glance at him and smile wryly. "What with you owning the company and all."

"Touché, Ms. Brooks. I'll rephrase. You endeavored not to let anyone stand in your way."

I cock my head, thinking about that. "Is that why you let Jackson back on? Because he did the same thing?"

"That's part of it." The admission surprises me.

"And the rest?"

"Because he's the best damn architect working." He takes one more sip of his scotch. "I guess talent runs in the family," he adds, and I bark out a laugh.

I swallow the sound soon enough. "Are you going to go public? You having a half-brother, I mean?"

He says nothing for a moment, and I wish I could take back the question. Then he sighs and swallows the whiskey that's left in the glass. "Honestly? I don't see that I have a choice. But I'd appreciate you asking Jackson to keep it quiet for the time being. I'd like to have some input from the PR team. For that matter, I'd like to get Evelyn's advice."

That makes sense. Evelyn Dodge, Damien's friend and former agent, has been around Hollywood forever. And nobody knows how to spin a story better than Evelyn.

"Anything else you need me for?" I ask.

"No. I think that's all for now."

"Okay. Then I'll see you tomorrow." I head toward the door.

"Actually, there is one more thing."

I pause and look back over my shoulder.

"You should give Nikki a call. I know she's been wanting to re-schedule your photography date. Maybe you two could find a time for that lesson with Wyatt."

I nod. "Sounds good." And then, because I understand that this isn't about business anymore, but about friendship, I add, "Thanks."

As soon as the door shuts behind me, Rachel squeals and runs around the desk. "Jackson told me. That's so great."

"I know," I say, succumbing to her hug. "Speaking of the men in our lives, what's going on with you and Trent?"

She presses her lips together, then hurries back behind the desk to catch a call. "A lady never kisses and tells," she quips, then hits the button on her headset. "Mr. Stark's office," she says as she winks at me.

I laugh, but I don't stay. I know Rachel won't hold it against me; I want to go see Jackson.

Since I have energy to burn, I take the stairs, stopping at my cubicle on twenty-seven to grab up my notes. Then I hurry down the last flight, my heels clattering on the concrete stairs, and slam, breathless, through the stairwell door.

I lean against the wall as I catch my breath. The stairs exit only a few yards from Jackson's office area, and I have an excellent view of him through the glass walls. He's sitting on a stool in front of the very same drafting table on which he'd fucked me so thoroughly. And though his head is bent, I can see enough of his face to catch his expression and it is both intent and rapturous.

He's in his element, and that simple realization makes me so giddy that I have half a mind to race back upstairs and wrap Damien in a hug.

I manage to restrain myself. Instead, I take a single step toward Jackson.

Despite his intense concentration, the moment I move, he inclines his head, as if sensing my presence. He doesn't look up, though, and so I continue on.

"I'm back," he says as I reach his doorway, still without looking in my direction.

My smile blooms wide. "Yes, you are."

He pushes away from the desk, the stool rolling easily on the concrete floor. As he does, I rush to him, practically flying into his open arms. I drop my notes on his desk then straddle him, and he spins us in the chair. When it stops, my back is pressed against the table, and I'm more than a little light-headed. But whether that's from dizziness or from being in Jackson's arms, I don't know.

"You're back." My whisper echoes his earlier words, and I press my hand gently to his crotch. "And I know just what you want to do now."

His brow lifts. "Is that so?"

"Mm-hmm." I bend forward so that my lips brush his ear as I murmur, very low and very seductively, "You want to work."

My other hand is on his back for balance, and the vibrations from his laughter roll through me. "Sweetheart, you do know how to turn a man on."

"You don't know the half of it. Did you see the folder I tossed on your desk?" I lean back so that I can see him, then thrust out my tits and slowly bite my lower lip in my best imitation of an X-rated movie star. "Building notes and specs," I say huskily. "It's like porn for architects."

His expression doesn't change, but I see the mirth in his eyes.

I reach back and grab the folder, then wave it slowly through the air. "Come on, baby. You know you want it."

"Oh, I want it all right." With one quick gesture, he wraps his arm around my waist and pulls me close, leaving me gasping. "But forget the porn," he says. "What I want is you. This project. This moment. And thank god I've got everything I want right here in front of me."

My heart flutters in my chest. "Me, too," I say as he pulls me down for a long, slow kiss. And though I mean the words with all my heart, I can't help but fear what tomorrow might bring.

That's okay, though. Because he's right; this moment is perfect.

And right now, that is enough.

thirteen

I'm kicked back in Jackson's Porsche, eyes closed, jamming to the latest release from Dominion Gate, a Finnish heavy metal band that Jackson says he wants to hear live when they tour in a couple of weeks. They're not bad, especially when they're turned up so loud that you're forced to move with the music because it's reached inside your body and grabbed hold of all your major organs.

When my phone rings, I don't actually hear it—because how could I?—and it's a wonder I even feel it vibrate, considering the way the car is shaking from the bass. But I'd taken it out to check the wiki on the band, and I've been holding it in my lap, and when my palm vibrates more than the rest of me, I realize that I've got a call.

I glance at the phone, see that it's Cass, and gesture for Jackson to dial back the music.

He does, but he punctuates the action with a grin and a mouthed *wimp.*

I roll my eyes and hit the speaker.

"Fucking awesome," she says, skipping preliminaries like "hello" or "how's it going?"

"I'll assume that means you got my message?" I'd texted her before we left the office about Jackson's glorious reinstatement.

"Not only did I get it, I have performed a ritual sacrifice to the gods."

"How very energetic of you."

"Naturally, the gods have showered their wisdom upon us and revealed their grand celebratory plan to me."

"Um."

I catch Jackson's eye. I can't tell if he's amused or if he fears that my best friend is a crazy person. "I'm not entirely sure if that's a good thing or a bad thing," I admit.

I can practically hear her rolling her eyes. "Where are you?"

I've been so overwhelmed by the decibel level inside the car that I hadn't been paying attention to our surroundings. I glance outside. "We're on the 10. Not to the 405 yet. Why?"

"Because we're going to celebrate. Or haven't you been listening?"

I laugh. "We're going home. Tomorrow's a full work day. Plus, I'm starving."

"That is such bullshit," she says. "You can have sex anytime. Westerfield's in thirty. No excuses."

Now I'm having no trouble reading Jackson. Definitely amused. But as for whether he wants to go get sweaty on a dance floor, I can't say. And since he's keeping his eyes on the road, he's not really helping.

"Cass. Seriously, I don't know."

"Bullshit. You're coming. There's a limited window of opportunity for celebrating something like this. I mean, unless Damien kicks him off again, how many times do we get to have a reinstatement party?"

"She has a point," Jackson says.

"See?" Cass says. "Am I on speaker?"

"No. You're just loud."

"Double bullshit. At any rate, Zee even said she was coming."

"Really?" Despite having met Cass at a party, Zee never seems to want to go out. So I know this is kind of huge.

"Really," Cass confirms. "So you have to come. It's like a rule or something."

I glance at Jackson, who lifts a shoulder. "If it's a rule . . ."

I shake my head, because I can't argue with both of them. "Can we at least run home and change?"

"Are you wearing clothes?"

"Shockingly, I did go to work dressed today."

"Then no. What you're wearing will do."

"Cassidy!"

"I'm serious! We haven't gone out dancing together in forever, and I am not running the risk that you'll back out. Which is why I'm hanging up now, and warning you not to be late. I don't want to have to stand in line, and you know they won't let me skip to the front of the line without you."

She hangs up without waiting for me to respond, and I know her well enough not to be surprised.

"Apparently we're going to Westerfield's," I say to Jackson.

"If the celebration gods have ordained it, I don't know how we can avoid it."

"True."

"You can bump her to the front of the line?" He exits the freeway and heads toward West Hollywood. "I didn't realize you were such a party girl."

"Not anymore," I say. More accurately, not ever. Party girls flitter and bounce, flirting and dancing with a number of guys before letting the evening take them wherever it leads.

But that was never me. I never flittered or bounced. On the contrary, I approached clubbing like a goddamn military maneuver.

Get in, get the guy, get off, go home. No attachments, and no surrendering the power.

At least not until I met Jackson.

He's the only man to whom I've ever willingly given up control. The only man with whom I've wanted to surrender. And though that revelation had terrified me at first, now I hold it tight around me, and it is as comforting as a warm blanket. Because he knows me. He understands me. And I do not doubt that he will protect me.

He glides to a stop at a red light and turns his full attention on me. "Not anymore?" he repeats, his voice low and even.

"Don't worry. Westerfield's was never like Avalon for me," I say, referring to the techno-centric dance club where I trolled for men before Jackson claimed me. "You know I don't need that anymore."

His right hand has been resting on the gearshift, but now he lifts it off and takes mine, twining our fingers. "I know." His words are soft, but firm, and I know they're true. He understands what I used to need.

More important, he understands why I don't need it anymore. "I love you," I say, my chest feeling full with the words.

I see the emotion in his face—a softness in his eyes coupled by an even deeper heat. He has not yet said these words back to me, and though my chest tightens a bit as the seconds go by—as he lifts our hands and kisses my fingers—I do not doubt that he feels them.

But, dammit, I still want to hear them.

"Jackson—" I cut myself off.

"What?"

"I can get into the club because it's a Stark property. A perk of being Damien's assistant."

From the way he looks at me, I can tell he knows that wasn't what I'd originally intended to say. But he doesn't press me, and I'm grateful. I know he loves me—I do. And when he does say the words, they will be all the sweeter if they come without my prompting.

"Stark-owned, huh? Does that mean you're comped at the bar?"

My chest feels a thousand times lighter, because whatever storm was threatening to build has dissipated, and I feel only the sweet warmth of sun between us. "Not just me," I say. "My entire party."

"In that case, this will be a celebration. Let's go partake of my brother's alcohol."

Traffic is uncommonly light, and we maneuver the surface streets easily. Before I know it, we're on Sunset, idling in a line of cars waiting for the valet. As I'd expected, there's a crowd waiting to get in, even on a Thursday. This is a Stark property, after all, and like all things Damien, it's done right, making Westerfield's one of the city's most popular nightspots.

"Just pass the line," I say. "We'll park in the back in the owner's slot." I'm looking ahead, pointing toward the turn into the driveway, and so I see Cass in line behind the velvet rope too late. I frown, but figure that's okay. We'll park, go through the building, and usher her in through the front.

The driveway leads to a small, gated parking area in the back. I give Jackson the code to punch in, and once the gate lifts, I point him toward the owner's slot, then take my Stark International parking pass out of my purse and hang it from Jackson's rearview mirror. As far as job perks go, that pass is one of the most useful. Parking in Los Angeles is a nightmare, but Stark owns enough property around the city to ease the pain.

"This will be staying here overnight," I tell Jackson. "But don't worry. The security on the lot is first rate."

"Are we camping out?"

"No," I say, grabbing his collar and pulling him toward me for the kind of long, slow kiss that makes my toes tingle. "But I intend to get you very, very drunk." I hold up my phone. "I'll text the office to send a car when we're ready to go. Okay?"

"So long as you're getting me drunk in order to have your wicked way with me, I have no objections at all."

"Then we're all good." I grin, delighted, and reach for the handle to open my door.

"Wait."

I pause and look back at him, expecting him to say something else. But all he does is reach out for the chain around my neck. He pulls out the vibrator and lets it hang outside my shirt.

"Jackson! What if someone realizes what it is?"

"It's a bold statement. It says you like sex. You do like sex, don't you?" His voice has dropped, and so has his hand. It's cupping my breast now, and I feel my heart flutter beneath his touch and my nipple harden simply from the feel of him.

"And since I'm the only one who gets to enjoy the pleasure of touching you, all it does is make people realize that I am a very lucky man."

I swallow, but I don't protest again. Even when we're not in bed, this thing between us—control and submission—is like a game. And I always play to win.

We enter through the rear service area. The kitchen and storerooms are back here, along with lockers for the employees. The area is relatively quiet and definitely not crowded, and going from this back area to the main floor of the club is like being thrust into *Fantasia*.

The music is loud, the dance floor crowded. The guests at the bar are stacked three thick, and the bartenders are moving with a controlled, exuberant efficiency. They're all excellent at what they do; to survive a night at Westerfield's, they have to be.

I grab Jackson's hand and tug him across the dance floor toward the front door, adding in a few moves as we make progress in that direction. Right before we get to the front seating area, he pulls me close, spins me, then dips me, just like in an old Ginger Rogers movie.

I laugh, even more so when the couple beside us starts applauding.

"Don't say I never took you dancing," he quips as we move counter to the flow of traffic toward the front door. Right now, it really just serves as an entrance, since it's early enough that no one is leaving yet. Which explains why the crowd waiting in line starts to buzz happily when Jackson and I step outside—two people leaving means two more spaces in the club.

I shatter their dreams, though, when I bend down and explain to the bouncer that we need to get someone halfway down the line inside the club.

To be honest, it would be easier to go in through the VIP entrance. But I forgot to tell Cass to go there, and now she'd have to walk all the way around the building to get to it.

There is a general grumble when we wave her up from the middle of the line, and she's allowed in past the dozens of people waiting ahead of her.

Honestly, if they'd had tomatoes, they probably would have thrown them.

"Okay, the waiting part sucked, but getting to pass everyone else up? That really never gets old."

"Great to see you, too," I say, then give her a hug.

Unlike me, dressed for work in nothing more interesting than a suit skirt and linen shirt, Cass looks amazing. Her hair is midnight black with a single streak of blue tonight. She wears tight jeans and a sleeveless shirt that shows off not only her ample cleavage, but the exotic bird tattooed on her shoulder, its colorful tail feathers trailing down her arm. All in all, she looks seriously hot, as confirmed by the interested looks of both men and women as we move farther into the club.

I lead the way around the dance floor toward the VIP room. Less crowded. A more easily accessible bar. A win-win as far as I'm concerned.

I'm flashing my Stark ID to the girl at the door when I realize that we're shy one person. "Where's Zee?"

Cass cups a hand to her ear and frowns. I motion for her to hurry up and go inside the VIP room so that we can hear.

"I asked you where Zee was," I say as the door shuts behind Jackson. The noise level is slightly more reasonable, but this area also has a dance floor, so it's still loud. Just not the kind of loud that qualifies as a sonic incident.

Cass makes a face. "I need a drink. They're on Damien, right?"

"I'll get them," Jackson says. He points to the one free table in the room. "You two go sit."

As Cass rushes to stake our claim, I kiss his cheek. "Thanks."

"She okay?"

I glance back at my bff. She looks like she's got her shit together, but Cass is good at putting on a happy face. "I guess I'll find out. Vodka martinis for both of us," I say, handing him my employee ID. "Extra olives."

"Yes, ma'am."

I watch him go, because I can't bear to miss the sight of his ass in those jeans. Then I sigh when the crowd swallows him and turn back to find Cass.

"Okay." I slide into the seat opposite her. "What happened?"

"She just said no. She said she was going to come, and then she just said no. That we should stay in."

"Did she say why? I mean, you told her you wanted to go out with us to celebrate, right? You told her it was your idea?"

"Every wretched bit of that," Cass says. "And she just looked at me like I was an idiot. And then—get this—she turns all sniffly and says, 'Well, if you don't want to stay with me.'"

"Oh, gag me," I say, and Cass nods vigorously.

"I know, right? I mean, I'm not imagining this? This is a very bad sign, right?"

"She's being manipulative," I say, despite my usual rule to not criticize anyone my friends are dating. Because, hey, as far as Zee is concerned, the word *bitch* is very loudly blaring in my head.

"I have to end it," Cass says. "God, I can't believe this spiraled down so fast."

"Better than dragging it out, though, right?"

She lifts a shoulder. "I don't know. I wish I hadn't met her in the first place. I thought—I mean, we clicked at first, you know? That first time we met at Jackson's documentary she seemed so cool and funny and totally into me. And I felt so comfortable around her, like I haven't with any girl since Siobhan," she adds, referring to the longtime girlfriend who broke up with her—and broke her heart—a few months ago.

"Maybe that was the problem? Maybe you were seeing what you wanted to see, instead of what was really there?"

"I don't know," she says as Jackson returns with a tray carrying three martinis. "But I know you got lucky with this one."

"I did," I agree, then lean over the table to kiss him. As I do, my new necklace clinks against the side of my glass, and Cass cocks her head.

"Oh my god," she says, emphasizing each word. "I saw that in a magazine. You're wearing a vibrator."

She doesn't lower her voice as she announces that little fact to the world. If anything, she's louder.

"Cass!" I look around to see if anyone has heard, certain that my face is bright red.

"What? I think it's totally cool. Or hot," she says, "depending on how you look at it. I thought about buying one." She shrugs, as if she's just told me nothing more interesting than that she'd tried a new brand of coffee, then glances at Jackson. "Did you get it for her?"

"It seemed both classy and practical."

"It really is," Cass agrees, nodding sagely.

"I'm going to die," I say. "I'm just going to melt here into the floor and die. And you," I add, pointing to Jackson who looks just a little too amused, "are going to pay. Big time."

His lips twitch. "I look forward to it."

"Incorrigible," I mutter. But, yes, I'm amused, too.

Cass leaps to her feet and grabs my hand. "Come on. I love this song. Dance with me."

I don't recognize the music, but I'm willing to dance. I extend my other hand to Jackson.

"Oh no," he says. "I already danced once. Besides," he adds before I can protest, "I need to stay here and guard the table. But you two go on."

"You sure?"

His grin is just a little devious. "What? Watching two beautiful women dance together? Trust me. That won't be a problem at all. But first," he says, then pulls me in for a long, deep kiss.

I let out a soft moan, then grin happily at him as I stroke the pendant that hangs between my breasts. "Later," I say in my most husky voice.

"You can be sure of it," Jackson says, with so much real heat in his voice that my mood shifts immediately from amused to aroused. He can see the change, and his smile is understanding. "Go," he says, nodding toward the dance floor where Cass is already moving to the music and motioning me over.

I obey. But where I really want to be right now is in his arms.

We dance for a while, moving with the music, following each other, just generally having a good time. But after six long songs I start to lose a little steam. I need a break and a drink, and so I nod my head toward the table, indicating that I'm going to fight my way back through the throng.

I've barely taken a step, though, when Cass pulls me back, her eyes wide.

"What is it?"

"Look." She points toward the table, but slightly to the left of Jackson. I follow her line of sight—and then gasp.

"Is that who I think—"

"Graham Elliott," she confirms, identifying one of the biggest stars in Hollywood at the moment. "Damn," she says. "If only I were straight."

Normally, I'd laugh. But right now, nothing seems funny to me. Because Graham Elliott is gunning to play Jackson in the movie that Reed wants to make and that Jackson wants to block.

And at the moment, Elliott is making a beeline for Jackson.

I am no longer even swaying to the music. Instead I am just standing on the dance floor watching as Elliott goes right up to Jackson, puts his arm around him, and greets him as if they are the best of friends while all around them, dancers pull out their cell phones and snap their Twitter and Instagram images.

Jackson remains as still as a mountain, his expression like thunder.

"I don't get it," Cass says. "Why's Jackson so down on the movie? Does the script make him look like an ass?"

"He knows the family. And what with the murder and the suicide, he's protective of their privacy."

"That's it?"

I'm certain that it's not, but I don't know the rest of it, and I tell Cass so.

She frowns.

"What?" I demand, and my voice is harsher than I'd like, because I'm touchy about the subject.

"I just figured he would have told you the real story."

"We haven't really talked about it." And that's technically true. But at the same time, the movie has come up every time we've talked about the assault on Reed. Because the movie is Jackson's sleight of hand—it's what he's willing to show the public even as he protects me.

And yet never once has he told me why he punched out that screenwriter. Why he doesn't want to see the movie come to life. And I have no clue what is so goddamn private within that family that the world would come crashing down if Hollywood looked through the lens.

And, most important, I don't know why it matters so much to Jackson, who wasn't even in the same state when the murder-suicide occurred.

So, yeah. I'm a little touchy on the subject. And all the more so now that even Cass thinks Jackson's silence with me on the subject is more than a little odd.

Right now, however, that's not what I'm focused on. Instead, I just want to get to Jackson, but that's getting harder and harder, because the crowd has realized that Elliott is nearby and it's moving in, circling tight around the two of them. And though I keep trying to see Jackson again, the crowd is just too deep.

"Dammit," I curse. And then, when there is a gap in the crowd and I finally do get a glimpse, I repeat the curse with even more ferocity as Jackson stands. And I seriously fear for Graham's very pretty movie-star face. Because at that moment, Jackson looks ready to explode.

"Cass." My voice is tight, urgent. I start to shove through the crowd toward him, but Cass gets in front of me. She's taller than me, and bulldozes a path through the swarm.

As soon as we reach the edge of the dance floor, I burst past her, no longer shy about using elbows to shove my way to Jackson. He's standing now, and his fist is clenched. And I have a sudden premonition of the front page of *Variety* showing him and me and Cass and Graham Elliott all in a sprawl with fists and feet and teeth and fingernails.

It's not a pretty mental image. And one I very much want to avoid.

I grab Jackson's arm, my fingers closing tight around him. "With me," I say. "Now."

For a moment, I think he's actually going to argue. Then he surges forward, pulling me through the crowd with him until we reach the end of the bar. We round the corner for the hall that leads to the restrooms, and the instant we are past the turn, Jackson lashes out, slamming his fist against the wall and, fortunately, not injuring the hardwood paneling.

I'm not sure if the same can be said for his hand, and I cry out in surprise and worry. "Jackson! Are you okay?"

I start to reach for his hand, wanting to make sure he didn't break the skin, but instead, he shoves me back so that I am pressed against the wall and his arms are caging me.

The unexpected motion has knocked the wind out of me, and I suck in a hard breath, then look up at his face. It's raw. Feral. I feel a bit like his prey. And though I know that he is angry right now—that he is wild—I cannot deny the excitement that is arcing between the two of us. That is filling me. Making me wet and hot and oh, so very ready.

And before I can even form a coherent thought, his mouth crushes mine, hot and hard and demanding.

I open to him immediately, almost instinctually. Tremors of excitement course through me, and all I can think is that I *need*. But even as I spread my legs in response to the silent demand of his thigh pressing against me, a small rational voice in my head is yelling for us to get out of there. It's reminding me of cameras and crowds and that this could be a very, very, very bad idea.

"Jackson." His name is ripped from me when he breaks our kiss for breath. "The crowd."

The word seems to bring him back to himself, and he takes a single step away from me. He is breathing hard—so am I.

"The office." He grinds out the words. "Where?"

It takes a moment for the words to make sense, but once my mind starts interpreting English again, I lead him to the stairs that head up to the club manager's office. It's empty now, and I punch in the key code, then draw him in. One entire wall is one-way glass and looks out over the main dance floor. Through it, colored lights now burst in, filling the otherwise darkened office.

Right now, though, I'm not thinking about the dance floor or the lights or anything other than Jackson's hands on me. His body pressed hard against mine as he slams the door shut with his foot.

He grabs me up, and I hook my legs around his waist. I cling to his neck as his mouth finds mine even as he stumbles backward, finally slamming us against that wall of glass.

I slide down his body until my feet find the ground. My skirt doesn't follow, and it's up around my waist, and somehow in the midst of all that, Jackson's hand ended up between my thighs. "Did you mean it?" he asks as his fingers push aside the band of my underwear. "Did you mean what you said about using you when I want to beat the shit out of somebody?"

"Yes." The word is hard and full of meaning. I want this—him. All I can think of right now is his hand inside me—and I shift my hips in silent, desperate invitation. "Oh, god, yes," I say again as he thrusts deep into me. Two fingers, then three.

His mouth is over mine again, then on my neck, my collar, my breast. We're pressed up against the thick glass, and I wonder if we cast a shadow, but I don't care. Right then, I'm not even sure that I would care if the glass were fully transparent instead of mirrored from the perspective of the club. All I can think of is this. Pleasure. Ferocity. Passion.

Jackson.

"Here." The single syllable is harsh and short, but I don't think I have ever heard a word so full of need.

He pulls me away from the window, turning me so that I am facing the desk that is behind us. It's large and the surface is mostly clear, just a few documents scattered about.

With one arm, Jackson sends the papers flying, then bends me over the desk so that my breasts are hard against its wooden surface. I'm still dressed—blouse, bra—and yet I feel the pressure of the desktop against my breasts so intimately that my nipples tighten painfully and red hot threads of sensation shoot from my chest all the way to my cunt.

"I have to have you," he says. "Christ, Syl, I have to fuck you."

"Yes." It's all I can say. All I need to say.

My skirt is still up around my waist, and now he yanks my underwear down so that it is almost to my ankles. I hear his zipper and spread my legs, and then his cock is right there and he is thrusting inside me with no foreplay, no teasing, no effort to get me ready.

It is hot and fast and frenzied, and dammit, I love this. This feeling of being needed. Of being used. Of being Jackson's release valve. Not violence, not anger. But me.

He is holding my hips, pounding hard into me. And though I have never orgasmed like this, without any attention at all to my clit, right now I am almost there. The pressure of his cock inside me. The rhythm of his thrusts stroking my walls. And most of all the wild excitement of knowing what he is doing and why he is doing it.

I feel his own release coming. Hear his muffled groan as he tries to hold back. The tightening of his grip on my hips when it can't be stopped and his release cuts through him. And I follow him over, exploding into a million tiny pieces even as he collapses, exhausted and spent, over my back.

For a moment, we are simply silent. Then he gently gets off me and uses tissues to clean us both up. He slides my panties back up and tugs my skirt down into place. Then he turns me around and straightens my blouse.

Once I'm put back together and well tended to, he takes care of his own clothes. Then he studies my face and says simply, "I needed you. Christ, Syl," he adds with rising emotion, "I always need you."

"I know the feeling." I pull myself up to sit on the desk, and he gets on beside me. I lean against him. We're facing the glass wall, and I look out at the crowd and lights below us. "Do you want to tell me what happened?"

He doesn't answer at first, and I tell myself that I shouldn't push him. A moment passes. Then another. And it is becoming harder and harder for me not to say anything.

Finally, he speaks. "He came up to me like it's a done deal." His voice is low. Even. But I can hear the anger underlying it. "Like the movie's going forward and there's not a damn thing I can do to stop it."

"You'll stop it," I say. "If it's that important you'll find a way."

He nods, but he doesn't look convinced.

I hesitate, then make myself go on. "But, Jackson, I still don't understand—would it really be that horrible if it was made? I get that it digs into the family's personal lives, but the papers have already covered the murder, right? And so did a lot of the news maga-zines and television news shows. So how much worse could a movie be?"

He turns to look at me. "Trust me. It would be worse."

I wait for him to continue—to explain—but he doesn't. Instead, he just turns back toward the window and looks out at the club.

I don't press him.

And I do trust him.

But still, the question lingers. And, yes, my heart aches a bit. Because though I don't understand why, I am certain that he is keeping things from me. Secrets. Big ones—big enough, at least, to eat him up inside.

I want to press, but I don't. After all, I'm keeping secrets, too. He knows the what about the stuff that happened with Reed, but he doesn't know the how or the why.

And those are both very big things. Big, important, emotional things.

My own words to Cass return to haunt me. *Maybe you were seeing what you wanted to see, instead of what was really there?*

Is that what I'm doing with Jackson?

Am I seeing trust because I want to see it? Because I crave his presence? His touch?

Am I fabricating depth to a relationship that isn't there?

And if I am, how do I stop?

More important, how do I tell the difference?

fourteen

"I am completely undrunk." Cass scowls at me as I take one arm and Jackson takes the other.

"Not drunk at all," I agree. "But we thought you might want to ride in the limo."

"Yeah?"

"It has a bar," I remind her. "In case you want to get more un-drunk."

She narrows her eyes, but she's too wasted to decide whether I'm serious or not.

We leave through the front entrance that faces Sunset Boule-vard, and I see that Edward has pulled the limo up by the valet stand. We maneuver Cass down the set of six steps, then move across the wide sidewalk. Beside us, a crowd is gathered behind the velvet rope, impatiently waiting to enter this popular hotspot.

We're walking slowly in deference to Cass's general state of in-ebriation, and when the first camera flash fires, I realize that we've been recognized. Suddenly, both the in-line crowd and the passersby are raising their phones and taking pictures. The rapid-fire flashes burst all around us, making me feel like we're arriving at a movie premiere rather than going home to nurse a drunk friend.

Usually, this kind of attention doesn't bother me. Damien attracts the paparazzi wherever he goes, which means it has little to nothing to do with me. I'm just the assistant in the background, much like the way Secret Service agents appear in so many candid photos of the president.

Tonight, however, is different. Tonight, we've already dealt with Graham Elliott's celebrity inside the club. Out here, we are dealing with Jackson's. Because this crowd wants pictures of the guy who bloodied the face of Robert Cabot Reed. And if they can get a shot of him with the former teen model that Reed photographed, then all the better.

Honestly, the thought makes my stomach curdle.

"Jackson! Jackson!"

"Why'd you punch him?"

"Sylvia! Why did you give up modeling?"

"What's the status of the movie, Jackson? Is it true you're trying to block production?"

"Someone just tweeted photos of you and Graham Elliott talking inside. Is he attached to the project?"

"How long have you and Sylvia been dating?"

The questions are coming on top of one another, and my initial calm in the face of the familiar has entirely evaporated.

I glance at Jackson, and it's clear that he sees my panic. "Go," he says, nodding toward the red-jacketed valet who is holding open the limo door for us. "I've got Cass."

At this point, I'm all about self-preservation, and I bolt for the limo. I get settled, then punch the intercom to tell Edward, the driver, that we're going to Jackson's boat. I start to give him the address, but he cuts me off. "Don't you worry, Ms. Brooks. I've got it under control."

A moment later, Jackson guides my unsteady best friend into

the limo and settles her on the back bench. He starts to cross the short distance to where I sit on the long side of the limo, but she tugs him down beside her.

He glances at me, but I just shrug, amused.

The moment we pull away from the curb, Cass peers around the interior. She looks at the bar, then looks to me sitting right beside it.

"Just one more," she says. "Pretty please?"

I roll my eyes, but grab a tiny bottle of vodka. I pass it to her, and I'm about to pass her a glass with ice as well, but she's already unscrewed the lid and is taking a sip.

"Was that such a good idea?" Jackson asks.

"Probably not," I admit. "But she's calling it quits with Zee, and I think she decided to drink away her angst while you and I were otherwise occupied."

"Hell, yeah, I did."

I grimace. "She's on a bender now, and not driving. Might as well let her finish."

Jackson tilts his head, and I see compassion in both his expression and the way he pulls her closer and gently strokes her hair. "I'm so sorry, kiddo."

"It's just not working with her," Cass murmurs. "I know it hasn't been that long, and she's going to say that we just need to give it time, but—"

"But you know," Jackson says. "You already know the way it is."

She shifts in his arms, her head flopping back a bit as she tries to look him in the eyes. "Yeah, I do. Is that dumb?"

Jackson shakes his head. "Not dumb at all. You can know the truth in a heartbeat if you're willing to really look." He turns to face me. "I'm really looking."

My chest feels suddenly tight, and I nod. Just one single nod of acknowledgment, but it fills me up. And all my earlier worry and angst seems to melt like cotton candy in the rain. Because though we may have secrets, there is nothing shallow or fake about what is between Jackson and me. It is real. It is right. It is us.

Cass glances between the two of us. "That was the most romantic thing ever." She turns her focus to Jackson. "Is there an XX chromosome version of you out there?"

"Sorry. Just the one brother."

She makes a face. "That you know of," she says, and both Jackson and I have to laugh.

She drifts off, her head tucked up against his chest and his arm around her shoulders.

"You look very parental," I say, and the light from the streetlamps as we turn into the marina must catch his face strangely, because for a moment it looks as though he flinches.

The illusion passes quickly as he smiles. "I'm hoping that I won't find any daughter of mine quite this wasted." But he strokes her hair as he speaks, and I can't help thinking that Jackson will be the kind of dad who'll protect his family with a wild ferocity, even if that means sacrificing himself.

And as Edward takes us the rest of the distance to Jackson's boat, I realize he's proven that already. Not for a daughter, but for me. Because god knows when he beat the crap out of Robert Cabot Reed, he did a hell of a lot more for me than my father ever did.

It's a nice thought—a comforting one. Because as the memory of all those camera flashes lingers, I can't help but fear what might be coming our way. The assault. The movie. Reed's photos of me. A whole shitstorm of gossip that we will inevitably have to face.

And though I'm not certain I'm strong enough to handle the storm—and although I know that Jackson's first instinct might be to beat the crap out of whoever is dishing it out—I know that whatever else he does, he will protect me. My knight on his shiny white horse.

Frankly, that is a damn nice feeling.

When we get on the boat, it's clear that there will be no after-party for Cass. "I'll take her down and put her in the guest room," I say.

"While you do that, why don't I open a bottle of wine? It's a clear night. How do you feel about the two of us sitting on the deck and watching the stars?"

"I feel exceptionally good about it. Give me five minutes to get her settled."

Fortunately, she's mobile, if wobbly, and I'm able to get her stripped down to bra and panties quickly. "In you go," I say, pulling the sheets back and helping her in. "I'll wake you in the morning before I go to work."

She mumbles something incoherent that I translate as "good night," and I start to tiptoe for the door. But just as I'm about to step into the hallway, her soft "Syl," calls me back.

"You okay?"

She holds out her hand. "Stay? Just 'til I fall asleep?"

I hesitate, thinking about Jackson and the wine and the stars above us. But this is my best friend, and she needs me, and there's really no debate to be had. I'm at her side in seconds. "Scoot over," I say, then lay down beside her. She spoons against me, and I close my eyes, realizing as I do that exhaustion has been creeping up on me as well.

"Thanks," she whispers.

"For what?"

"For taking care of me."

"I think Jackson doled out the most care tonight."

"Not tonight. Forever. For being my best friend."

I smile, touched. "Yeah, well, it's a little self-serving. I get a great best friend in return."

"Aren't we lucky?"

"We are," I say. "We really are."

My eyes are closed, and I wait for Cass to say something else. But there is just silence, and after a few moments, the rhythm of her breathing changes and I feel the steady rise and fall of her chest against my back.

I tell myself to open my eyes and get up, but then I tell myself that if I just lay here quietly for another minute or two I'll be all re-energized. Since that sounds like a fabulous plan, I keep my eyes closed and just let myself drift and drift and drift. . . .

I startle awake, gasping a bit, and then immediately relax when I see Jackson sitting in the room's single chair opposite me. "Oh, hell," I say. "I'm so sorry. I guess I fell asleep."

"You needed it."

I start to sit up.

"No. Don't wake her."

He stands and crosses to me. I shift enough so that I can look up at him as he reaches down to brush my cheek with the oddest expression. "What?"

"Nothing," he says. "I was just thinking about the look on your face."

"What about it?"

"Peaceful. Content." He pauses. Just for a heartbeat. "I don't like seeing it when you're in anyone's arms but mine."

I frown and start to push up out of the bed. "Jackson, I—"

"No, no." He gently holds me in place. "I just want you all to myself. But I'm a big boy and I'd never begrudge you your friends. Stay," he says. "She needs you."

"Jackson . . ."

But he just presses a kiss to his fingertips and then brushes them over my lips. "Good night, sweetheart."

I try to fall back asleep after he's gone, but I can't seem to manage it. And so I very carefully slide out of Cass's embrace and go across the little hall to Jackson's room. He's not there, but I find him on deck in one of the oversized lounge chairs, asleep under the stars.

I slide in next to him, then pull up the blanket from the foot of the lounger to protect us from the cool night air.

He rolls over, then pulls me against him, enveloping me with his warmth. "I meant what I said," he murmurs sleepily. "She needs you. You could have stayed."

"I did stay," I say. "And then I came here. Because you need me, too."

He is silent for a moment. Then the arm that he has swung around my waist tightens just slightly. "Yes," he says. "I do."

fifteen

I'm pretty sure the items on my to-do list are breeding.

There's no other explanation as to how I can spend the entire day tackling task after task after task and still have no end in sight.

Even so, I love it.

One of the Stark International drivers drove Jackson and me in to work together, and I spent this entire Friday morning on a conference call soliciting requests for proposals from five of the largest food service companies in the country. I've got an intern pulling the names of the top twenty chefs across the country, each of whom I intend to contact about the possibility of opening a signature restaurant on-site at the resort.

I've negotiated a tentative deal with the FAA to allow a short airstrip on the island, and I have even scheduled a meeting with the local EPA office to discuss my most favorite topic in the world— endangered cave crickets.

More specifically, endangered cave crickets that might actually hold up construction if we don't get the little buggers squared away quickly.

All in all, I'm feeling pretty damn smug when Trent Leiter eases around my cubicle wall and leans against my filing cabinet.

"Heard the news," he says. "Jackson's back on the project. What did you do? Bribe Stark?" He frowns. "No, wait. Hard to bribe the man who owns half the world."

"I think Mr. Stark just realized that the press from the assault doesn't have to negatively impact the project."

His brows lift as he grins. "Negatively impact? What, did public relations send around a memo?"

"Actually, yes." The PR department had circulated a memo that morning addressing how anyone on staff who is not me, Damien, or Aiden should respond if approached about Jackson's arrest. "The proper responses are 'no comment,' 'no comment,' and 'no comment.' I came up with the part about the lack of negative impact all on my own."

"Catchy," he says. "Wish I knew the whole story."

He eyes me speculatively, but I just shrug. "I've worked directly for Mr. Stark for five years, but that doesn't mean I'm in his head. And since when did you become such a gossip hound?"

"Just making conversation."

"Yeah, how's this? Jackson's better than a good luck charm. Three problems tackled in just one morning. The FAA came through. I got the guest ferry all squared away—we can launch from San Pedro and Long Beach, and unless I miss my guess, I'll have a launch site from Marina del Rey set up soon. And, I scored a meeting with the EPA dude."

"That's great," he says, but he sounds distracted.

I can't really hold that against him. It's not his project, and I'm sure he's got plenty of problems of his own to deal with. "So how's the Century City site going?" I ask, more out of politeness than interest.

"Not as smoothly." His smile doesn't quite reach his eyes. "I guess I need to find my own good luck charm."

"I'm sorry." Though Trent isn't my favorite person, and I don't understand what Rachel sees in him, he is a colleague, and I don't wish him ill. "Can I help?"

He shakes his head and makes a motion with his hand as if he's waving away smoke. "No, no. I didn't mean to make it sound dire. I'm distracted by something else. Everything in Century City is moving forward." He takes a paper clip from a bowl on my desk and starts to unfold it. "Honestly, once you've been in this business a bit longer, you'll realize that bumps in the road are just part of a day on the job."

I lean back in my chair and nod, not sure if he's trying to be helpful, or if this is his backhanded way of telling me I'm too new and raw to actually be managing a project, even with Aiden's help.

That's hardly a question I'm going to ask, though, and so I opt for that time-honored tactic of conversational diversion. "So, you and Rachel are going out?"

He lifts a shoulder as he focuses on the star pattern into which he's bent the paper clip. "She's a lot of fun."

That is hardly the most romantic endorsement, but I know that Rachel is happy. I hope that Trent just isn't the kind to over-share about his relationships, and for the time being, I'm sticking with that assessment. Because so far, today has been awesome. And nothing—not cave crickets or irritating co-workers or the fear that another friend's relationship is on the skids—is going to spoil my mood.

Fifteen minutes later, my cell phone chirps, and when I glance at the text from Cass, I realize I should never have tempted the gods.

Check out the pics. Not viral, but lots of shares. I look drunk, but hot. U look hot, and sober. Jackson looks like sex, but he always does.

There's a link, and I click through. She's right—we both do look hot. And Jackson, who is holding up Cass on the other side, looks good enough to eat. To be honest, if Cass didn't look so wasted it would be a good picture to frame for my desk. Both Jackson and I have soft expressions, and though we're clearly focused on keeping Cass upright, the moment is so gentle and sweet that I want to bend down and kiss his photo since the man himself isn't right beside me.

I'm about to send her back a text thanking her for the link when she sends another message.

Zee saw pic and freaked. Said it looked like I was screwing both of U.
Be proud. I stood firm. Told her we were over.
It's done. Holy fuck.

I respond immediately:

I am proud!!!!! U did good. Hold fast. We'll find the right girl for u.

It takes a moment, but her reply when it comes through makes me smile:

In time for Halloween party wld be nice. And thx. XXOO.
And here are some more for your computer wallpaper.

There is another link, this one to images of Jackson and me. There is one of us at the table, just looking at each other, but the heat in our eyes is palpable. Another is positively awesome, and I hope that I can find a high-quality version so that I can print it. Because someone actually caught our dance—right when Jackson dipped me. The picture is slightly blurred, suggesting motion, and we both look like we couldn't be having a better time if we tried. Frankly, that's how I always feel with him.

These images come with captions, too, and I'm now the official subject of celebrity gossip, because I have been identified on social media as starchitect Jackson Steele's girlfriend.

Honestly, I can't say that I mind.

Love these, I text to Cass. *Thx.*

Her reply makes me frown.

:) But there are other pics, too. These might not make you happy. Is J around? Has he been online?

As far as I know, Jackson is on twenty-six with Lauren Crane, who has recently been promoted from the file room to work as his assistant until his secretary arrives from New York. If everything is going well, he's walking the floor with her and giving both Lauren and the construction staff directions on where to put up walls and doors, where to set up drafting tables, and all the other minutiae that comes with getting his area built out the way he wants it.

Since a couple of guys from his New York staff are arriving in ten days with his secretary, he's been crazy busy, and I would be seriously surprised if he's noticed anything happening out in cyberland.

I don't say all of that to Cass, though. Instead, I just text back, *I doubt he's seen any pics. What up?*

She responds with two links. The first leads to more advertising photos of me, some of which have been merged with recent images of Jackson and turned into social media graphics. *Great.* My childhood trauma has become someone else's social media pastime. Isn't that wonderful?

The second link is more immediate, and just as disturbing. On this site, I find a picture of Graham Elliott, his arm hooked buddy-buddy style around Jackson's shoulders.

Well, hell.

My fears are confirmed when I get Cass's next text:

Buzz is that the movie is a go and Graham is playing Jackson.
Tell J not to blow a gasket.

I roll my eyes. Easier said than done.

I tell Cass I need to get back to work, which is technically true. But instead I scour the internet. Sure enough, the speculation is back about the movie, with the press opining that Graham was the go-between, healing the rift between Reed and Jackson Steele, who was recently arrested for assaulting the producer-director.

Isn't that just so sweet?

I consider giving Jackson a heads-up, but decide that he has enough to worry about. Since there's nothing he can do about the pictures and comments, I might as well wait until work is over and he has a drink in his hand.

I'm just settling back into work when my intercom buzzes. "Mr. Stark asked me to tell you that you and he and Mr. Ward and Mr. Steele are scheduled to have dinner at Cut 360. Seven tonight with Dallas Sykes. I've already told Mr. Ward," Karen adds, referring to Aiden. "And he said to tell you that Mrs. Stark will be joining you."

"Wait, slow down." I click frantically on my computer to open my calendar. "I don't know a thing about this."

"Apparently Mr. Sykes is in town and wants to meet Mr. Steele. Mr. Stark said to apologize, but that you two need to be there unless it's absolutely impossible."

Which, I know, translates to *just be there*. Dallas Sykes is a gorgeous, brash, tabloid-friendly department store mogul who is also the primary investor in The Resort at Cortez.

"Okay," I say, because what else is there to say? "I'll let Mr. Steele know."

"Great. And you have a call holding on three. He says he's your brother."

That's odd, since Ethan has my cell phone number, and knows I prefer not to take personal calls through the office number. I answer warily, but it really is my little brother.

"What's up?" I ask, immediately on alert. "Are you okay? Why aren't you calling my cell?"

"Hey, Silly," he says, using the nickname he's called me since he was three and I was six. My full name is Eleanor Sylvia Brooks. But that's what came out of his little baby mouth. "Great to hear your voice, too."

"My darling little brother. How wonderful to hear from you on the phone you never call me on, thus making me worry. And then teasing me about worrying."

"I'm fine." I hear the laughter in his voice. "I lost my phone and couldn't remember your number."

I shake my head, but I am smiling. That's Ethan. My scatterbrained brother, whom I absolutely adore.

"Do I need to arrange to have your phone surgically attached to your body?"

"I think I'll just scour the apartment again. The place is a mess from all the packing. It's probably under a box."

Since his stuff is being shipped from London—and that process takes weeks—I hope it didn't accidentally end up inside a box. But I keep my thoughts to myself. No point in being the voice of doom.

"I saw your picture this morning. You and Cass look great. But what's the deal with Jackson Steele? He's the guy you dated for a while in Atlanta, right? You guys are back together?"

"We are," I say, "and I'll tell you all about it—and introduce you—on Wednesday. You're still getting in around four, right?"

"Yup. I have to go through customs, so do you just want me to text you when I'm heading outside?"

"That'll work. And are you sure you don't want to go with me to Jamie's Halloween party on Friday? Stark keeps a suite at the Century Plaza and it's empty right now. You could have it through the weekend."

"That would be sweet, but I want to get down to Irvine and hang with Mom and Dad."

"Fair enough, but I was really hoping to spend some time with you."

"Well, they're your parents, too. You can hang out down there with us."

The thought makes me shudder. "In case you forgot, I have work. In another city." I say all this brightly, as if that is the only reason I don't want to spend time with my parents.

"Well, it's not like there won't be more chances," he says reasonably. "Considering I'm moving back to California, we'll see each other a lot." He's been living in London, so I can't argue with that. "And as for the rest, you're staying for dinner at Mom and Dad's on Wednesday night, so we'll have some time then."

Just the thought of going to my parents' house makes me edgy. "Listen, there's been a slight change of plans."

"Don't you dare blow me off."

"Work is insane right now, so I thought I'd send a limo for you. Get you to Irvine in style."

"You are such a liar. We just agreed that I should text you when I get out of customs."

"I meant text the limo," I say, lying again.

"Bullshit. Come on, Syl. Mom says she never sees you. That you came back from Atlanta, landed your high-paying job, and fell off the planet."

To be fair, I fell off the planet as far as my parents are concerned when I moved into an exclusive Beverly Hills boarding school for my sophomore year of high school. I don't say that to Ethan, though. Instead, I just say, "Work is crazy right now."

"Are you ever going to tell me what the big drama is between you and them?"

I frown. "No. Sorry, but no. But there *is* drama. Isn't that enough?"

He exhales loudly. "Look, I know how much they sacrificed when I was a kid. And I know some of that lashed back on you."

I hug myself, feeling suddenly cold. *Lashed back?* Hell, yeah, it lashed back.

"I just can't help but feel like this rift between you and them is my fault. And it would make me feel a hell of a lot better if you'd just come, okay?"

I close my eyes, because I know I'm going to cave. Because in so many ways he's right.

And in so many ways he's wrong.

But the biggest truth is that I'm not going to tell him the truth. So, yeah. Maybe I do need to suck it up.

"Fine," I say. "Dinner. But I'm not staying late. I've got to work on Thursday, and—"

"Whatever you say, big sis."

I frown, but it's affectionate. "I love you even if you are a pain in the butt."

"Of course you do. See you Wednesday."

I end the call, then head to the reception desk to ask Karen if anyone called while I was tied up. Since I'm approaching from behind her, I can see her computer—and that she's scrolling through the pictures of me, Jackson, and Cass. Not to mention Graham Elliott. Yesterday I saw her looking at some of the old ad photos of me that are circulating.

Wow, gee. How great is that?

"Oh. Hey." She coughs as she clicks her computer back to a word processing screen. "Need anything?"

"Yeah," I say. "I think I need a coffee." And since that is absolutely true, I head down to the lobby for caffeine and the chance to clear my head.

My parents. My pictures.

For a day that had started out great, it's going downhill fast.

sixteen

Even though it is days before I have to see my parents, just the conversation with Ethan has made me antsy. And though I like to think that I'm capable of standing on my own two feet, the truth is that I balance a lot better when I have Jackson beside me.

So instead of heading straight to the lobby, I detour to twenty-six. The construction crew and Lauren are there, but Jackson is not. When Lauren tells me he had an errand to run outside the building, I remember that we left his car at Westerfield's. Considering how much he babies the Porsche, I'm certain he went to fetch it.

Without a coffee companion, I continue down to the lobby on my own. It's a swift descent, but I still have enough time to chastise myself for being edgy and out of sorts. After all, it's not as though anything has changed. Ethan told me over a week ago that he was coming, and I've been looking forward to seeing my little brother.

But now that his arrival is closer, it's harder to ignore the fact that I'm going to be seeing not only him, but my parents. I'm going to have to sit at the dining room table in their house. I'm going to share wine and Mom's meat loaf. And I'm going to have to make conversation with my dad.

That would be gut-wrenching enough all by itself. But it's a billion times worse now that my past is assaulting me from all angles, with Reed in the news and old advertisements featuring my likeness popping up all over the place.

Hell, even Jackson is a reminder, because now every time the press mentions him—even if it's not in connection to the resort—it's *Architect Jackson Steele, recently sentenced to community service for his assault on producer-director Robert Cabot Reed.* And I hate, hate, hate that their names are now linked in the public's mind.

And, goddammit, in mine.

The line at Java B's is long, but they also have an outdoor coffee cart that I can see through the glass front of the building, and despite it being a gorgeous day, there are only three people waiting to order. Since that seems like as much of an invitation to enjoy the day as I'm likely to get, I head out. I end up with an extra-large latte and a chocolate chip cookie that is about the size of a salad plate. I will either keel over from sugar shock or be so hyped up for the rest of the day that I accomplish all my tasks without even blinking.

I'm hoping for the latter. After all, if I'm busy burning through my various work tasks, I'll have no time to think about the impending torment of a visit with my family.

The cookie is about the best thing ever, and I have to talk myself out of buying another one as I stand and crumple my napkin. The only trash can is by the coffee cart, and as I head in that direction, I'm facing the loading area, a small section of road set off from the main traffic flow along South Grand Avenue to allow for cars to pick up and drop off passengers at Stark Tower.

I'm not really looking for anything in particular, but as I'm turning to head back toward the building entrance, something familiar catches my eye. I shift back around, and see that it is Jackson. He is standing by the passenger door of a small, red sedan.

I take a step toward him, but then he opens the door, and a tall, slender redhead steps out. She's familiar and vibrant and lovely, and she puts her hands on Jackson's shoulders and brushes his lips with a kiss.

My delicious cookie suddenly turns to acid in my stomach. Because I know this woman. True, I've never formally met her. But I know her name. I know he cares about her. And I also know that he has slept with her.

Megan.

I stand frozen to the spot, as if my feet are anchored by the weight of my jealousy.

He hands her the keys and she circles the car, then gets in on the driver's side and pulls away.

Jackson starts walking toward the building, and I pivot back toward the coffee cart, then reach out and grab the edge of the condiment bar because I'm now feeling even more unsteady than I was after the conversation with Ethan.

Megan.

Megan?

I'd seen her at the premiere of *Stone and Steele,* the documentary about Jackson and his work on the Amsterdam Art and Science Museum, but that was weeks ago. I hadn't met her then, though. I'd only seen her from a distance, first approaching Jackson, and then as the two appeared in heated conversation.

After that, she'd been gone. I'd had no idea who she was, and it hadn't really seemed relevant. At least not until I'd seen a picture of her with a darling little girl hanging in Jackson's houseboat.

Hanging on *his bedroom wall* in the houseboat.

He'd told me that she was a friend. That they'd slept together once, but that had been a one-off. A mistake. And I got that. After all, I'd slept with Cass once, but that didn't mean we were ever a couple or that anything was still going on.

But if what he said was really true, then why hadn't he told me she was still in town? Why had she kissed him so intimately?

And why did it suddenly feel as if the world as I knew it was shifting beneath my feet?

"Syl?" His voice, as warm and gentle as a summer breeze, drifts toward me from a few feet behind me. I stay put, motionless, then close my eyes and draw in a breath when his hand closes over my shoulder. "Coffee break?" He brushes a kiss to the back of my ear. "Good idea."

I turn to face him, then realize that I'm still holding the coffee I'd bought at least fifteen minutes ago. "I—no. I'm done with it." I lick my lips and toss it into the trash, even though there's still half a latte left.

I start to head back toward the building, and Jackson falls in step beside me. If he realizes my mood is off, he doesn't show it. And though I should be grateful, that little blip of reality has the opposite effect. It pisses me off. Because, dammit, Jackson *knows* me. Hasn't he always been able to read me?

And if he can't read me now, doesn't that mean that his head is full of another woman?

Oh my god, I'm turning into Super Bitch.

I pause just before we get to the revolving door that is the entrance to Stark Tower. "I was looking for you earlier. We're having dinner tonight with Damien and Dallas Sykes. Nikki and Aiden, too."

"All right," he says. "What time?"

"Seven. Just down the street at Cut 360."

The conversation seems strange and stilted, but I can't tell if that's because something is truly off, or because I'm filtering it through my own little cloud of angst.

"Sounds good. Why don't you come down about six forty-five. We'll walk over. Should be a nice night."

I nod. And then, before I can stop myself, I blurt out, "You weren't in your office earlier."

"No," he says. "I went out."

"So I gathered. Where'd you go?"

"Nowhere special."

"With Megan." I try to sound normal, but my voice is flat.

He looks at me, and his head tilts just slightly. I think his eyes might have narrowed, but that may just be my imagination. "Yes," he says evenly. "With Megan."

We're blocking pedestrian traffic, and a tall man in a very expensive suit shoots me an irritated glance. I don't care. Because now I'm certain the conversation is stilted, and I don't understand it and, dammit, it scares me. Because this isn't the way it's supposed to be. Not between me and Jackson. Not ever.

I force a casual tone. "I didn't realize she was still in town from the documentary."

"She came back."

"You never did tell me what you two were arguing about at the premiere."

He meets my eyes. Mine, I'm sure are needy. His are as cold as arctic ice. "No, I guess I didn't."

He might as well have slapped me. "You know what, Jackson, screw it." I see him take a step back as if in defense against a blow, but I'm too far gone to care. "You want to hold on to your secrets, then you just fucking do that."

I storm off, feeling like an idiot, and not at all sure if he's the one who's off or if I am.

Back in my cubicle, I try to concentrate. Try, but don't succeed.

I know that I'm being jealous, but dammit, I don't care. I wanted him today—needed him. And he wasn't there. Because he was with the one woman other than me that he'd not only slept with, but that he'd cared about.

So, yeah, maybe it's stupid or bitchy or unfair, but I'm going to wallow. Because so long as I'm pissed off and moody about this, then at least all the shit with my father and brother stays buried under a load of irrelevant angst.

Fuck.

"Bad day?"

I spin around in my chair to find Karen standing at the edge of my cubicle holding a vase full of yellow roses.

I grimace. "Did I say that out loud?"

"Don't worry. I've heard way more colorful language on the floor."

"Sorry. And yeah, this isn't the best of days."

"Maybe these will help." She passes me the flowers. "They just came for you."

"Really?" I suppose I should have clued in; it's not like Karen wanders the halls with roses. But I guess I assumed she was walking them to the coffee station to fill the vase with water. "Who are they from?"

But that's a question that I ask only for form. Of course I know who sent them. And the heart that had been feeling so heavy flutters a bit in my chest.

Just to be sure, I peek at the card.

I'm just one floor away, but it feels like worlds apart.
I'm sorry.
J.

I tuck the card in my purse, and smile at Karen. "You're right. They helped."

"Glad to hear it." She takes a step back toward the reception area, then pauses. "If Jackson shows up, should I send him straight back?"

"Yeah," I say. "You do that."

I'm about to type out a quick *sorry I was a bitch* text, but before I even start typing, I get a call from Cass.

"Hey, what's up?" I ask.

"That's what I want to know," she says. "Do I need to come over there and bitch-slap your boyfriend?"

Either my best friend has completely lost it or—"What are you talking about?"

"I'm talking about the redheaded twit. Who is she? Have you seen this shit? Hang on."

She's rattling her words off so fast I can barely process them, and I've just opened my mouth to ask her to please slow down when she sends me a text with a website link.

"Did it come through? Click on it."

"Hang on." I don't want to—I really don't want to. Because whatever it is, it's not going to be good. But I need to know, and so I click. And then, yes, I curse.

"Oh, *fuck*."

The site is one of the eight billion celebrity gossip sites. But this one is operated like social media. So someone can start a story, and then site members can add to it with comments or photos. This one starts with an image of Jackson, his head bent close to Megan's, his face full of so much affection that I really just want to throw up.

There's a headline, too. *Starchitect Jackson Steele: Hollywood's newest member of Club Bad Boy?*

"Oh, god," I say.

"I'm so sorry," Cass says. "Do you know her?"

But I'm too busy checking out the images and text that follow the headline to answer. There are five pictures. The first of me and Jackson at Westerfield's. Beneath that is another image from last night, only this one shows me and Jackson with our arms around Cass as we lead her to the limo. The last three images are of Jackson and Megan. The first is what I saw an hour ago—her kissing him in front of Stark Tower. The second is the two of them seated across a table from each other, apparently having lunch. And the final one shows the two of them on the deck of his boat. It was obviously taken with a long lens from the dock. They're facing each other, his hands are on both of her shoulders, and from the angle, it looks like he's about to pull her to him and catch her in one hell of a lip-lock.

And the most horrible thing? I recognize the green flag of the yacht that's moored right next to them. Because it arrived this morning as Jackson and I were leaving for work. Which means that this fucking photograph was taken today. *Today.*

"This isn't—" I try to form a sentence, but my brain is frozen. All of me is frozen. I'm cold. So very, very cold. "It can't be—"

"I sure hope the hell not," Cass says. "I mean, they're making shit up about the three of us, so hopefully the crap about the redhead is bullshit, too."

"Her name's Megan." I sound shell-shocked. "What do you mean the three of us?"

She answers me, but I don't even hear her words. They're just so much background noise. Because I've found what she's talking about all on my own. The text under the headline that talks about how Jackson is working for Damien. About how he's new to Hollywood, and he's settling right in. Getting into fistfights. Fucking lots of women. Me. Me and Cass as a nice little girl-boy-girl sandwich. And this new woman that the writer can't yet identify, but who Jackson took back to his boat after an intimate lunch for an even more intimate dessert.

This can't be right.

I scroll down and find images of Jackson with other women, all taken over the course of the last five years. There aren't many—it's not like he's some mega movie star and the paparazzi is glued to him—but whoever wrote this article did their homework, and for each gala Jackson has attended, there is a different woman on his arm. And the commentary makes clear that Jackson pretty much fucked his way across the United States, and is continuing to do exactly that. With Megan. With me. And with God only knows who else.

"Don't completely freak until you talk to him," Cass warns, which is a little ironic considering she'd called me in full freak-out mode, and I tell her as much. "I know, I know. And I'm sorry. It's just—well, I like Jackson, but I love you, and I don't want you to get hurt. And I swear if he does hurt you, I will cut his balls off with a hacksaw."

I cringe. But I don't disagree.

"You're going to talk to him, right?"

"Yeah," I say. I don't say when, but I know it won't be soon. Right now, I'm feeling just a little too raw.

"Okay, listen, my four o'clock just walked in. But you call if you need me."

I promise that I will, then end the call. I sit and stare at the computer screen and then—because that really isn't helping my mood—reach over and turn off my entire goddamn computer.

Shit.

How the hell could a day that started out so well have spiraled down so quickly?

I stare at the vase of flowers on my desk—lovely roses that should add some cheer to my day, but instead are only making me miserable. *"Fuck."*

I pick up the vase, and before I can talk myself out of it, I drop the whole thing—glass and flowers and water and all—right into my trash.

It's not as cathartic as I'd hoped, but I do feel slightly better.

The truth is that I should just haul my rear downstairs and talk to him, but I feel too ripped up inside. I'm afraid that I'll start shouting at him. Or, worse, that I'll burst into tears. I need time to get my shit together. I need to not think about Jackson or Megan or those stupid photos and just let it all settle.

And since the best way to do that is to lose myself in my work, I turn the computer back on, pull up my phone list, and start returning calls.

That's what I'm doing when he arrives, as silent as a cat. But it doesn't matter. I know he's there, and the band around my heart that had started to loosen tightens once again.

"I look forward to getting your proposal," I say into the phone, then hang up. I wait one beat, then another. Then I swivel in my chair to face him.

I don't want it to, but the sight of him takes my breath away.

He's not dressed any differently than he was earlier. Casual slacks and a button-down shirt, the top two buttons open to expose the indentation at the base of his neck. Nothing special about the outfit. Nothing formal about his posture. On the contrary, he is leaning negligently against my cubicle wall.

But it is the expression on his face that has knocked me flat. Passion and penitence and desire so strong it almost pulls me out of my chair. So help me, I want to enfold myself in his arms and press my head against his chest. Because isn't Jackson the one person who has always been able to make me feel better? Who can soothe and reassure me?

Not today.

Today, I have no one.

Today, I steel myself as I look him in the eye. "This really isn't a good time."

He glances down, and I cringe as I realize that he's looking right at the flowers in my trash. I start to rise—I want to explain—but I force myself to stay seated. Right now, I'm not the one who needs to apologize or explain. Jackson is. And if this evidence of how frustrated and pissed I am doesn't prompt him, then maybe nothing will.

When he lifts his head and looks at me again, his eyes are flat and unreadable, just like his expression. Only the tightness in his jaw—as if he is clenching his teeth—evidences his dark mood. And it is only because I know him so well that I can see his rising temper. "I'll let you get back to work." The words are flat and measured and completely cold.

"Jackson—" His name is past my lips before I can call it back, and I sit there, slightly flummoxed, because I don't know what I intended to say.

He had taken a step backward, but now he pauses.

I curse myself, because I am not ready to talk about this. So I just say, "Seven o'clock. Don't forget. I'll see you at the restaurant."

He meets my eyes and holds my gaze for a moment longer than is comfortable. "Seven," he finally says. Then he turns and walks away.

And though I rise and watch him move toward the stairwell, Jackson never once looks back.

seventeen

"Considering you're the man of the hour, you're awfully damn quiet, Jax." Dallas Sykes leans back in his chair and pushes his dinner plate away before polishing off his third martini. The department store magnate is pretty much the walking definition of a sexy bad boy, complete with half-naked women often found draped casually over his arm. Jackson and I both crossed paths with him when our trip to the Cortez site fueled gossip, and we ended up in the tabloids alongside Dallas and his very married girlfriend.

"It's Jackson, and I apologize. I have a lot on my mind." He doesn't look at me. Not that I expect him to. We've been managing to not look at each other for the last ninety minutes, ever since we arrived separately at the restaurant.

We're at a round table, and I'd taken the chair next to Nikki. Aiden had to cancel dinner—apparently Trent took a long weekend, but there are issues at the Century City project that require immediate attention—so that means that we are at a five-top. Nikki, Damien, and I arrived first, and when Jackson came a few moments later, he had the choice of the seat next to me, or the seat next to Damien.

He chose to sit next to me. And though I have avoided his eyes all evening, I can't avoid the tension that fills the air between us, so thick that I am amazed that no one else is drawn into it, like a black hole that sucks in everything that drifts too close.

I try my best to steer the conversation toward the resort in general. But Dallas—one of the primary investors—has heard it all before, and keeps his focus laser-sharp on Jackson.

"Bet you never knew you'd be such a celebrity when you were sketching your way through your childhood." He grins. "I saw your documentary."

Jackson smiles politely. "I hope you found it interesting."

"Fascinating," Dallas says. His eyes are as green as Jackson's are blue, and he looks so earnest, that I can't help but wonder if the bad boy, playboy thing is an act. The man is managing a multibillion dollar company and doing a damn fine job. Plus, he's no slouch intellectually. So what's his story?

That's going to remain a mystery, of course. It's very bad form to poke into the personal lives of your investors. At least it is if you want them to keep investing.

The general topic of bad boys, however, is very much on the table as Dallas leans closer to Jackson. "I have to say, I thought I had one hell of a reputation for playing fast and loose. But you certainly did a number on that Reed guy. I gotta know. What was that about?"

"Just having a bad day." I can almost see the tension pouring out of Jackson, like a red haze staining the air.

"We've started thinking about retail on the resort," I say brightly to Dallas. "We want to keep it very high-end, boutique oriented, but I thought you and I should sit down at some point and talk about you possibly opening a retail space."

"Happy to," he says. "It's the celebrity thing that gets me," he continues to Jackson, undaunted. "Documentary. Feature film. I saw the pictures with you and Graham Elliott. Hell, you could star in the thing if you wanted. You've got the look."

"Dallas," Damien says firmly. "I think that considering the fact that Reed still might file a civil action, we should not expect Mr. Steele to talk about this."

My stomach twists. Now that the criminal case has been resolved, I thought the courtroom drama was over. And I can't help but wonder if Damien knows something, or if he's just trying to shut Dallas up.

I hope it's the latter. And, frankly, I applaud the effort.

"Hey, we can drop it. I was just curious about the movie. Of course, if you do want to star in it, probably best not to beat the shit out of the producer. So what was that about? You just didn't like the script? When's it hitting theaters, anyway?"

Beside me, Jackson's posture stiffens. His left hand is in his lap, and now he moves it to my knee. He has barely brushed my skin when he seems to realize what he's doing, and he yanks it away as if my body is on fire.

I don't even hesitate. I reach for him and clutch his hand with mine. Because no matter what else might be between us, I won't have him be alone right now.

"I'm afraid you've been misinformed," Jackson says, his voice stiff but polite. His hand is clenched so tight with mine that I have to actually grit my teeth. "There's not going to be a movie."

"Uh-huh." Dallas has the look of a dog with a bone, and I'm certain that he's going to pursue this line.

Damien, thank goodness, comes to the rescue, asking Dallas about an arson claim in one of his Chicago-based stores. Apparently that arose from a huge drama between the store manager and a street gang, and Dallas is interested enough in the soap opera aspects to stay on point.

As the conversation finally shifts away from Jackson, he eases up on my hand. And when the conversation shifts again, and Nikki mentions that Wyatt called her, Jackson releases me entirely.

I deflate, as if that simple loss of touch is more profound than the distance that has been growing between us all afternoon.

I force myself not to show it, though. Instead, I focus on Nikki. "Oh, good. I'm glad he called. I meant to tell you tonight. I called him this morning. We're all set for Monday evening."

"Hot date?" Dallas asks.

"Photography lesson," I say. "We had to postpone the last one." Nikki kisses Damien's cheek. "It was worth it."

Since Damien surprised her with New York theater tickets, I'm sure it was, and Nikki tells us all about the trip before we backtrack the conversation to planning the specifics for our Monday photography lesson. "I'll meet you in Santa Monica," she says. "Around seven? And then maybe Damien and Jackson can join us after for a drink?" She says the last with such a question in her voice that I am absolutely positive she has noticed the rift between Jackson and me.

I'm about to say that it might not be the best night for socializing, when Jackson responds. "I think that's a great idea." He looks at me as he speaks, his eyes soft with apology. And though I cannot say for certain that we will be fine come Monday, I do know that I am done being completely mad at him. It's time to talk about this.

And so I nod. "Yes," I say. "It's a great idea."

I'm surprised to learn that Dallas knows a bit about photography, and we talk about Wyatt's work, including his prints that hang on some of the Stark International walls. The conversation meanders from there to Damien's tennis career and then back full circle to Jackson's assault.

This time around, however, Dallas isn't quite as pushy. "I heard you were serving your community service at the Stark Children's Foundation."

"I start Sunday," Jackson says. "There's a fund-raiser that I'll be working, and I'm looking forward to it. Not something most of us criminal types say about our community service obligations, but I'm glad to have the chance to work with the kids. And it is a good cause," he adds, looking at Damien. "I should be volunteering for a place like that even without the gray cloud of incarceration hanging over my head."

"You should," Damien says. The foundation, which helps abused and at-risk kids through sports therapy, is a relatively new charity that Damien founded, but one that I know means a lot to him. It means a lot to me, too, though I've never told Damien why. But I identify deeply with the kids that he has set out to help.

The waiter comes with a dessert menu, and the meal finishes easily, with the conversation never drifting back to anything too touchy. I skip dessert and opt only for coffee. And when we all finally head back outside, Jackson pauses at the restaurant's valet stand and hands the college-aged attendant his ticket.

"Dallas? Where are you heading?" Damien asks.

He points generally to the left. "I've got a suite at the Biltmore," he says. "Care for a nightcap?"

"We would," Damien says, his arm around Nikki's waist. "Sylvia?"

"She's with me." Jackson turns his attention from Damien to me. "We have some things to discuss. About the resort," he adds, though the addendum is clearly a lie.

Damien nods and both he and Nikki say that they will see us at the fund-raiser on Sunday.

I turn to Jackson. "I'm with you?"

"I damn sure hope so," he says. "Because having you not be with me is brutal."

The valet arrives, then parks the Porsche in front of us and gets out, holding the door open for Jackson.

Jackson steps to the passenger side and does the same for me. "Please, Syl. We need to talk. More than that, I think I need to apologize."

I get in the car. Honestly, there was never any doubt.

And though I don't know what exactly we are going to say to each other, I do know that there are things that must be said.

eighteen

Traffic is light, and we manage to get from downtown to Jackson's boat in less than half an hour. During the entire drive, Jackson says nothing, and we both just sit back, lost in the ear-blasting sounds of Dominion Gate, as Jackson continues to play the album we didn't finish the other night during our drive to Westerfield's.

When we arrive at the marina, he maneuvers to his parking slot in front of the *Veronica*, kills the engine, and turns to me. "I miss you. And I'm sorry."

I swallow, then blink back tears. "I need to hear you say it. Are you sleeping with her?"

"No." The word is fast and harsh. "God, no. I told you. Once, and that was a long time ago. She's a friend, Syl. She's only a friend."

I nod, then open my door. "Come on."

He still looks a bit wary, but he follows me out of the car and then onto the boat.

As soon as we're on deck, I go to him. I slide my arms around his waist and press my cheek against his chest. His arms surround me, and I breathe deep, feeling content for the first time in hours. We stay like that, feeling the boat sway beneath our feet, until I finally pull away, then go to sit on one of the lounge chairs.

"Is that all that's bothering you?" he asks. "Megan?"

I shake my head, trying to articulate what I haven't even really worked out in my own head. "I was pissed," I admit. "Because when I met you in front of the office, it was clear you were keeping secrets. And—no," I say as he starts to speak. "Let me get this out. And I didn't like the way I felt when she kissed you. I—I was jealous." I lick my lips. "And then I saw the other pictures."

His brow furrows. "What other pictures?"

"On social media. You on the boat with Megan today. And you with other women you've dated over the last few years. Usually at parties and stuff."

"I haven't seen them."

"No? Well, they pissed me off. And I know that it's stupid, and I know that we weren't together then. And I know that you told me they didn't mean anything to you—"

"I told you that because I meant it."

"I know. You just fucked them. Except for Megan, you didn't care about them. Not like that. I get it. I really, really do." I shrug. "But I'm still jealous. Especially when I think about, you know, the other stuff."

"Other stuff?"

I can feel my cheeks turning pink, which pisses me off because I don't want to be embarrassed or uncomfortable. I want to keep a tight grip on this conversation, and I'm afraid that I'm doing a piss-poor job of that. "You like control, Jackson. And we've done stuff. In bed, I mean. And I like it—I do. I like it a lot." As I speak, I'm rubbing my wrists, thinking about the leather cuffs he'd used on me not so very long ago. "And you've got that whole trunk of stuff in your bedroom, and I don't think it's been sitting there just waiting for me to come along like Christmas Day, and I can't help thinking of all the other—*shit*."

I cut myself off because I'm saying too much. And honestly, I didn't intend to say any of this. Hell, I hadn't even fully processed any of this until I started talking. All I know is Megan. Jealous. Other women. Jealous.

Apparently I have unplumbed jealous depths. Who knew?

Jackson has been sitting beside me on the lounger, but now he moves to kneel in front of me. He rests his hands on my knees, and the contact is warm and comforting. "There's only you. There has only ever been you. Even before I met you, it was just you." His smile is a little crooked. "And there will only ever be you."

He leans forward, then kisses me softly. "Wait here."

My lips are still tingling as he descends below deck. I have no idea what he is doing, and so when he comes back up carrying the trunk, I actually gasp with surprise. "Jackson?"

He looks at me just long enough to smile, and then he moves to the side of the boat and—before I have time to realize what he's doing—he drops the entire trunk over the side of the boat.

"Jackson!" I leap to my feet and hurry to his side, just in time to see the dark water settle. I turn to him. "Why—"

"Only you," he repeats, then pulls me to him. "And I assure you, we'll have a very good time filling a new trunk."

I can't help it—I laugh. But when the laughter fades, I have to shake my head. "I don't like this part of me. The jealous part. It's shrewish and icky and all sorts of things I don't like. But I don't want to lose you. And I see things like that. Pictures. Or you keeping secrets. And I just get scared and twitchy, and I'm sorry." I take a deep breath, because those words spilled out of me fast and furious.

"I'm sorry I didn't tell you I was going out with Megan today."

"No, no. I'm the one who's sorry. Really. I was just being bitchy. And I'm sorry."

"Oh, baby." He strokes my cheek. "Come with me."

He takes my hand and leads me below deck to the small galley.

I sit at the table, and he comes to join me, bringing a bottle of wine, two glasses, and a box of Chips Ahoy cookies. He takes one, then holds out the box to me. I don't really need it, but I take it anyway, then take a tiny bite as Jackson leans back in his chair and starts to speak.

"I didn't know Megan had come back to town," he says. "She went home after the screening, and I just assumed she was still in Santa Fe." He pauses to wash his cookie down with wine. "She called before lunch. Said she was downtown and needed to talk. Her husband died about a month ago."

"Oh." Now I feel even more like a bitch. "I'm sorry."

"It's been . . . hard on her." He sighs and presses his fingertips to the bridge of his nose. "I told you she was a friend, and that's true. But it's not just Megan I'm close to, it's the whole family. Especially Ronnie."

"The little girl."

"She's three going on thirteen." His smile is broad and it's clear he adores her. "Smart as a whip and as sweet as she can be. She's—" He drags his fingers through his hair, and I can't help but think that he looks completely exhausted. He shakes his head and smiles sadly. "She's a very special kid."

I frown, because his words don't match the sadness I see on his face and hear in his voice. "Something's wrong." I get out of my chair and circle the table until I'm beside him and leaning against it. "What's happened? Is Ronnie okay?"

"Yes, yes. Ronnie's fine. It's Megan." He takes a deep breath, then drains the last of his wine. He runs his fingertip over the rim idly as he speaks, and I don't think he's even aware that he's doing it. "You asked why I don't want the movie made. Well, Megan's a big part of the reason."

"Megan?" I don't understand what this redhead has to do with a movie about a house Jackson built in Santa Fe.

Santa Fe.

"It's her house? She's a Fletcher?" The Santa Fe house—the one that pretty much launched Jackson's career—was commissioned by Arvin Fletcher.

Jackson nods. "He's her dad."

"Oh." Arvin Fletcher is one of the biggest land developers in the country. He started out ranching in New Mexico and was smart about his investments. He's not worth as much as Damien, but I bet it's close. And when he hired a then relatively unknown architect to build him a residence just outside of Santa Fe proper, he put Jackson on the map. Afterward, the house grew in notoriety. Because one of Fletcher's three daughters murdered her twin and then killed herself. Megan, I realize, is the surviving sister.

Wow.

I stand and start to pace, trying to get my head around this. "So you don't want the movie to happen because you're close to this family. Fletcher gave you a huge break and you want to protect them?"

"That's part of it. But only a small part. Megan's bipolar. She's a lot of things, actually, but that's the easiest label. She's been steady for years—the drugs help and she was good with Tony. But since his death, it's been harder. She's off-center, not taking her meds the way she should."

"Oh." I'm not entirely sure what to say. "That's a shame."

"It's a lot of things. That's one of them." He presses his fingers to the bridge of his nose. "I worry about her raising Ronnie. And I worry about the press getting a peek at all the family skeletons. And they will, you know. If they make this movie, the family will become an open book. Even if the screenwriter doesn't poke and prod, the media will. And I don't want it to get out about Megan's illness. About how bad it can get. Or about the fact that Amelia had issues, too."

"She's the one who killed herself and her twin?"

He exhales, then nods, but it's clear that talking about this upsets him. "Yes. She shot Carolyn. Megan is their older sister."

"The script suggests Amelia went crazy because of you," I say gently. I haven't actually read the script, but I heard that from Jamie who heard it from her Hollywood sources.

His expression darkens. "She was infatuated, yes. But I wouldn't want to guess as to why she did anything."

I just nod, realizing that I've struck a nerve.

"The bottom line is that I don't want Ronnie growing up in the midst of high drama. She's had enough trouble, and now with Tony passing it's hard enough for Megan to focus."

"Can she take care of Ronnie? I mean, if she's not taking her meds?"

"We've had a few heated discussions about that very thing. But I'm not family, so there's not a lot I can do. Not legally, anyway." His voice is bitter. Harsh. After a moment, he looks straight at me. "Syl, I need to tell—never mind."

I move to him and take his hand. "What?"

"I just need to fix this—and I don't know how."

"Fix it? You mean, get Megan better? Back on her meds?"

There is a long pause before he nods.

"You can talk to her," I suggest. "To her family."

He draws a deep breath. "I do. But she swears she's going to take them religiously. And she says she has enough help."

"Does she?"

"How much is enough? Megan's grandmother helps out. And there's some extended family in the area, too."

"Arvin?"

"No."

I don't ask. From the way Jackson said the word, I can guess that the circumstances surrounding Megan's pregnancy didn't meet with her father's approval.

"At any rate, now you know most of it. There's more, of course. But the bottom line is that I want Reed to keep his nosy, voyeuristic ass away from the people I care about." He reaches for my hand. "Can you understand that?"

"Yeah." I squeeze his fingers. "I do. And I really am sorry I was such a bitch earlier."

He chuckles. "You weren't."

"Oh, I totally was."

He moves his hand to my cheek and I lean against it, soaking in his warmth. I look up at his face, and his expression is fierce. "No," he says. The word is firm.

He sucks in air, then runs his fingers through his hair before pushing out of his chair and walking across the open space to a window that overlooks the open sea. He looks out at the darkness, and I can see the tension in his shoulders. I want to go to him, to hold him and help him ease his worry about his friends. But I force myself to stay seated. To wait until he's said everything there is to say.

"I don't want to keep secrets from you." He is still facing the window, but now he turns. "I don't. But at the same time, things will come out when they come out. Does that make sense? Do you understand?"

"You know I do," I say. "I said so when you told me that Damien is your brother. I don't have a right to your secrets. And it's wrong of me to get bitchy and make it worse for you." I think of my own secrets—painful ones that I've held close. That I haven't yet shared with this man I love. This man I trust.

I draw a breath for courage. "Honestly, I'm not really sure how much of today was even about you or Megan or any of those other women. I was in a pissy mood, and on any other day I might have actually handled the whole thing like a sane person."

Immediately, his eyes sharpen. "Why? What happened?"

"Nothing specific," I lie. "Just a bad day."

The truth is that I've realized that I do want to tell him everything about Reed and my dad and the whole shebang. I want to spill it all out. I want him to hold me close and soothe me and tell me that the storm inside me will subside. That he will help make it so.

But I don't want to tell him today. Not when I've just seen so much evidence of his own worries and fears.

Mine can wait. They've already waited years. Another day won't matter.

He is watching my face, his expression knowing. "Now who's the one keeping secrets?"

"Me," I admit. "But it can wait." I reach out and take his hand. "Truly."

His brow furrows as he moves closer to me. He's right there in front of me, and I can feel the power and concern radiating off him, and all of it is directed at me. "Don't ever think that."

I blink, confused. "Think what?"

"That you need to pull your punches with me."

"Pull my—what?"

"Don't think you have to coddle me if I've had a bad day."

"I'm not," I say, then realize it's a lie the second the words spill out. "Okay, maybe I am, but what's wrong with that? You want to take care of Megan and Ronnie, right? Well, I want to take care of you."

"Sweet," he says. "But it doesn't work like that." He sits down again and tugs me into his lap. "You tell me what's on your mind so that I can help you, too."

He pulls me closer and I curl up against him, feeling warm and safe. Ironically, this was the way my dad used to cradle me in our big armchair. But that was when I was young. Before things went bad and I didn't even want to look at him, much less touch him.

"I don't know where to start," I admit.

"The beginning is usually a good place. Or you could tell me what happened today."

"My brother called." I draw a breath, relieved at how easy that was.

"Ethan, right? The one moving home from London?"

"He gets in Wednesday. I'm picking him up and driving him down to Irvine." I swallow, because just saying that makes my mouth go dry. "I was hoping you'd go with me. Because—well, because I don't want to go alone."

"Of course I will."

"Thank you." My relief is so intense it almost knocks me over.

Jackson is studying me, the concern evident in his eyes. "What happened with your parents, Sylvia?"

I'm so used to not talking about it that I start to push the question away, even though I've already decided that I want to share my past with this man. I regroup, nod, and gather my thoughts.

And then, slowly, I begin. "It . . . it was all okay when I was little. Good even. Normal."

"So when did that change?"

"When Ethan got sick." I stand up, because I really have to move, and I pace the length of the small table. "He was the most precious kid. Everyone adored him. My parents thought he hung the moon, and I didn't mind, because I did, too."

"You're older?"

I nod. "By just under three years. And my favorite thing in the world was taking care of him. Playing mommy, you know? I'd feed him, change him, play with him. And when he got older, we were best friends."

I wait for Jackson to ask me what happened, but he is calmly watching me, clearly letting me go at my own pace.

"About the time he was ten, he started getting into fights with the bigger kids at school. They were picking on him and—anyway, the reasons don't matter. The point is that the bruises didn't heal as fast as my mom expected. So she took him to the doctor."

"What was wrong with him?"

"Nothing," I say. "At least that's what the pediatrician told us. So for a year, nothing happened. By the time my parents found out that it was an aggressive and rare blood disorder that attacks the organs, a lot of damage had already been done, and they said he'd probably only survive a few more years."

"Oh, Syl."

"It was horrible, and I was so scared, and suddenly he was getting weaker every day. I would wake up and it would be like he'd faded in the night." I squeeze my eyes shut, not wanting to remember. "And it felt like we were just waiting for him to die."

A shudder runs through me, and Jackson is on his feet in an instant, his arms tight around me. I burrow against him, letting his strength push back these horrible memories.

"But he's alive," Jackson says gently. "How did he get better?"

"Money." My face is pressed against his chest, and the word is muffled. I force myself to lean back so that I can look up at him. "The doctors all said there was nothing we could do. The damage was done, and there was no cure, anyway. But my mom was relentless. She heard about an experimental drug—K-27—and she applied for the trials. They wouldn't take him—I don't know why. I think it was because he was too young, which is stupid because he was dying anyway."

I force myself to stay on track. "My mom learned about a doctor in Central America. He was using K-27 to treat patients like my brother, along with some other drugs in a cocktail. And according to everything she learned, his patients were getting better. Like, completely better."

"The damaged organs?"

"Repaired. Somehow this drug encouraged the growth of healthy tissue to replace the bad, necrotic spots."

"She got your brother to this doctor," Jackson says, continuing the story.

"Yes."

"But it was expensive."

I meet his eyes. His are sad, and it's clear he has some idea where this story is heading. "Yes. Very. And my mom didn't work. And my dad was just a technician for one of the studios. A cool job that paid well and had great Hollywood perks—but nowhere near the kind of money that he needed."

"That's where you came in."

"He was asking everyone if they had extra work for him, and Reed used to do some of the on-set photography during shoots. Production photos, candids to use during press junkets, that kind of thing. He told my dad he did model shoots on the side. That he was looking to build up that end of the business. He'd seen me before— Dad took me to work with him a couple of times and got me on the set—and told Dad that he could use me."

I push away from him, because I have to move. I can't stand still and talk about this. Because it was the first step to horror. But it was also the first step to saving my brother.

I go to the window and look out, wishing that I didn't have these memories. That I could just skip over the bad parts and be healed. But that's not possible, and so I press on.

"We got the money."

"*You* got the money," he says. He's still by the table, as if understanding that I need space right now.

"It was a lot of money," I say. "It took about a year to earn enough. But I told myself that was okay, because it was for Ethan. And he's better now, so it was worth it. What I did, I mean. It was worth it because it was for Ethan."

I see my own pain reflected on his face, and then I see the decision—and it's clear there's no way he's letting me stand over here by myself. He is at my side in seconds, and I slide gratefully into his arms.

"My dad knew, of course. He never said specifically, but I told him I wanted to quit. That I'd model if we needed the money for Ethan, but I wanted to go to someone else. He told me that no one else would pay what Bob did. And that's how I knew. My dad knew exactly what Reed was doing to me, and he was whoring me out. Damaging one child for the sake of another."

Even as I say them, the words resonate with me—wasn't that what Jeremiah did to Jackson? Sacrificed him at the altar of his brother.

"Your mom?" Jackson asks. "Did she know?"

"I don't know. She just went along with whatever my dad said. And even though she saw Ethan's bruises, she never saw my pain." I shrug. "I don't—I don't like being around either of them. I'm angry around them. Hard. I don't like myself when I'm with them, and I don't like the memories that come back."

"And yet you're going down there on Wednesday."

"For Ethan. He doesn't know any of this, and there's no way I'm going to tell him. So he just thinks I had a teenage falling-out with our parents."

"You don't have to go," Jackson says gently. "You can spend time with Ethan here. If he knows there's a rift, he'll understand."

"Maybe. But he really wants me there. And there's not much I wouldn't do for him."

Jackson is looking at me, and then he says, very slowly and very carefully, "Including letting a predatory photographer molest you?"

The tears that I have been holding back burst out of me with the force of a breaking dam. "Yes." My voice is harsh. Choked. "I could have walked. I could have stopped. I could have done something— anything. But I didn't."

"Oh, baby." There is grief in his voice, but I don't hear pity, and I am grateful.

"I blame my dad, but it's on me, too." My voice is shaky and thick with tears. "All this shit that has colored my life. It's my fault, too."

"*No.*" The word resonates through me, as violent as an earthquake. "You were a child with a sick brother you loved. Your parents should have taken care of you, not used you. And none of it—*none of it*—falls on you. *Christ.*"

He pushes away from me, and I see the rage rising inside him. He wants to break something, that's easy enough to see. And I think that given the slightest provocation he would reduce the furniture in this room to splinters.

"Are you okay?" I ask, and he responds with a self-deprecating laugh.

"Am *I* okay?" He closes the distance between us, and I can feel the power and heat—the rage and compassion—rolling off him. "Sweetheart, right now I only care about you."

He brushes a kiss over my lips. It's soft and it's gentle. But I know that's only an illusion. Inside him, there's a volcano of my making, and I can't help but wonder when it will explode.

nineteen

"Jackson."

That's all I say, but it's enough. He scoops me up, then holds me tight against his chest, his strong arms as firm as iron bands. "Yes," I murmur as my pulse kicks up simply from the rightness of being in his arms. "Whatever you need. However you need it."

I expect it wild. Wicked. I imagine that he will spread me on the table and fuck me hard in a frenzied rush to drive out his own demons by banishing mine.

By claiming me. By controlling me.

I do not expect the sweetness of his kiss. The butterfly-soft touch of his lips against my eyes, my cheek, the corner of my mouth. "You," he says, and the word is both gentle and firm. "All I need is to touch you. All I need is to make you feel. To take you softly and gently. And to make you forget."

"Jackson, I—" But I can't get any more out. My throat is too thick, and his name cannot slide past the emotion that fills me.

He carries me down the stairs, pausing before he does to open a small control panel on the side of the stairs and press a button. I look at him with curiosity, but his mouth just curves up in an enigmatic smile. I know better than to ask—he'll tell me when he's ready. And I hold my tongue as we continue down toward his bedroom.

It's a small, narrow hallway with Jackson's bedroom on one side and a guest room on the other. At the end of the hall is the bathroom—a simple toilet and shower. At the other end of the hall, just by where we are now standing at the foot of the stairs, is a storage closet. Or, at least, I had always assumed that it was a storage closet. Now, Jackson turns in that direction.

"Where are we—?"

But I stop talking the second he opens the door. It's another bathroom, only this one is dominated by a luxuriously deep tub and beautiful, gleaming fixtures.

The water is already running in the tub and the lights are dim. Soft music plays through speakers—a low, slow saxophone piece that I'm not familiar with, but that is sweetly seductive.

"Oh my god," I say. "How did I not know this was here?"

"I've been having it remodeled. It's still not quite ready," he adds, pointing to some unpainted trim and some exposed wiring for light fixtures. "It's been a work-in-progress, and once we got back together I wanted to wait until it was ready to show you. But I think it's ready enough."

"It's fabulous," I say, as he carries me to the tub and sets me on the side. It's pushed up beside a wall of glass bricks against a blue background, and though I know that this is not an actual window to the sea, the color is such that it suggests the ocean beyond. The tub itself is surrounded by dark wood that forms a three-sided box, with steps leading up to the top where I now sit. Though the front has room only to sit on the ledge, both sides are as wide as a couch, providing a flat sitting area outside the tub.

"Teak?" I ask, running my finger along the polished wood.

Jackson nods as he begins to undress me, very slowly and very tenderly. He unfastens each button, then eases the blouse off my shoulders. Then he traces the swell of my breast against the line of my bra cup. I arch back, my body going limp from the pleasure of such sensual caresses. Gently, he reaches behind me and unclasps the bra. Then folds it and the shirt neatly on a nearby table.

Now I am wearing only my skirt, underwear, and shoes. He moves down a step so that I am still seated on the edge of the tub, naked from the waist up, but he is below me on the second step. My body tingles in a state of sensual overload as the cool air from the room brushes against my bare left breast even while the heat rising from the bathwater teases my right.

From below, Jackson caresses my calf, then eases my shoes off. He strokes a gentle finger under my foot, so light that it is almost a tickle, but instead sends sensual threads darting up my inner thigh to settle at my sex, making me tremble with anticipation and delight.

He guides my feet to the step upon which he sits and tells me to stand, taking my hands to steady me. I do, and he releases his grip long enough to reach behind me and unzip my skirt. He tugs it down over my hips, taking my panties with it, so that I am now standing naked in front of him.

His eyes drift slowly over me, and I force myself not to cross my arms over myself, but to simply let him look—and to enjoy the heat that I see on his face, and the knowledge that it is directed at me.

"In," he says, nodding at the tub.

I step in slowly. The gently bubbling water is hot, but not scalding, and it's scented with lavender. I breathe deep and let the water take me. When I'm submerged to my neck, I look up at Jackson. "Coming in?"

I expect him to say yes, of course, and am surprised when he shakes his head.

"But—"

"Shhh. Close your eyes."

I consider protesting, but I do as he says. I hear him moving behind me, then feel his hands upon my body, slick with some sort of oil. He rubs my shoulders and arms, his touch firm but gentle. He slides his hands down over my shoulders, then massage my breasts, and as he does, arousal swirls through me.

"Stand up," he says. "But don't open your eyes."

I comply, and while my damp skin cools in the touch of the air, he keeps me warm with the sensual strokes of his oil-soaked hands. Over my belly, my hips. Then down my thighs to where my calves continue beneath the water.

He is not touching me sexually, and yet my body is on fire. My breasts feel tight and heavy. My nipples craving a nip of his teeth. My lips are parted, silently begging for a kiss. And the muscles of my sex throb and clench, desperate for penetration, even as my swollen, sensitive clit begs for his touch.

He doesn't satisfy, though. His hands slide up my thighs, yes. And though I shift my position so that my legs are parted—though I go so far as to actually whimper—he does not touch me intimately. Instead, his fingers stop their climb just shy of where I so desperately want to feel him. He's teasing me, of course, taking me to the edge. Heightening my arousal.

And while I curse him, I can't deny that it's working. I am beyond turned on. So excited that it feels as though I am floating, all the more so because I am light-headed simply from the heat of this deep, wonderful tub.

"Back in. But keep your eyes closed." He speaks in a whisper, as if this is a ritual, and it feels that way. As if he is worshipping me. Or readying me to present to an eager god. Either way, the focus is on me. On my pleasure. And I am delirious with the power of it.

Once I'm back in the water, he has me sit on the lowest step so that the water hits my shoulders. He leaves me for a few moments, and when he returns, he tells me to tilt my head back, then uses a cup that I hadn't noticed to sluice water over my hair before massaging my head with a rosemary-mint shampoo that makes my scalp tingle even as I breathe deep, then sigh with pleasure.

His fingers are strong, and the pressure on my temples and at the base of my neck is just enough to keep me relaxed and happy, and when he rinses the lather out of my hair, I can't help but wish that we could stay like that just a little bit longer.

As if reading my mind, he massages conditioner into my hair, then gently combs through it, and I'm thankful my hair is short because it so rarely tangles, and the attention is wonderfully sensual rather than potentially painful.

When I'm all bright and shiny and clean, he helps me out of the tub, finally letting me look around. I watch steam rise off my naked body as Jackson urges me to lay down on a towel he's placed on the side of the tub, along with a small inflatable pillow. Along the edge, there are rows of tea candles, filling the room with a warm glow and soft shadows.

"Jackson." I say his name on a breath. "The room looks magical."

"Looks? Sweetheart, I want you to feel magical. Lay back. Close your eyes."

"What if I want to see you?"

"See me in your imagination, then."

"I always do," I admit, and am rewarded by both tenderness and heat shining in his eyes.

"I want you to feel," he says. "And I want the feelings to send you someplace extraordinary."

He helps me down, so that I am on my stomach, my head turned sideways and my eyes closed. The towel I am on covers something soft, and I feel as though I am enveloped in warmth. My arms are at my sides, and the damp heat of the room is making me both sleepy and aroused, and the combination is surprisingly potent and erotic.

He starts at my shoulders, using that same scented oil to stroke and massage, not too intense, but enough to be both soothing and relaxing. I've had a few sports massages, but none compared to this. His touch seems to fill me, and all of the stress of the day is just melting away under his persistent, incredible attention.

Slowly, he massages my shoulders, then down lower until his hands are cupping my waist, then my hips. He moves lower still, his clever hands kneading my thighs, and I spread my legs, my body craving more. He doesn't take the hint, however. Instead, he continues lower, rubbing my calf, and then repeating the process on the other leg, working his way slowly up until his fingertips are teasing the sensitive skin between my ass and the top of my thigh.

I am a warm bundle of contentment, and it only gets better when he—*yes, finally*—eases my legs apart. I'm so wet, so aroused, and the brush of air over my sex makes me moan, and that sound turns even deeper and more needful when his oiled hand slides down between my legs to stroke me, his fingers sliding almost lazily into me.

But I want more, and I push back, trying to make the contact harder, deeper. I'm so turned on, and I am craving release, and the only word that fills my mind is please. *Please, please, please.*

I don't even know that my lips have moved or that I have spoken, but I must, because he turns me over, and my legs are spread wide and he's telling me not to open my eyes. To just float. To just feel.

What I'm feeling is his fingers inside me again. Thrusting hard. Thrusting deep.

And his body above me, his clothes brushing my bare skin, the cotton rubbing my sensitive nipples. He brushes a kiss over my lips and I whimper when it is all too short.

He starts trailing kisses down even as his fingers continue to stroke me, to tease me. Lower and lower, deeper and faster. His mouth on my breasts, on my belly. His tongue teasing my nipple while my hips arch in wild abandon as he finger-fucks me hard and deep.

Then his mouth is there, his tongue dancing over my clit, and oh my god, he's right, it's magical, because I swear that I am rising up, carried away on a storm of golden pixie dust as these sensations that had started so warm and tender have turned hard and hot and demanding and oh so very wonderful.

And then the spell shatters, breaking me apart, sending bits of me swirling off as electricity seems to arc through me, making me sizzle and glow and cry out from the wonderful, incredible, overwhelming pleasure of it all.

"Oh god." I am gasping, trying to catch my breath. "Jackson—oh, dear god, Jackson."

"Hush," he says, and I realize that while I've been off in another dimension, he has picked me up. He's holding me close, and my arms are around his neck. I'm completely exhausted, and sleep is pulling me under. He's carrying me out of this truly exceptional bathroom and down the hall to his bedroom. He slides me into the bed, then gently tucks the covers around me.

Then he takes off his own clothes, and though my eyes are drooping, I can see his erection. I try not to drift too far, because I expect another round. An intimate touch. After all, he is so hard that he must be about to burst. But that touch doesn't come, and I roll over so that I am facing him and blink sleepily. "But don't you want—"

He presses his fingertip to my lips. "Right now," he says as he pulls me closer, "I have everything I want in the world."

twenty

"This," Cass says, stepping back from the overstuffed clothing rack and holding up what looks like nothing more than some see-through pink gauze with a shiny, sequined band.

I cock my head. "What is that supposed to be?"

"A harem girl outfit. Duh." She holds it by the sequined band, which apparently would sit on the unfortunate wearer's hips. As far as I can tell, though, there is no top. Not even a sparkly festive one a la Barbara Eden in *I Dream of Jeannie*.

When I mention that to Cass, she just shrugs. "Maybe they're going for authenticity?"

"Maybe, but I'm not. Veto."

From a few racks over, Jackson looks up. "Don't I get a say?"

"Absolutely not."

We're spending Saturday morning doing our Halloween shopping. Right now, we're in Burbank at a consignment store that sells mostly old costumes from various television shows. I don't know what show that came from, but it wasn't that classic sixties sitcom.

"It's Halloween," Jackson says. "I think a harem girl is a great idea."

"You just want to see me half-naked."

"It's expedient," he says. "Less to deal with once I get you home."

"Goodness, Mr. Steele." Cass fans herself. "How you make a girl blush."

"Cassidy, I may not have known you for long, but from what I can tell, there's very little that makes you blush."

She looks at me. "I'm not sure if I should be insulted or impressed with how astute he is."

"Impressed," I assure her. "Definitely impressed."

A few more moments pass, and then Jackson calls me over. "What do you think?" He is holding up a tiny pink cowboy hat and a matching tiny pink denim jacket.

"I'm petite," I say, "but that's toddler size."

"Thanks for the tip. I was thinking about Ronnie."

"Oh!" I'm now with the program. I think of the dark-haired little girl I've seen only in a photograph. "I think she'd be darling in it, but Halloween's just a week away. In my experience, parents usually have toddler costumes lined up about eight months before the blessed event."

"In that case, it can just be for dress up. At any rate, it'll be fun to give it to her tomorrow. She loves presents."

"Who doesn't? But what's tomorrow?"

"She's still in town with Megan—they don't leave until Monday. I invited the two of them to the fund-raiser," he says, referring to the open house and charity auction for the Stark Children's Foundation. Jackson decided to serve out his community service there, and his time starts tomorrow. "There's a petting zoo and Ronnie is crazy for animals. What?" he adds, obviously confused by my growing smile.

I shrug. "It's not every man who'd invite his friends to his community service."

Jackson chuckles. "I'm not every man."

"No," I agree. "You definitely aren't."

"Plus, I thought it would be a good time for you to meet them."

"Yeah?" I pull him in for a kiss, which he enthusiastically returns before taking the pink toddler outfit to the counter and asking the clerk to hold it while we continue shopping.

"And what about you?" Jackson asks Cass as he heads toward the men's racks.

"Oh, now that Zee and I broke up, I'm back to my regular costume. I wear it every year," she explains.

"You should mix it up," I say.

"What costume?" Jackson is looking between the two of us, clearly intrigued.

"Straight girl," we say in unison, and he laughs.

"I wear a skirt and a blouse and I ogle the men. It's hilarious."

"Fair enough. But if you don't need a costume, why'd you come shopping with us?"

"What? And miss the chance to help that one pick out something seriously hot?" She points to me, then holds up her hands in a gesture of self-defense as Jackson raises his brows. "For your enjoyment only, of course. I'll be ogling the straight boys, remember?" She flutters her eyelashes, clearly working hard to look innocent.

She turns to me. "Speaking of, why don't you convince him to go as Superman? Man of Steel, right? And I have a feeling he'd look seriously fine in tights."

Jackson laughs. "Ogling men. Me in tights. Are you certain you're gay?"

She snorts. "Just because I don't want to sample the merchandise doesn't mean I don't recognize quality when I see it." She turns to face me. "You appreciate a woman's tits, right?"

"I am so not having this conversation." I look to Jackson for help, but he only shrugs.

"Don't look at me. I definitely appreciate a woman's tits."

"Careful or I will make you wear tights." I slide into his arms and rise up on my toes to kiss him. "And you know I can be very persuasive."

"*Your* tits," he says quickly. "Only yours."

My effort to find a witty comeback is thwarted by Cass's enthusiastic cries of "Oh! Oh!"

She's moved a few rows over, and now she thrusts a cutoff leather jacket into the air. "Biker chick! And Jackson can go as a biker. It's perfect."

It actually does sound fun. Not to mention comfortable, which is always my big complaint about Halloween costumes.

"Not bad." Jackson palms my ass and squeezes. "What do you say, baby? Want to be my old lady?"

"Mister, I think that sounds just about perfect."

Once we have a plan it doesn't take too long to put together the basics of our costumes. We're at the register waiting to pay and debating pizza or burgers for lunch when my phone rings.

I have every intention of ignoring it, but when I glance at the caller ID, I see that it's Reggie Gale, my old boss from my very first real estate job, five years ago in Atlanta. "How are you?" I ask after the preliminaries. "I'm so glad to hear from you. I've been meaning to call."

"Been too long," he says. "I thought if you were free we could have dinner."

"You're in town?" *Reggie*, I mouth, in response to Jackson's questioning glance.

"Santa Barbara. But I'm heading down to LA in a bit. Should be there in plenty of time for a drink or a bite if you have the evening free."

"I'd love it. I'm with Jackson, though. Do you mind if he tags along?"

"Steele? I haven't seen him since Atlanta. It'll be like old home week. The two of you. Trent."

I frown. "Trent? Trent Leiter? Is he coming to dinner?"

Reggie laughs. "No, I just meant I'm seeing old friends. You two in LA. Him up here. I've known Leiter since that San Diego project I worked on with Stark right before I hired you."

I can't think of any business that Trent has in Santa Barbara, and I make a mental note to ask Rachel on Monday if he's taken her away for a romantic weekend. That would be a treat for Rachel, who usually works Damien's desk on weekends. But she's been covering for me so much lately that Damien gave her the weekend off and staffed his desk with one of the floating secretaries.

We make plans to meet at six-thirty at the wonderful Restaurant at the Getty Center, one of my favorite places in Los Angeles.

"Which means you want to skip lunch," Cass says after I explain the change in plans to both of them.

"Pizza," I say. "One slice. And then you and I should go change," I add to Jackson. It's already almost two, and there is no way I'm going to such an elegant restaurant in jeans and a Dr. Who T-shirt.

By four, we are both cleaned up and changed. Me into a wrap-style dress that clings in all the right places, and Jackson into one of the suits that he's left at my apartment.

"We still have time," he says as I finish up my routine by brushing mascara on my lashes. He slides a hand around my waist. "I know just how to fill it."

"Do you?" I turn in his arms, feeling his heat seeping into me.

"Two words," he says, then bends low to murmur, "Getty Center," before claiming my mouth with his own. I melt into the kiss, my body tingling from my toes all the way up to my lips. And honestly, it's not just his touch that has set me on fire. It's the fact that he knows me so well.

"Why, Mr. Steele, you do know the way to a woman's heart."

"Hopefully into her bed as well."

"I'd say your chances are very, very good."

We spend the time before meeting Gale exploring the Getty Center property. The center is off Sepulveda Boulevard and high enough in the hills to boast stunning views. More than that, though, the entire property is a testament to the thing that both Jackson and I love—fine architecture. And as we stroll through the grounds, we discuss not only the fine work that the architect, Richard Meier, accomplished with the structures, but how it works in harmony with the surrounding land and other natural elements.

"Even the stone that he chose," Jackson says, pointing out the fossilized feathers and leaves that decorate the travertine stones that make up so much of the center. "These are the kinds of elements we need to look out for on the Cortez project," he adds. "Shells, driftwood, fossils. The rocks that have been beaten and carved by the sea. The more we can work those elements into the design—incorporate them as part of the building materials—the better."

We continue like that, chattering on about the Getty, the resort, and the beauty of the space in general until it's time to make our way to the restaurant.

Reggie is already there, and he shakes Jackson's hand enthusiastically and then pulls me into a crushing hug.

"I like the beard," I say. He's always been a big man with a Paul Bunyan build, but now he looks more like Santa Claus with the full, graying beard and mustache.

"Thought I'd try something new. Always good to keep them on their toes."

"Who?" I ask.

"Everyone," he says, and then winks.

We get settled at the table and order drinks, then fall into a convivial conversation full of reminiscing, catching up, and lots of laughter.

"So what were you doing in Santa Barbara?" I ask as I finish the last bite of my seared scallops.

"Visiting family, primarily. My nephew is the concierge at the Gateway hotel. He and his wife wanted my advice on an investment property, and I wanted to get away from Houston. Seemed like a win-win situation."

"So the investment is a good one?"

"Some land outside the city. Lots of growth potential. So long as they can afford to keep those assets tied up, I think it's a good deal for them. And speaking of good deals, you certainly had the right idea," he says, his attention focused on me.

"What do you mean?"

"I've been paying attention to your Cortez project. A resort that is spread over the entirety of one of the channel islands. Honestly, Syl, it was inspired."

"Thank you."

"Even if the Lost Tides Resort gets up and running before Cortez, it still won't have that aspect going for it."

I glance at Jackson, who doesn't appear to understand, either. "What's Lost Tides?" I ask.

Reggie leans back in his seat and sighs. "Well, shit. I assumed you'd heard. A developer in the Santa Barbara area is trying to bring a resort to one of the islands. Hasn't managed to acquire all the square footage, but as far as I've heard, they're moving forward with development."

"Who's the developer?" I ask even as Jackson asks about the architect.

"Not sure. Apparently, they're being as anonymous as possible until they're ready for the big announcement. I guess the plan is that the more drama they can drum up, the more press they'll get. And the more press, the more interest from the tourism industry."

I feel a little sick to my stomach. "So how do you know?"

"My nephew's boss," Reggie says. "He keeps his ear to the ground."

I glance at Jackson and grimace. "Well, a little competition never hurts anything."

He puts his hand over mine. "Don't worry," he says gently. "Our resort is fine."

I sigh, then nod, relieved that he can read me so well.

"He's right," Reggie says. "Santa Barbara's a long way from Los Angeles."

"Besides," Jackson adds. "Santa Cortez has a lot more going for it."

"Yeah? Like what?" I'm playing along, expecting him to cite himself.

Instead, he says, "You."

"Oh." My heart flutters as he squeezes my hand, and from the look in his eyes, I see that it is not a platitude. "Thank you."

Across the table, Reggie is watching us. "I wondered if the two of you had gotten back together. I'm happy to see that you have."

"Me, too." I whisper the words, my throat too full of emotion to speak clearly.

"Ironic that you're both working for Stark," he continues, and I feel Jackson stiffen beside me. Hell, I feel myself do the same, suddenly fearful that Reggie has somehow learned about Jackson's relationship with Damien.

But that's not what he means.

"I mean, the man saved all our asses, didn't he? Hell, I should probably take a job with him and complete the circle."

"What are you talking about?" Jackson asks.

"The Brighton Consortium, of course."

The Brighton Consortium consisted of a group of real estate investors and professionals who had been in the process of developing four hundred acres of land for commercial purposes. Jackson had been their intended architect, and had it gone through, he would have been responsible for a massive complex, including every building in the development. At the time, it would have been his biggest job yet, and he undoubtedly had expected it to be the project that truly launched his career.

Jackson lets go of my hand. Now he's gripping the edge of the table. Hard.

"Stark screwed me out of Brighton," he says. "He swept in, acquired key parcels of land outside of the consortium's agreement, and killed the whole goddamn project."

"Damn straight he did. Like I said, he saved our asses." Reggie peers at Jackson's face, then exhales. "Oh, son, didn't you know? That project was dirty."

"What are you talking about?" His words are measured and wary.

"I'm talking about fraud. The criminal kind that gets the feds involved waving claims like RICO and securities fraud."

Jackson says nothing, but I am relieved to see that his grip on the table has loosened just slightly. "Go on."

"I didn't realize when I got involved, and I got out as soon as I saw what was happening. Brighton's the reason I decided to retire. Leave Atlanta." He lifts a shoulder. "Of course, retirement didn't stick."

Jackson says nothing.

"I've known Damien for a while, and when I realized what I'd gotten in the middle of, I confided in him. Apparently someone else in the thick of it did, too. He had no reason to stick his nose in, and he sure as hell wasn't going to turn a huge profit, but he found a way to acquire those key parcels. As soon as he did, that was the end of it. Brighton went up like a puff of smoke, and so did the risk that we'd all end up with federal convictions hanging around our necks. All of us," he adds, looking at me.

"Sylvia? She was just your assistant."

"And she may have walked. At the very least, they would have latched onto her as a witness, made her testify. And you—"

"I would have been hard pressed to avoid a conviction," Jackson says slowly. "I was all set to get an extremely lucrative commission. It would have been hard to prove I wasn't completely hooked in." He closes his eyes and runs his fingers through his hair. "Shit."

"Sorry to be the bearer of bad news. I assumed you knew."

"I didn't," Jackson says. "But I appreciate you telling me." He turns to me. "I flat out accused him of knocking my career offtrack. And he didn't say a thing."

"Damien's not a man to justify himself to anyone." I meet Jackson's eyes. "Reminds me a little bit of you."

The fund-raiser for the Stark Children's Foundation is scheduled to start at eleven, with a lunch buffet, activities for the kids, and then a speech by Damien and a live auction, complete with a cattle auctioneer that Damien found in Texas.

Cass and I arrive at about eleven thirty, and I immediately start looking for Jackson, who's been here since eight.

The fund-raiser is being held at the Greystone Mansion, a popular event location in Beverly Hills. The 1920s mansion itself is huge—over forty thousand square feet—and is tucked away in rolling hills and lush landscaping.

The event is being held in conjunction with Stark Sport Camp, and the entire property is dedicated to the kids who are staying the full weekend for a variety of games and other activities. For camp, the foundation has rented the entire property. But the fund-raiser— which is only a few hours out of the weekend—is being held primarily on the main floor of the mansion, with a few activity stations set up outside on the portable sport courts.

I see a basketball court set up off to the left as Cass and I head into the mansion. "There it is. Jackson's community service."

"That's what he's doing?" Cass asks. "Basketball?"

"Honestly, I don't know. Let's find him and ask."

We enter the main area with the polished checkered floor and stunning grand staircase that has graced so many movies. Along the sides of the room, buffet tables are set up. Adults and children are going through the line, then taking their food to the small cafe tables that are provided both inside and out.

"I don't see him," I say, though I do see several familiar faces. Evelyn Dodge, for one, a Hollywood agent and friend of Damien's.

She's a dynamo with publicity and I recall that Damien was going to ask her advice about releasing news of his relationship with Jackson to the public. As far as I know, though, they haven't discussed it yet.

I also see Charles Maynard, Damien's attorney who also represented Jackson on the Reed assault case and negotiated community service in lieu of a conviction. Ollie McKee is here, too. He's one of Maynard's associates, and he's been helping Cass with her plan to franchise her tattoo parlor.

I point him out. "Oh, good," she says. "A familiar face."

I laugh. "What am I?"

"About to abandon me to go find Jackson. And you know it."

"True," I admit. "Catch up with you later?"

"Absolutely."

She heads off to Ollie, and I start to make the circle. I check the buffet tables first, because I think it's very likely that he got stuck serving food. But he's not there. In fact, he doesn't seem to be anywhere.

I follow the crowd and end up in a wonderfully colorful garden out back. But there is still no Jackson. I'm starting to think that with the size of this place, I'll never find him.

Finally, I see someone I recognize, and I catch up with Stacey, the assistant director of the S.C.F. "Do you know where Jackson is?" I ask after the standard greetings.

"He's down by the petting zoo. His friend with the little girl can't stay, so I gave him an hour off to hang out with them."

"Can't stay?" My heart sinks for Jackson. I know he was looking forward to spending some time with Ronnie. And I was looking forward to meeting both the child and the mother.

As Stacey had said, I find him at the petting zoo that's been set up at the rear of the gardens. He's kneeling beside a little girl with curly black hair as dark as his own. She's wearing the little pink cowgirl outfit, and I can't help but smile.

I look around, but don't see Megan, so I move closer, approaching from the side. I don't want to disturb Jackson's moment with Ronnie, but at the same time, I want to meet her.

I'm at an angle where I can see her face now. Her huge blue eyes and little cupid bow of a mouth. She has her hand out, and Jackson puts a few pellets of goat food in her palm.

"Okay, just hold it out, and he'll eat."

She does, but as soon as the very eager goats approach, she slants her palm, and all the food falls off.

Jackson laughs. "No, sweetie. Keep it flat."

"They'll bite me."

"What? Like this?" he asks, then moves in close making *num num* noises as he pretends to eat her all up.

She squeals and squirms. "No, Uncle Jackson! That tickles!"

"That's the idea, squirt. Okay, ready to try again?" His eyes flick up and he sees me. For a moment, I feel like I'm intruding, then his smile widens to include and welcome me.

I come over slowly, because Ronnie has gotten with the program and I don't want to accidentally scare off one of the goats as she thrusts her little hand out, then giggles as goat lips brush her palm.

When I finally arrive, Jackson stands and puts his arm around me. "Do you know who this is?" he asks Ronnie.

"Sylvie!"

I squat down so I'm eye level with her. "Very good. How did you know that?"

"'Cause Uncle Jackson said you're pretty."

I tilt my head up to see him. "Oh, he did, did he?"

"Yup. Who am I?"

"You are Ronnie."

"Yes!" She holds out a hand covered with goat spit, clearly wanting a high five.

I happily oblige.

"More food?" Having finished the greetings, she's ready to get back to the goats. I stand and slide into Jackson's embrace. "She's darling."

"She really is."

From a few yards away, I hear a woman calling, "Jackson! Finish up, okay? The taxi's waiting."

"That's Megan?"

"Yes. Stay with Ronnie a minute?"

"Sure." I take the bag of goat food and join the little girl.

And though I'm honestly not trying to eavesdrop, I can't help but overhear bits of their conversation, which consists of Megan insisting they have to go, and Jackson asking her to reconsider, promising to bring Ronnie to the hotel in plenty of time for them to catch their evening flight.

Megan sticks to her guns, though, and after a moment, Jackson calls me over, indicating that Ronnie can stay at the pen. I join them, and as he introduces us, I try to form an opinion of this woman. I know she's a friend of Jackson's, I know he cares about her, and I know she's dealing with a lot of problems. But I'm also seeing a woman who seems overly harsh, problems or not. After all, the poor kid has only been to the petting zoo and the grounds are practically a fairground of children's activities today. So my desire to like her is tempered by my feeling that she's being unreasonable.

And, yeah, that whole jealousy thing still lingers.

After the introductions, Jackson goes back to gather Ronnie, and I hang behind. "If you're worried about him watching her while he does the community service thing, you don't need to be. I'm happy to help."

"No. That's not it. She just needs to come with me."

"But if he's willing to watch her and bring her—"

"That's not his job." She snaps out the words, and I decide that I should probably keep my nose out of this.

I go with Jackson to put them in the taxi. I give Ronnie a big hug and get a sloppy kiss on my cheek in return. Jackson does the same, and is similarly rewarded. He hugs Megan, and we stand back as the taxi pulls out, watching the little girl waving at us from the window.

"God, I adore that kid."

"I'm not surprised. She's pretty adorable."

"I'm sorry you didn't meet Megan at her best. She's under a lot of stress."

"I get it," I say. "Single parenting must be hard. What about Ronnie's biological dad?"

Jackson hesitates, then shakes his head. "He wasn't in the picture."

"That's a shame."

Jackson leads the way down a stone path, and I walk beside him, holding his hand.

"Is it?"

I look at him, confused. "What?"

"It's just that everyone says it's hard to grow up without a father. But look at you and me. We probably would have been better off."

I consider what he says, and I can't deny there's merit. "I guess it's the kind of question that can only be answered in the specific. How can we say which would be better for Ronnie without knowing all the details? As for you and me—" I cut myself off with a shake of my head. "These are the kinds of big philosophical questions you shouldn't discuss without wine. Because if I grew up without a dad, does that mean Ethan would have died?"

He looks at me, then kisses my forehead. "I guess all we can do is live the life we have."

"Together?"

"Absolutely."

"Good answer," I say.

We pause to watch some kids playing catch with parents and volunteers. I lean against him, and he wraps his arms around me. It feels nice. It feels comfortable. And though I don't want the moment to end, I can't help the way my mind wanders, thinking about this place, these people. Ollie. Charles.

"You tensed up," Jackson says, and I frown for being so transparent. "What are you thinking?"

"About what Damien said Friday night," I admit. "About Reed bringing a civil lawsuit now that the criminal one is wrapped."

"Mmm."

"I saw Charles. Have you talked to him about that?"

"That and other things," Jackson says. "He thinks it's likely Reed will use the threat of a civil suit as leverage. And since I pled guilty to assault, it's pretty much a lock."

"You'd end up paying him damages."

"Or I let him do the movie and he drops the case."

"Asshole."

"I agree. Of course, I had Charles relay that I'll pay the damages. I can't predict what they'll be, of course, but my bank account is doing fine. And I'm not one to bend over to blackmail."

I shudder. "It's all such a mess."

"There's some good news, at least. Charles told me that Ollie is working hard with Cass. He thinks it's a good business for franchising and she's asking all the right questions. Doing her homework. Playing it safe even while making the leap."

"That is good news."

He tells me more about who he's chatted with as we continue down the stone path. We've gone quite far before I realize that Jackson is supposed to be working this function. When I call him out for slacking off, he just laughs.

"I still have a few minutes of my free hour. Plus, I'm on my way to my next job."

"Which is?"

He gives me a flat-eyed stare. "Apparently, I get to be my brother."

I'm baffled until we arrive at the portable sport court that has been set up as a small tennis court. Damien is there, hitting a ball back and forth over the net with a boy who looks to be about eight.

He sees us and waves, then calls over one of the volunteers to take over for him. He says a few words to the kid, then joins us.

"Thanks for doing this," Damien says. "I think you'll enjoy it. The kids get so excited when they hit the ball."

"So do I," Jackson says dryly. "Trust me when I say that tennis skill doesn't run in the family."

"You'll do fine." Damien takes a step back toward the court. "Come on."

"One second, okay?"

Damien eyes him, then nods. "What's on your mind?"

Jackson nods toward me. "Sylvia and I had dinner yesterday with Reggie Gale." He draws a deep breath. "I owe you an apology."

"Do you?"

"I blamed you for Atlanta. Turns out I should be thanking you."

"I made a business decision," Damien says, still in pure business-mode. "Nothing more."

Jackson studies him for a moment. "All right." He starts to move toward the court. "Ready?"

"Wait."

Jackson stops. I stand perfectly still, feeling a lot like an intruder, but I'm afraid if I leave, I'll disturb whatever is happening between these two men.

"I want to show you something." Damien pulls out his phone, finds something on it, then passes the device to Jackson.

Jackson reads, then frowns. "The press is lambasting you about cave crickets?"

"An internal email was leaked this morning," Damien says, which is something I hadn't yet heard. "In it, I said that we weren't going to shut Cortez down because of a species of crickets that the EPA says is protected."

"And somehow the press got your email."

"And they're taking it out of context. The discussion was with my staff and the goal was to research whether or not the species really is endangered. It isn't."

Jackson passes the phone back to Damien. "Why are you showing me this?" It's the same question I have—especially since the EPA has already told me that we're now in the clear and that Cortez is on track.

"The cave cricket issue has been resolved. But the release of this email doesn't look good for the resort. And the timing of this new round of sabotage so soon after your return to the project is very telling."

I watch Jackson's posture go rigid. And my stomach does a few flips of its own.

"What exactly are you saying, Stark?"

"I'm saying that someone is fucking with us. With both of us."

For a moment, Jackson doesn't react at all. His face is as unreadable as Damien's during a board meeting. Then finally, cautiously, he says, "You don't think it's me."

"I did," Damien admits. "I don't anymore. But I do think the timing is key."

"So who's doing it? Jeremiah?"

"He's definitely at the top of my list."

Jackson shakes his head. "I don't believe it."

"Then don't believe it. But you need to know something. Whether or not Jeremiah Stark is behind the sabotage, he's not a good guy. He's not a victim. He's a manipulative narcissist. The sooner you realize that, the better."

"What is it you think?" Jackson asks. "That I'm wearing rose-colored glasses? I know damn well that Jeremiah's not an innocent man."

"I'm glad your eyes are open."

"Wider than they used to be," Jackson admits. As if to illustrate the point, he looks around at this camp and the fund-raising activities to benefit abused children. "I read the press after your trial."

"Did you?" Damien's voice is cool. Though Damien is intensely private, he'd gone public recently with some of the horrific shit that had tainted his childhood. It was a seriously brave thing to do; I'm not certain I would have had the courage.

"Did he know?" Jackson asks. "What Richter did to you? Did our father know?"

For a moment, I don't think that Damien will answer, and to be honest, I very much want to leave. But I don't think that either man realizes I am there anymore.

Time seems to slow, and Damien says nothing. Then he looks Jackson in the eye. "He knew."

Jackson closes his eyes. When he opens them again, his expression is harsh, and I can practically feel his desire to hit someone. "He hurt us both, Damien. He wrapped us in a web of lies and deceit."

"Do you think I don't know that?"

Jackson drags his fingers through his hair, looking at me as he does. "That's not the kind of thing a father should do. You expect a parent to do the best for a child. To take on the burden, no matter how hard it might be. And definitely not use the kid as a pawn."

He turns his attention back to Damien. "We were pawns, Damien."

"And now we're not," Damien says.

"No," Jackson agrees. "We're not."

Jackson holds out his hand to me, and I go to him, relieved that he doesn't mind that I just heard that entire exchange, and also pleased that he wants me at his side.

"I never thought I'd say this, but I like you, Stark. If it weren't for all the shit around us, we might have been friends."

Damien's smile reaches his eyes. "Nikki said the same thing, more or less."

"Really? When?"

"When we met in the Bahamas and you turned down my first offer for a resort project. I told her I couldn't read you. That I couldn't decide if I liked you or hated you. She said I liked you."

"Did she? Why's that?"

Damien grins. "Because you're one of the few people who's managed to say no to me."

Jackson laughs, and I bite back a laugh of my own.

"Don't make a habit of it," Damien continues.

But Jackson just cocks his head toward the court. "Come on, little brother. Let's go play some tennis."

twenty-one

This week, I'm back on Damien's desk for Monday since Rachel is out for the day. Damien's out of the office until almost five, but that doesn't mean I get to coast. His desk is nonstop busy. Mostly because the man is seriously freaking busy all of the time, but part of it is because Rachel is still pushing aside the projects and tasks she's not completely comfortable with.

That wouldn't be a problem if I were away on vacation. But she's supposed to be training as my replacement. Which means I have to add talking with Rachel about her job parameters to my ever-growing to-do list.

I don't, however, consider my pile of work to be a bad thing. It keeps my mind off all the social media speculation about me and Jackson, Jackson and Megan, Jackson and the movie, Jackson and his assault on Reed. Plus, my mind keeps drifting to Ethan and dinner with my parents.

All things considered, I'm happy for the distraction that comes with Damien's very busy desk.

I'm on the phone with the president of Stark Manufacturing in Hong Kong when Damien walks in. I mute the call as I hand Damien a stack of mail. "I've got Mr. Cheng on the line. Shall I transfer him to your office?" Since it's the middle of the night in Hong Kong and likely urgent, I expect Damien to say yes, and I already have my hand on the proper button on the phone.

Damien, however, surprises me.

"Tell him I'll call him back in half an hour, then come in. I've got a couple of things to discuss with you." He doesn't sound angry, but he also doesn't sound pleased. I can't imagine that I did something wrong, because surely I would have heard about it by now. Has Rachel messed up something I need to fix? Has there been more bad press about the resort?

I'm a bit on autopilot when I finish the call with Mr. Cheng, then pick up a notepad and head into Damien's office. He's behind his desk reviewing correspondence, and he points at one of the guest chairs, indicating that I should sit. I do, then cross and recross my legs as I wait for the gauntlet to fall.

Finally Damien puts down the document, then looks at me. He says nothing for so long that I have to fight the urge to fidget. After what feels like way too long, he gets up, then moves around the desk so that he is now in front of me. He leans back against the desktop, and though his posture is ostensibly casual, I know him well enough to see that the opposite is true. His motions are planned, his air of relaxation intentional.

What I don't understand is why.

Finally, he reaches behind him and pulls a folder from the corner of his desk. "There's something I think you should see."

I take the folder and see that it is from Pratt & Associates, the private investigations firm we routinely use for employee background checks. I glance up at Damien, but I don't yet look inside.

"I like Jackson," he says, as if we're just having simple cocktail conversation. "And I no longer believe that he's behind the problems we've been having at the resort."

"But?"

His eyes dip to the folder in my hands.

It's clear I can't avoid whatever is inside. I take a breath, flip open the folder, and then jerk back as if I've been bit by a snake.

It's a petition to establish paternity and parental rights filed by Jackson Steele regarding Veronica Amelia Fletcher.

Veronica. Ronnie.

The boat. Of course. Jackson's boat is called the *Veronica.*

She's his daughter.

Oh, dear god, Jackson has a child.

And never once has he so much as hinted at this new, harsh reality that is now staring me in the face. Even after the night on the boat. Even when he told me all about Megan, he still said nothing.

Oh, god.

My skin feels hot, my throat tight.

I swallow and flip through the document. Attached to the end is exhibit A: a positive paternity test based on DNA analysis. And although the petition was filed recently, the paternity test is several years old.

Nausea wells inside me, and I sincerely doubt that I will get out of this room without throwing up. It takes every ounce of strength I have to remain calm, my expression even.

"I wasn't sure if I should tell you." Damien's voice is gentle. "For all I knew, Jackson might have told you himself. Or it might be the kind of thing you just don't want to know at all. But considering the press attention both of you have been getting lately, I thought I should show you."

I look down at the document again so that Damien can't see my face. I'm angry and hurt and confused.

Mostly, I feel betrayed. And numb.

I pass the file back to Damien. I really don't want to touch it. "Why do you have this?"

"We do a background check on everyone who works for the company. You know that."

"We don't pull pleadings from other states," I say.

"Actually, I believe the policy is clear that employees or contractors who also happen to be my half-brother are subject to a deeper investigation."

I lean back, surprised.

Damien shrugs. "I wasn't searching for dirt. I just wanted to know more about my brother."

I want to hug myself, because I am cold—so very cold—but I don't want my veneer to fall. I don't want Damien to see what a wreck I am, or how much those few pieces of paper have sideswiped me.

I nod, then force a smile. "Well, I appreciate you telling me. I really do. It means a lot that you thought to do that. That you were concerned about me. But the truth is that I already knew. Jackson told me."

"He did?"

"Of course," I say, as if there could be no other answer.

How very much of a lie that is.

I push myself up out of the chair, hoping I don't look as freaked out as I feel. "I'm leaving early today, remember? I should probably go make sure whoever human resources sent up is all set."

He nods, looking at me in that way he has, as if he can see right into my head and reveal the lie.

I really hope that's not true.

He watches me for so long that I'm afraid he's going to start cross-examining me. But then he smiles, all charm and goodwill. "All right," he finally says. "So I'll see both of you in Santa Monica in a few hours?"

Drinks. After the lesson with Nikki and Wyatt.

Shit.

"We'll be there," I say brightly.

He moves back behind his desk, nods in dismissal, then dives back into his correspondence.

I exhale slowly and head toward the door leading out of his office and to my area. I expect to find one of the floating secretaries behind my desk.

Instead, I see Jackson.

"Hey," he says. "You almost ready?"

I hesitate just past the open doorway. *I'm not ready for this. I am so very, very not ready for this.*

At first I just stand there, numb and uncertain. But then the door shuts behind me, and when I hear it click shut, it's as if I've been pushed back into action. I take a step toward my desk. "We're rescheduling the photography thing," I lie. I keep my eyes down, as if the notes on my pad are the most important scribbles in the history of the world. "There's something going on in the Hong Kong office. I'm going to work late with Damien."

"That's too bad."

As I slide behind my desk, I catch a glimpse of him and manage a disappointed smile. "Yeah, well. Rain check. But you should head out."

"That's okay. I'll stay. I have plenty to do on twenty-six. We can grab some dinner when you're done."

"I'll probably eat at my desk."

I'm talking to him, but I'm still not looking him in the eye. I can't, because I don't want to cry or scream, and I'm afraid if I look, I will do exactly that. Right now, I just want him to go. And that simple fact makes me want to cry the hardest.

"Syl?" His voice is both gentle and wary, and I realize that I can keep very little from this man. "What's wrong?"

I know I should tell him, but I can't. He's held on to his secret; I can hold mine for a little bit longer.

"Nothing. Hong Kong. I'm distracted."

It's clear he doesn't believe me—smart man—but he doesn't call me on it. "All right," he says carefully. "I'll be working on twenty-six. We can drive home later together."

"I'll use one of the company cars."

"Not necessary. I have plenty to do." He looks right at me, and

I know that he doesn't believe a word I'm saying. "I'll drive you home. It'll be nice to have time to talk."

He goes to the elevator without waiting for me to reply. He pushes the call button. And he doesn't once look back.

Shit.

I don't even realize I've made a decision until I reach the elevator, too. It's just arrived, and as he steps on, I do as well. And as soon as the doors close, I turn on him, letting all of the temper I've been holding in fly. "Goddamn you, Jackson Steele." I feel hot and cold at the same time, and so full of fury I could burst. "You put on this big act. Tell me you don't want to keep secrets. And yet when the opportunity is staring you right in the face, you don't say a single goddamn word."

"What are you talking about?"

"I'm talking about Ronnie!" I shout, shoving him in the chest and making him stumble back a step. "I'm talking about the fact that you have a daughter."

He goes completely gray as every ounce of blood drains from his face. He reaches behind him as if he needs the solidity of the elevator wall to steady him.

I stand frozen, waiting for him to deny it. To tell me I have it wrong—so very wrong.

He doesn't.

Instead, he asks, "How do you know?"

I lift my chin. "The paternity test. It's public record, Jackson."

"Public record? Only if someone's looking. Who'd be—that son of a bitch." He meets my eyes, his flashing with anger. And with hurt. "Damien."

I say nothing, but it doesn't matter. I'm sure the truth shows on my face.

"That fucking prick."

I wince, realizing that whatever detente Damien and Jackson have reached, I've clearly just destroyed it.

He takes a single, wary step toward me. "Syl, we need to talk."

His voice is softer now, as if he has put the anger away in a box. For a tiny moment, I'm proud of him, because I have a feeling all he really wants to do is hit something.

I'm not, however, proud enough to go with him. Not now. Not when I need to be alone.

"No," I say. "Maybe we do need to talk, but I can't right now. I need to think." I feel myself sagging with sudden, horrible exhaustion.

"Syl—" He is reaching out for me, and those damn tears are welling in my eyes again.

"No," I repeat. "I'm sorry, but I am going to Santa Monica tonight." I meet his eyes. "And, Jackson, I need you to not go with me."

"Here's to excellent students and negative spaces," Wyatt says, lifting a beer in a toast.

We're in Hard Tails, a relatively new bar on the Third Street Promenade just a few blocks down from my condo. Damien and Nikki are on one side of the booth, and Wyatt and I are on the other.

It's odd not to be sitting by Jackson, but I try not to think about him. I've been trying not to think about him all evening.

So far, I'm not managing that task too well.

"So a good report card on these girls?" Damien asks.

"Oh, yes. A-pluses all around."

"I'm so proud," Nikki teases, then passes her camera to Damien so he can check out the photos she's taken.

"These are great," he says. "I especially like the one with the pier."

"That one was Syl's idea. But I think we both nailed it."

Wyatt points a finger at both of us. "What did I tell you? Negative space."

We don't meet with Wyatt as regularly as I would like to, but he always has a theme for his lessons. Today's was composition. Using negative space—or the empty part around the object—to tell part of the story.

My passion is taking pictures of architecture, and after taking a number of shots of buildings near the beach, I'd finally looked out toward the ocean, then realized what so many photographers have discovered—that the famous Santa Monica Pier is a great subject for a photo.

I'd placed the pier down and to the left in the image, leaving a great deal of negative space filling the frame—the darkened ocean, the dimming sky. I'd shown it to Nikki, and even though she prefers to photograph faces, she'd taken a similar shot.

Now my mind is stuck on the idea of negative space. On seeing what's not revealed and making meaning out of it.

Jackson and I were both keeping secrets—our personal negative space. And I suppose that Wyatt is right about the negative space telling the story, because god knows there was a lot of story hidden in both our secrets. My father and Ethan. Megan. Ronnie.

Does that mean that negative space in relationships is about trust and secrets? And is there ever a time when there is no negative space to be found?

In a photograph, that would be crowded and horrible.

But in life?

In life, don't we want the secrets revealed and the negative space filled?

I don't know, and when the waitress arrives with another round of beer and a huge basket of cheese fries, I'm happy to abandon my philosophical moment.

The conversation turns to nothing in particular. The shows Nikki and Damien saw in Manhattan. Wyatt's upcoming trip to Chicago. Soon enough, we have to call it a night. Damien has an early morning overseas call, and I'm ready to be alone.

"I need to hit the ladies' room," Nikki says. She looks at me. "Come with?"

It's a totally transparent invitation, but I accept it nonetheless.

"I heard about the paternity action," she says as soon as we are alone in the small bathroom. "You okay? You seem a little shell-shocked."

"I guess Damien didn't believe me when I said I already knew." I grimace. "And I thought I was hiding it so well."

A small smile touches her lips. "I just got a peek." She reaches out to touch my arm. "Seriously, if you want to talk about it."

I do, I realize. *I really do.*

"It's just—I mean, the man has a daughter. He didn't think maybe that would be important to mention?"

"Does it bother you? That he has a kid?"

"No," I insist. "It's the fact that he didn't tell me when there were so many times that it would have fit right there into the conversation."

"Believe me, I understand. I'm married to a man whose natural state is to keep secrets."

"And you're okay with that?"

Nikki shrugs. "I won't deny it drives me crazy. But I'm not in his head, you know. And especially before we were married, I think I wanted to know things to prove to myself that he and I were okay. But that doesn't mean I had a right to those secrets. Not unless they affected me, too."

"Oh, I think having a kid affects me."

She lifts a shoulder. "Maybe it doesn't. Or maybe he's scared to tell you."

I just shake my head, not sure what to say to any of that.

"Come on, Syl. You guys are amazing together, but that doesn't change the fact that you pushed him out of your life five years ago. Maybe he's afraid you're going to do it again."

"No." The word is vehement and full of certainty. I look her straight in the eye. "No way. There's nothing that would push me away." Even this, I realize. It's a bump. A fight. But in the end we'll work our way past it. Won't we?

"And he knows that?" she asks.

"Of course."

"Fair enough. Maybe he doesn't want to tell you because there's nothing to tell. Damien told me that his attorney hasn't gotten a court date. Maybe he's not going to pursue it. Or maybe he was planning to tell you tomorrow or next week and you jumped the gun. I don't know, Syl. But neither do you."

"You think I shouldn't be mad."

"I didn't say that. Be mad all you want. Just don't be unfair."

I think about that. Have I been unfair?

She leans back against the porcelain sink. "The thing is, I've seen you two together, and it's intimate, you know? You fit. And I'm guessing that it's even more intimate than you've let on. But that's not—I mean—oh, shit."

"What?"

"It's just that intimacy's not a key, you know? You don't just get close to someone and expect that to open a door and everything comes tumbling out like an overstuffed closet."

I have to sigh. Because she's right. And I know that. It's just that this secret is so big that it seemed like a game changer. But maybe it's not. Maybe the game stays the same.

twenty-two

Jackson's not answering his phone, which probably means he doesn't want to talk to me.

Honestly, I don't care. We need to talk, and if he wants to send me away or lock me topside on the boat while he goes below deck, he can do that.

But until he takes those extreme measures, I'm doing whatever it takes to get to him. To talk to him.

To tell him how I feel.

And, yes, to tell him that I was wrong.

Which is why I am now pulling into the marina and parking my car. And when I do, I realize that the reason I'm able to park so close to Jackson's boat is because his car isn't in its assigned slot.

Fuck.

I try to think where else he could be, but the fact is that I just don't know. LA is a big city, and he could be anywhere.

I pull out my cell phone and dial the office, checking in with both the night receptionist and the security staff, but I am assured across the board that Jackson isn't at Stark Tower.

He wouldn't have gone to a club—not even to blow off steam.

And while his usual modus operandi is to fuck his way through moments like this, even after a fight, I do not believe that he would find another woman.

Then again, that's not really his MO, is it? I'm the one who begged him to use me when he felt out of control. When he had to lash out.

It's not a fast, hard fuck that he'll be gunning for.

It's a fight.

Shit.

I close my eyes and try to figure out what to do. I'm certain that I'm right, but that knowledge doesn't do me a whole lot of good. This is LA, after all, where hard bodies rule, and that means there are more gyms in this city than Damien has dollars.

I haven't got a clue where to start.

And since I don't know where to go, I'm going to have to settle on going nowhere.

I make my way onto the boat, grateful that Jackson has given me a spare key.

I get a glass of wine and settle on the couch in his office area, thinking that I'll take my mind off his absence by watching a movie or something, but I'm way too distracted for that. I'm actually considering calling Ryan and getting that intelligence agent friend of his to track Jackson's OnStar when I realize there's one thing I haven't tried.

I stand up, trying to remember the name of the friend who was hooked in to where all the underground fights took place. Butter? Cutter? No, *Sutter*! I do a little fist-pump, because I'm certain that I'm right.

Not that the name does me any good on its own, but if Jackson has Sutter's contact info . . .

I head over to his desk and poke around for a Rolodex or address book. But like all the rest of us, Jackson is living very squarely in the twenty-first century. Which means his contacts are filed electronically. Which means they are on his computer.

Which means I can't get to them unless I can figure out his password.

Which I am absolutely going to try to do, despite personal privacy and all those buzzwords. Because, frankly, I'm worried. And, yes, because I need to see him.

I try the basics first—his birthday, his social security number—which I get by calling the security team at Stark. The license plate number of his car. When those don't work, I try the name of his projects. His company. His boat.

Nada.

Finally, I try my name, and am disappointed when that doesn't work, either.

But it does give me an idea, and instead of using the *Veronica,* I simply try *Ronnie.*

And, voilà, the computer buzzes to life.

Since I'm really not trying to snoop, I go straight to his contacts and do a search for Sutter. I find him, Clay Sutter, easily enough, and scribble both his office and mobile numbers onto a scrap of paper. Then I log out, pull out my own phone, and dial.

There's no answer at the office number, which doesn't surprise me as it's already past ten at night. I hang up when the answering machine clicks on, and try Sutter's mobile number. Voice mail there, too.

Well, hell.

I hang up, because I'm not prepared to leave a message. Will he hear it tonight? More important, will he deliver it?

I've just decided that I don't have a choice, and am about to call back, when it occurs to me to text him. After all, voice mails require logging in, opening the message, listening to it. Lots of people ignore voice mails, myself included, unless I absolutely recognize the number.

But a text will flash across his phone screen, and that's what I want.

So I tap one out, then revise, then tap some more.

Finally, I send my message:

Looking for Jackson-911. This is Sylvia. Please, do you know where he is?

It will either work or it won't, but I figure it's my very best shot, and I hold my phone in both hands and say a silent prayer.

Less than a minute later it rings, and I practically drop the thing trying to get to the button to answer the call. "Hello? Sutter? Hello?"

"You're Sylvia? His girl?"

I'd been standing, but now I collapse into Jackson's desk chair, my knees suddenly weak. "Yes. That's me. I've been looking everywhere for him. Do you know if he's—"

"He's at my place," Sutter says. "Or he was when I left him an hour ago. My boy was a wreck. Needed to work off some energy. So I gave him the extra key and told him to lock up when he leaves."

I run that through my addled brain. "So, he's not in a fight? One of those underground rings?"

"Not tonight, he's not. Hell, I don't think anyone's got a fight going on tonight."

"I need to see him. Can I go? Will you tell me where to go?"

He hesitates.

"Please." My voice cracks as I beg.

"There's not another key," he finally says, "and I doubt Jackson would hear you knocking. Park in the back and go in through my private office. There's a keypad lock."

He rattles off the lock code and the address, and I am so grateful that I would have kissed this man if I could.

I use my phone to map the address and end up in a run-down

strip shopping center by the airport. Most of the signs for the businesses are broken and the windows covered with brown paper, but three still remain in business. A thrift store, a liquor store, and the gym.

That's all the sign on the facade says—GYM—but that's all I need to know I'm in the right place. That, and the sight of Jackson's Porsche parked in front, looking vulnerable in this seedy neighborhood.

My car, a simple Nissan I've had since I started working for Damien five years ago, isn't as sexy or fancy as the Porsche, but it looks vulnerable as well when I park it all by itself behind the gym. It has a car alarm that I rarely use. Tonight, I activate it.

Fortunately, Sutter was thorough in his instructions, and it's easy to find the door to his office, and once I've punched in the code and entered, I pull the door shut and lock it. The office is bare bones but neat, with what looks like an army surplus desk, a couple of filing cabinets, and lots of awards and certificates framed on the wall in plain black document frames that you can buy at any drugstore.

The gym is as simple as the office. It is mostly mats and free weights. Nothing like the gym at work with row after row of weight and cardio machines. Here, there is a treadmill for cardio, and that's about it. There's also a boxing ring, slightly raised and padded, and I imagine that's some pretty serious cardio, too.

But it's the far left corner that interests me as I stand in the doorway between this main area and the office. Because that is where Jackson is, shirtless and in loose gym shorts. His back gleams with sweat, and he is pounding away at a punching bag.

I don't know how long I watch him—a minute, an hour, a year?—but finally he seems to run out of steam. He turns away, breathing hard, and as I step backward into the shadows, I see that the ferocity in his punches isn't reflected on his face. Instead, he looks tired and a little lost. And that, I think, is because of me.

He walks to the locker room, and once he has disappeared inside, I step out of my hiding place. I follow him, slowly entering the plain white room that smells of soap and antiseptic. I see rows of lockers, and then off to the left there is a line of shower stalls with thin plastic curtains. Jackson is in one. He thinks he's alone, and the curtain isn't closed. He is facing the tiled wall, letting the water pound on him. After a moment, he leans forward and puts his hands on the tile, his head down, his posture full of defeat.

No.

I toe off my canvas shoes, then peel off my jeans and underwear. I leave them on the floor, then pull off and discard my shirt and bra as well, so that by the time I have reached the shower, I have left a Hansel-and-Gretel-style trail of clothes across this tidy, mopped floor.

I pause for a moment behind him, afraid that this is a mistake. But even if it is, I'm going forward. Whatever the consequences, I have to talk to him. I have to apologize. And I have to know the story; I have to know about Ronnie.

I enter the stall, then slide my arms around his waist.

He freezes at first, and I have a split second to think that perhaps sneaking up on a naked man from behind in a shower stall is a very bad idea.

Then his body relaxes. He says nothing, but turns in my arms. His eyes meet mine before I glance down and see his cock go hard, as if matching the intensity of his expression.

His gaze slides over me, and I start to speak, but he shakes his head. Just the slightest movement, but it silences me. Then he pushes me back so that my now-heated skin is pressed against the tile. There is heat in his eyes. Hunger. And in one fast, almost violent movement, he claims my mouth, his hands on the tile on either side of me.

We touch nowhere except our lips, and yet I feel him throughout my entire body. My skin tingles. My cunt throbs. My breasts seem to beg for him to touch me, rough and wild. To take and to claim and to—

He spins me around so that now I am facing the shower stall, and he pulls my hips toward him, holding on to me so that I don't slip. Again, he says nothing, but he puts my hands on the tile, so that now I am bent forward at the waist, and he is behind me. He strokes his hands over my back, then over my ass, then he urges my legs apart and slides his hand between them. I am completely wet, and desperately aroused. I want him to use me. I want him to fuck me.

And then he is over me, one hand cupping a breast as the other guides his cock to my core. When he's positioned, he doesn't hold back, just cups my breasts and slams hard into me again and again, deeper and deeper.

I am on fire, wildly turned on by not only the way he feels pounding inside me, but also by this reality. By coming to him, giving myself to him in both apology and passion, and then knowing that he needs this. That he needs *me*.

This will be fast, I know, for both of us. I can feel the pressure building inside of him just as it builds inside me. I'm close, so close to the edge as he slams harder and harder into me, and when he finally cries out in release, I join him, my body clenching tight around him, drawing it out so that he clutches my breasts tight and I moan in the complete, decadent, wild pleasure of this moment.

It was fast and brutal and incredibly powerful.

Most of all, it felt right. It felt like an apology and a promise.

He holds me while we catch our breath, his lips brushing the back of my neck. Then he urges me up and under the shower spray. He stands close to me, using a washcloth to clean us both before turning off the water. He grabs a towel from a pile near the stall and dries me, then wraps me in a dry one. He dries himself next, then wraps the towel around his hips.

"Sylvia," he says. And it is the first word he has said since I arrived.

I close my eyes and draw a breath. "I'm sorry I lashed out at you. I put you on the spot and I punished you for not telling me a secret, and that was horrible of me, especially since I've already told you that I understand about secrets. They're yours, not mine, and I don't have any right to demand them."

"You have every right to this one," he says. "A child affects you, too."

I draw in a shaky breath. "You didn't tell me—and, and I guess I thought that meant that I don't mean to you what I thought I did."

From his expression, you would think that I'd landed a physical blow. "Oh, sweetheart, no."

"Then why not tell me?"

He drags his fingers through his wet hair, then leads me back to the lockers. I gather my clothes as we go, and as Jackson opens his locker, then starts to dress, I do the same. "Everything's happened fast with us, and I've only recently made up my mind about Ronnie—to push the action, set a court date, and bring my little girl home."

I frown, because something about what he says doesn't make sense to me. But I can't put my finger on it.

"More than that, though, I think I was afraid to tell you."

"Afraid?"

"You didn't sign up to be with a man with a child."

The words are flat and hard and they weigh heavy on me. "Sign up?" I repeat. "Like we all pick a queue for our lives and our loves and that's where we go and we never veer out of our line? It doesn't work that way, Jackson."

I'm dressed now, and I go to him. He's in jeans, but he hasn't buttoned his shirt, and I press my palm against his bare chest, letting his heartbeat resonate through me. "I love the man, Jackson. Architect, lover, father. And I'm not saying that a child won't change things between us, but we can make it work. I want to make it work." I meet his eyes, overwhelmed by the tenderness I see looking back at me. "I don't know a thing about toddlers. But I love you, Jackson. And you love Ronnie. That makes it a no-brainer for me."

"Oh, baby." He pulls me close and kisses me, long and lingering and so wonderfully sensual that when he finally breaks it, I have to sit on the wooden bench or else fall to the ground in a puddle.

"You are amazing, you know that, right?"

I grin. "I like to think so," I say, making him chuckle. "What did you mean when you said you'd bring her home?" I've finally realized what is bugging me. "What about Megan?"

"Megan's not her mother. She's her legal guardian."

"Oh." I frown. "Who is?"

"Amelia," he says, and everything clicks into place.

"The screenplay is right. She was obsessed with you."

He finishes buttoning his shirt and sits on the bench beside me, then takes my hand. He looks down at our joined fingers as he speaks. "I was dating Carolyn, Amelia's twin. Not seriously, but we enjoyed each other. She was easy to be with and I—I wasn't looking for anyone permanent. I was raw after you, Syl. I just wanted a woman in my bed. Someone to take the edge off."

His words are painful to hear, all the more so because this is a chain of events I set in motion, but I say nothing. I just sit and I listen.

"Amelia had a crush, but I never cared for her. They were identical twins, but looks were the only thing they had in common. Amelia was narcissistic and had a cruel streak. A selfish streak. And one night she came into my bed dressed as her sister, wearing Carolyn's perfume. She said nothing, and she woke me up with kisses and touches and—at any rate, I wasn't thinking clearly. I thought Carolyn had come home early from a trip. It wasn't until after I'd fucked her that I got my wits back and realized she was Amelia. It was that one time, but it was enough."

"She was pregnant."

"She was. And she tried to pressure me into marrying her. I said no. I didn't love her—I despised her, actually. Or pitied her. And I didn't love Carolyn, either."

He takes a deep breath, and though I have a million questions, I force myself to stay quiet.

"I told her I wasn't even sure the baby was mine—and that was true. Amelia slept around. But she insisted that it was, and part of me believed her. But I wasn't about to be pressured into marriage, and when the house was done, I left. A few months later, she had the baby. And a week after that, she lured her sister into a work shed. Used a revolver to put five bullets in her, and then used the last one to kill herself."

He is speaking evenly, almost matter-of-factly. But he is gripping my hand hard, and I can tell that every word is painful.

"Megan got custody of the baby."

"She did. And she called me. She knew—as much as anyone did—that Ronnie was mine. She also knew—and now Arvin was involved—that the whole thing would be a huge scandal. She was awarded legal guardianship, and the family asked me to not claim the child. At the time, I thought that was best. I was shell-shocked. Confused. Lost. Hurt. I don't even know. And I was traveling so much, working twenty-four/seven, that I didn't think I could be a good dad. A solid father. I sent money regularly, started college funds, bought presents. Then I started visiting. Megan and I became friends—and, yes, we slept together once, but there was nothing real there. But there was something real between me and Ronnie. I grew to love her. And though I didn't need a paternity test to know she was mine, I had one anyway."

I think about the little girl's eyes and hair, and I feel like a fool for not having seen it before. "It was positive," I say, stating the obvious. "When did you take it?"

"Ronnie was about eighteen months old."

I frown a little as I nod. I know that, of course; I'd seen the test attached to the court documents. "Why didn't you file a paternity action then?"

"I thought about it," he says. "But Ronnie's well-being has always been my chief concern. At the time, that meant me being her uncle. She had Megan and Tony, and though they hadn't adopted her, they stood as Mommy and Daddy."

He runs his fingers through his hair. "So she had stability. Care. She also had Megan's maternal grandparents around to help. Still has them, of course, even though David, Megan's grandfather, had a small stroke last year. He's bedridden. But her grandmother, Betty, is a rock. I'm pretty sure that woman is invincible."

"What about Arvin? For that matter, what about Megan's paternal grandparents?"

"Dead," he said. "And Arvin was having none of it, and his wife passed away a while back, so he had no wife to soften his stance. Even so, staying in Santa Fe with Megan and Tony and Betty was a much better situation than bouncing all over the world with me and growing up in the care of a nanny."

I nod, taking it all in. And I understand the decision he'd made. "It must have been hard," I say.

I can hear the loss and longing in his voice when he says simply, "It was."

"But now you're pushing to establish parental rights?"

"I want custody now. It's what's best for Ronnie."

"Because her life was stable when Tony was alive, but now with all of Megan's problems . . ."

I trail off, and he picks up the thread. "Exactly. I hate it, but I can't deny that Megan's losing her grip—and I need to keep Ronnie safe. I need to be her dad, not her uncle." His voice gathers force. "More than that, I want to be."

"And Megan's okay with that?"

"Yes and no. When she's level, she is. And so is her family, especially Betty, who's been a huge ally to me."

"And when Megan's not level?" I ask.

"She wants me to stay the hell away." He frowns, his expression all kinds of sad. "Even when she's level, though, she's concerned. When you first saw her at the screening, we argued, remember?"

I nod.

"Megan was chewing me out about bringing Ronnie into the thick of this shit. She's going to be surrounded by enough scandal with the movie, Megan said. But how much worse will it be if we add to that by revealing that I'm her father?" He frowns. "The thing is, all of that is true."

I draw in a breath, because he is absolutely right. The kid will be the focal point of a media shitstorm.

"That's why you don't want the movie made."

He squeezes my hand. "That's why it *won't be* made," he says, "and that's what I told Megan. There's not going to be a movie. There are two people in this world that I will protect no matter what. You and Ronnie." He meets my eyes. "I'm not letting that movie get made, Sylvia. There's been enough trauma in that little girl's life. Whatever it takes," he says, "I'm shutting Reed down."

"Do you know what I'd like to do tonight?" Jackson asks. We're in the Porsche, just pulling into the marina parking lot.

It's after eleven, and we're both exhausted. Big emotional revelations will do that. "If you say go out dancing, I will have to hurt you."

"I want to sit in bed with you beside me, a drink in my hand, and the television playing some mindless program. Possibly with a book, but that depends on how mindless the show is. What?" he says, apparently realizing that I'm staring at him.

"Nothing," I say. "Just that I only this minute realized how absolutely perfect you are."

A shadow flickers across his eyes. "I worry, you know. That I'm doing the right thing for her even without factoring in all the bullshit with the movie. I mean, what do I know about being a dad?"

I take his hand. "I think worry is one of the signs of a good father. I think that worry is part of the package." I brush his cheek with my thumb. "You're going to do great. She's a lucky girl to have you."

I don't know if I've eased his concerns, but the shadow fades, replaced by a slow smile. "And you?"

"Me?"

"Are you lucky to have me?"

My heart twists. "Luckiest woman in the world."

He holds my gaze; his is so intense and vibrant that it not only steals my thoughts, but makes my body hum.

"What?" I finally manage.

"I'm just looking forward to our lazy night in bed."

"Oh." A flicker of disappointment cuts through me.

"In the interest of full disclosure," Jackson says. "I should probably tell you that I have every intention of fucking you awake tomorrow morning."

"*Oh.*" I lick my lips. "Thank you for the heads-up, Mr. Steele. I look forward to getting fucked."

It is, frankly, a truly wonderful night. *Law & Order* isn't mindless, but we've both seen the episode before so it might as well be. I flip through a photography magazine while we watch, and Jackson reads the book that *Psycho* was based on, then tells me we need to watch it over Halloween weekend.

"Maybe after Jamie's party?"

"It's a date."

I am actually going so far as to write the movie date into my phone's calendar when it rings—and the caller ID shows Siobhan O'Leary. I frown, but answer. "Siobhan?"

"Hey, Sylvia. Long time, huh?"

"Yeah. Hey. What's up?"

"I saw the pictures of you and Cass. The ones that have been going around after you guys were at Westerfield's. And, well, I've been meaning to call her, so I thought that was like a sign."

I smile. Siobhan always said signs were bullshit.

"Anyway, I tried to call, but I think she's blocked my number."

"Yeah," I say. "She did."

"Oh." I hear a clicking, and imagine that she's tapping a pencil near the phone. "So I figure I have two options. I can get a new phone number, or you can ask her to unblock. I figure the second option is better, because I'm pretty attached to my number. And if I get a new one and she hangs up on me, I'm just going to be out the cost of a new number. Not that she's not worth it, but it seems a little wasteful."

Okay, she's made me laugh. And that's always a good sign.

"All right," I say.

"Really?"

"No promises, but I'll ask her. Wait a couple of days before you try again. She might have to talk herself into it."

"That's okay," she says. "I'll wait as long as it takes." And she sounds so sweet and enthusiastic and just genuinely happy that I am grinning when I end the call.

"What's up?"

"Cass's old girlfriend wants to get back in touch. I told her I'd tell Cass to unblock her number."

"This is a good thing?"

"I think so," I say. "Siobhan and Cass always clicked. I mean, they fit together like watch gears, you know?"

He smiles just a little. "I do."

"It blew me away when they broke up—it was for all the wrong reasons, too. Siobhan's bi, and her parents were pressuring her to get back together with an old boyfriend."

"It didn't work."

"Guess not," I say. "But now I'm a little worried. I don't want Cass to get her heart broken again."

He rolls over and kisses my shoulder. "If they click—if it's right—then Cass will be fine. After all," he adds gently, "that's what second chances are for. And you and I should know that better than anyone."

twenty-three

I spend the entire next morning running around like a crazy person at work, and so I feel perfectly justified taking a small break in the early afternoon to bring my camera down to the graphic design department so that I can pull the memory card and print out a poster-size copy of my photograph of the pier.

Not that I think I'm Ansel Adams—or even Wyatt Royce—but I'm proud of it, and I think that Jackson will like it, too. Maybe it's silly, but I want to surprise him with a present. Something unique. Something me.

Which explains why I'm about to use work resources for my personal gain.

Thankfully, no one in the graphics department has a problem with this. In fact, the manager, Joan, thinks it's such a great idea that she offers to help me so that I'm certain to get all the various settings on the printer right.

She also offers to print off the rest of the images on my card so that I'll have hard copies. Of course I agree, and while she copies my files, I hang out in the department talking with the artists and looking at the preliminary sketches of the proposed logos for the resort.

"I'll have a messenger walk them up to you when the slew is printed," Joan says as she hands the memory card back to me.

I thank her profusely, then head up for a meeting with Aiden followed by a telephone conference in Damien's office with Dallas Sykes about that boutique that I'd mentioned at dinner. Turns out he thinks it's a great idea.

I want to go down to twenty-six and see Jackson, but he dropped me at my car this morning before heading on to a warehouse in San Bernadino to look at samples of various building materials and won't be back until late.

When I return to my desk, I'm pleased to see that Joan has come through. There's a thick clasp envelope with my name on it lying on my desktop, and I can't wait to see how the photos turned out.

I open the clasp, dump the contents on my desk, and then back away as quickly as if I'd been attacked by a snake.

I stand there, my back pressed to the fabric-covered wall of my cubicle, my stomach roiling.

These aren't the photographs I've taken of structures around Santa Monica. Instead, the pictures are of a teenage me. Half-naked. Arching back for the camera. Touching myself. Arranged in all the poses that Reed dictated. And I'd complied, because that was the job—to do what he said. To get the money.

To save my brother.

What did it matter that I'd been ashamed? That I'd hated it?

I realize with a start that I am standing there frozen. But this is a cubicle, and anyone can pop by and stick their head through the door.

With a small, panicked cry, I burst forward, then start to shove all the photos back into the envelope. As I do, I find a small, white envelope mixed in among them. It has no address, just my name.

I stare at it, certain that whatever is in the envelope is worse than those photos.

I don't want to open it. I don't want to know.

Roughly, I shove it to the far side of my desk, and then scoop the photos back into the big envelope. I seal the clasp. I cram the whole thing in my purse.

I want to run to the shredder, but I know that I can't. I have to keep them.

And, dammit, I have to know what the letter says.

Slowly, I open it. Inside the envelope there is a small piece of paper with just a few words, but they are enough to send me falling into my chair as my knees buckle.

The public sees the movie or these pictures. Tell Steele it's up to him.

Oh god oh god oh god.

I sit there, my hands on my knees, trying desperately to remember how to breathe. I'm not doing a very good job, and I'm afraid that any minute, I'm going to pass out. But I know that I have to hold it together. I'm in a fucking cubicle and I don't want anyone to see me like this.

I try to think what to do, but my mind doesn't seem to be working right.

Jackson. I need Jackson.

I fumble for my phone, then have to resist the urge to fling it across the room when it rolls to voice mail. I try again and again, but there is no answer. I start to send a text message, but my hands are shaking too much.

I need to get out of here. If I can just get out of here, then maybe I can breathe.

I take my tote bag and my phone and I head toward the elevator, then ride it all the way to the lobby. When I arrive and have cell service again, I text Rachel. I'm proud that I've calmed enough to manage that small task. I tell her that I'm meeting with a list of contractors and will be out of the office for the rest of the day.

Then I get back into the elevator and descend to the parking garage. And then, when I'm finally in my car, I clutch the steering wheel, close my eyes, and cry and cry and cry.

Enough.

After a good ten minutes lost in a crying jag, I grip the steering wheel, squeeze my eyes shut tight, and force myself to calm the fuck down. This sucks, yes. It's completely, totally, one hundred percent fucked up.

But that doesn't mean I have to go spiraling down into hysterics like some doe-eyed twit from the seventeenth century.

I am not a weak woman. *I'm not.*

I saw what I wanted with the Cortez resort, didn't I? And I went after it.

I found the strength to walk away from Jackson five years ago when I thought I had to. And, yes, I had the mettle to later admit that I still wanted him, and that we could battle my nightmares together.

All of which translates into strong, right? So what the hell am I doing breaking down in my car?

I already melted down once over this asshole's pictures of me. I'm not going to do it again just because there are more. Even if these new pictures are a billion times more horrible.

I'm not weak, I tell myself again. Because the more I say it, the more I believe it. *I'm strong.*

Hasn't Jackson told me so over and over and over?

Jackson.

Christ, I've been selfish. Wanting him beside me to help me find strength, when the fact is that he's just as deep into this as me. More, maybe, since at the end of the day what Reed wants is to make the movie, not release the pictures. Jackson's going to be just as angry as I am scared. And he's going to need me just as much as I need him.

Even while the thought makes me sad, it also comforts me. Because we're in this together, he and I, and the truth is that we're a pretty damn good team. Not only are we planning an entire resort together, but we've survived a hell of a lot of shit.

We can do this.

Granted, I don't know how, since Reed has put us at cross-purposes—but we'll figure it out. That's what we do.

But I need Jackson beside me to do it, and so I rub my hands over my eyes, tell myself very sternly that I cannot break down over the phone, and dial his number again.

This time—*thank you thank you thank you*—he answers on the first ring.

"Good afternoon, Ms. Brooks," he says in the kind of voice that suggests that he's happy to hear from me, but deep into business-mode. "I'm just sitting down with Mr. Pierce to talk price on a couple thousand tons of burnished copper plating. Can I call you back in a few?"

"I—yes. Of course."

There is a pause, and when he speaks again, his tone is low and careful, as if he's treading over broken glass. "I'll leave right now. Where are you?"

I close my eyes, a little ashamed that I'm so relieved, and that he knows me so well.

"In my car, but I'll meet you at the Stark suite at the Century Plaza hotel," I say, referring to the suite that the company keeps open for visiting clients. I happen to know it's currently unused. And while it's foolish, I don't want to show him those horrible pictures inside either of our homes.

I close my eyes and shudder as, once again, the memory of those images washes over me. "Actually, the bar," I say, because right now, I really want a drink.

I hear him curse softly under his breath. "Are you okay?"

"No," I admit. "But I will be when I see you."

"What's happened?"

But I can't tell him. Not like this. And the truth is that I don't want to have to tell him at all.

I sigh. "I'll leave something for you at the front desk. Get it, then come find me."

I know he wants to argue, but all he says is "I'm on my way."

He clicks off, and I close my eyes, letting the relief wash over me.

I take a few moments to pull myself together and fix my make-up before I pull out of the garage and start the trek west from downtown to Century City.

There's a wreck on the 10, so it takes me longer to get there than I'd planned, but Jackson is coming all the way from San Bernadino, so I know that he has not arrived before me. I get the key to the suite from the girl at the front desk, then leave the envelope for Jackson. I hesitate before handing it over to her, not liking the fact that it is out of my hands.

Somehow, that seems like a metaphor for the whole damn situation.

I consider going straight to the room, after all, but the lobby bar is too appealing to pass up. It's not quite four, so the post-work crowd hasn't yet arrived and there are tables to spare. Even so, I sit at the actual bar, my back to the main lobby area, and order a glass of pinot.

The bartender is not a chatty type, and I appreciate that. I have worked through panic and nausea, and now I am just drifting. Not in a happy place so much as an away place.

I'll come back down to earth when Jackson gets here. Until then, I'll drink wine and pretend like there's nothing wrong in my world.

I finish my first glass and then another. I've just taken the first sip from the third glass the bartender slid in front of me when I realize that he's there.

I haven't seen him. Haven't heard him.

I am simply aware of him. His heat. His intensity.

He is like a radio emitting a low, powerful frequency, and right now, I am completely tuned to him.

Slowly, I put down my glass, then look over my shoulder to find him. He is only standing at the edge of the carpet that separates the bar area from the marble flooring. He'd gone to work in casual dress, appropriate for spending the day in a manufacturer's warehouse.

There is, however, nothing casual about him.

Even in jeans and a simple white button-down shirt, he projects power and ferocity. He holds the envelope with the photos and threatening note in his hand, and though it hangs loose at his side, the knuckles on the hand that hold it are white, and I can see the tension in his arms.

His face tells a similar story. His jaw is so firm that I am certain his teeth are clenched. As for his eyes—they burn with the heat of a man about to go to battle, and I am certain that a similar fire reflected in the eyes of ancient warriors before they went out to decimate a village.

In other words, Jackson is holding it together—but his composure comes at a price.

I open my mouth to say his name, but he shakes his head and holds up a finger. Then he steps to the bar and puts down a hundred-dollar bill. He takes my hand to help me from my stool, and the shock that runs through me from even such simple contact is enough that I must hold on to the edge of the bar for a moment in order to keep my knees from collapsing out from under me.

He is tight with contained energy, and the thought that I will be the woman in his arms when he lets himself go makes me wet with anticipation.

Dear god I want this. Want him. I want the release of abandonment. The safety of giving myself to him. I want the delirium of being swept out of myself.

And I want the hours of bliss in which the photographs and the threat and the horror that surround us are, if not forgotten, at least pushed aside. Diminished by the power of the explosion that will erupt between us.

As he leads me through the hotel toward the elevator, I practically vibrate with need. I feel it from Jackson as well—the intensity and effort with which he is holding back—and I fear that we will both succumb before we even make it to the room.

I'm far from wrong, and the moment that we are through the doors, Jackson slams me against the wall with such force that a picture falls from its hook to the floor. His hands cage me, and though he doesn't touch me anywhere else, he is so close that my entire body sizzles from the heat of him.

"Tell me you want this."

"I want it. Please, Jackson, you know I want it."

"Tell me what you want."

I swallow, but I know that I have to say it, because he will not touch me until I do. And so help me, I cannot stand to wait even another second to feel this man against me. "I want you to take me. To use me. You feel out of control because of what that bastard is doing to us? Then take control now. Take it from me, Jackson. I want you to."

As I finish speaking, I hold my wrists together and out to him.

He tilts his head and breathes softly. I can almost see him thinking—and I can definitely see the desire rising in his eyes. And when he unbuckles his belt and rips it off, I know that I have won—and my body throbs in anticipation.

Every part of me is sensitive now, as if my entire body is simply one erogenous zone waiting for his touch. So much so that when his fingers brush my arms as he wraps the belt multiple times around my wrists and forearms, a wild tremor cuts through, and I know that I am on the verge of having the most explosive orgasm of my life.

He takes his time making sure the belt is secure, and when my wrists are bound tight together and there is no way that I can wriggle free, he gently eases them up above my head. I hold them there, understanding what he wants, as he gently traces his fingers over my still-clothed body.

I tremble, wanting so much more than this soft pleasure. This sensual tease.

"Now tell me why." He pulls me close to him so that I feel his erection against my abdomen. I am breathing hard, my senses on overdrive.

Why? Because right then I think that I will die if he doesn't take me.

I don't say that though. My mind is a whirl, my thoughts scurrying.

"Tell me," he repeats. His voice is a low tease, a gentle whisper. But there is a hard undercurrent, and it is a demand. Either I answer, or he backs off. "Why," he repeats. "Tell me, baby."

He runs his hands up my side, and then along my arms that are stretched above my head. His fingers reach the belt that has bound my wrists together and he grabs hold, jerking it upward so that I gasp and rise up onto the balls of my feet. "Why give yourself to a man like this?"

"Not a man," I whisper. "Just you. Only you."

I watch his face, and I see the way his mouth curves up in a flicker of a smile in response to my words.

The smile doesn't reach his eyes. They are still hard and hot and demanding. "Why?" he repeats.

I know what he wants to hear. He wants me to tell him about my need to feel in control. About how I need to surrender it to him—I need to give it, rather than having it ripped from me. He wants to hear me speak about fear, and about how submitting to him is our way of giving me back control and battling the nightmares that these horrible photos will unlock.

And all of that is true.

But there is one reason that is more so.

"Because I love you."

He closes his eyes and draws a long, deep breath. And his cock, already hard against my abdomen, pushes almost painfully against me.

I'd worn a dress to work today, and the low neckline dips to a V between my breasts. He draws his fingers down over the swell of my breasts, following the path of material and flesh. His eyes are on mine, as blue and deep as the sea.

"Mine." The word is hard and harsh and full of passion and power. And in one bold, wild move, he fists his hands into the material, and rips the dress open, exposing my breasts and my stomach, all the way down to the band of my thong.

I gasp. I'd liked that dress, but I like this feeling—wild and abandoned and taken by Jackson—a hell of a lot more. And right now, I'm certain that I have never been so wet and so aroused in my life.

He strokes my breasts, finding and releasing the front clasp of my bra. He pushes the cups to the side, exposing me, then takes a single step back from me, breaking contact.

His eyes skim me, and I shiver from the slow inspection. "You're so lovely." His voice is rapturous, and there is something about such tender words said in a wild moment, that makes the words that much sweeter.

Sweet, however, isn't what Jackson wants or what I need, and I am breathing hard when he puts his hand on my shoulder and urges me down until I am on my knees in front of him.

I know what he wants—hell, I know what *I* want. My wrists are still bound, but my fingers are free, and I manage to unbutton the top, then tug down the zipper on his jeans. I free his cock, hard and thick like velvet-encased steel, then use my tongue to tease up the length of him, all the way to the tip and the salty drop of pre-cum. My cunt clenches as I taste him, and my nipples—already tight with need—are almost begging for attention.

"Go on, baby." His voice is raw, and I know that he needs this as much as I do. He needs it hot. Wild. But most of all, he needs *us*. "Suck my cock."

The command, spoken with such precision and force, seems to ricochet through me, all the more powerful because those were the same words that Jackson said to me on his lot in the Palisades the day he told me that I couldn't fight my nightmares unless I gave up control and submitted.

And that is exactly what I'm doing now.

I take him in, just a little at first. Teasing and tasting. Sliding my tongue along its length. Teasing the tip, then drawing him in. Playing and sucking and finding a rhythm that has his hands fisting in my hair and rough noises of pleasure escaping his throat. And though this started with the illusion that I have some control over this moment, that is all that it is—an illusion. Because soon enough, he has me at his mercy, and instead of me teasing him, he is fucking my mouth. Going deeper and harder until I have to concentrate to breathe. To take him in. Because I cannot move back or adjust, I can only submit to him and to this supremely intimate moment.

I've never really loved giving head, but this is different. Hotter. Wilder. I'm subjugating myself for his pleasure, and that is strangely powerful, and supremely arousing. I'm so desperate for him. But not to fuck—not yet. Instead, I want him to take this all the way. I want to feel him explode. To have him lose his grip completely.

I want that bite of pain when the fingers he has twined in my hair tighten. When he loses all reason and simply lets go.

Most of all, I want to know that I am the one who caused that.

I can tell that he is close—his body is tight and stiff, his cock throbbing with the need for release. And though I have very little use of my hands, I manage to squeeze his balls, and am rewarded when that added touch sends him tumbling over. He explodes in my mouth, clutching my hair tight. And as he does, hot threads of pleasure shoot through me to pool between my legs, bringing me that much closer to my own release.

I manage to swallow, and when he pulls out, both of us breathing hard and satisfied, I cannot deny that despite my submission—despite being held in place and fucked hard—I am absolutely light-headed from the power of this moment.

"Christ, sweetheart. I think you just about destroyed me."

My body tingles with the praise. "In a good way, I hope."

"In the absolute best way." He scoops me up and holds me close to his chest as he bends to kiss me. When he straightens, I hold my still-bound hands up, then lift my brows in question.

"Oh, no," he says. "Not even close."

And the words, said with such potent ardor, send a fresh shiver of anticipation coursing through me.

He carries me to the bedroom and puts me gently on my feet in front of the mattress. "On your knees." He gives the order as he peels me the rest of the way out of my destroyed dress. "Facedown. Elbows on the bed. And, baby," he adds as he tosses my bra toward a nearby chair, "I want to see your ass up high."

I am now clothed only in my thong, the vibrator necklace that I have worn daily as ordered, and my shoes—black slides with three-inch heels. I do as he says, and as I climb onto the mattress, I catch a glimpse of myself in the mirror over the dresser. My skin glows, and my eyes sparkle. I look radiant with pleasure, and when I meet Jackson's eyes in the reflection, his stern, commanding countenance breaks for just a moment to reveal a small smile of approval.

"You were made for this," he says. "For me."

He nods toward the bed as he steps toward me, and I look away, positioning myself as he asked. He steps behind me, then strokes his palm lightly down the line of my spine before cupping the globe of my ass.

"You are mine, Sylvia. From the first moment I saw you in Atlanta, I knew that there was no other woman for me. Not before, and not ever again. You are the light that fills my days and illuminates my nights." I close my eyes, lost in both the meaning of his words and the passion with which he speaks them. "You are the rhythm of my heart."

He slides the thong's thin strip of material aside, then slips his fingers into my cunt before stroking my perineum. He teases my ass, and I bite my lower lip. The sensation is incredible, and when he presses against me, I feel my muscles clench, then relax as he gently slides a finger inside me.

"Oh yes," he says, as I gasp from the unexpected pleasure of this new invasion. "You belong to me. But I'm yours, too. Wholly and completely."

He is sliding his finger deeper inside, and his words, so sensual and soft, are in direct contrast to this deeply prurient touch. He orders me to stay still as he continues to tease my rear as my body adjusts. And, yes, as I crave more.

Too soon, he slides out, and I whimper. "The lady liked that," Jackson says, still standing behind me. "One day, we'll try more than a finger."

The promise excites me, and when he lightly smacks my bottom, the impact sets off a chain reaction inside me. I shiver as electric sparks seem to spread out from my clit, like a tiny preview of a massive orgasm to come.

"Don't move," he says, and then leaves the room. I immediately mourn the loss of contact, and it is all I can do not to beg him to return.

I hear him moving in the suite. Drawers opening. Things rattling. Is he in the kitchen?

Then I hear his footsteps as he returns, and I start to turn my head to look at him, but am stilled by his sharp, quick, "no."

I stop, then move only long enough to face forward.

Soon enough, he is behind me again. He rests a possessive hand on my back, and I am surprised by how much this calms me. As if the world is simply not right without the brush of Jackson's skin against my own.

"I spanked you once and used my hand, and loved the way the sweet sting lingered on my palm. But this isn't entirely about me, and I'm wondering if you might enjoy something just a bit different."

Oh. He is stroking me now with something slightly rough. Not leather. Not metal.

Wood, perhaps?

I'm not sure, and when he lifts it from my ass, then smacks it lightly down again, any potential for further analysis goes right out of my head. There is just this sensation—a light sting, and not nearly enough.

"Do you want more?"

"Yes."

The word bursts out of me far too fast, and Jackson chuckles. "As you wish."

He repeats the smack, this time harder, so that my ass burns with a deep red pain that thrums and throbs with each additional spank. Between each blow he rubs me, and that sensation—a gentle touch over tender skin—is both soothing and arousing, as if each sweet touch sends the deeper pain further inside. It builds and builds, until there is no longer any pain at all, but a floating kind of pleasure that spreads out from my ass to bathe my entire body, sensitizing me and making me wild and hungry for more.

"Are you sore?"

"Yes," I whisper, as he slips his hand between my legs and strokes me slowly, teasing my clit before slipping two fingers inside me. I am still wearing the thong, and the sensation of the material rubbing against me as he enters me is one more piece to this puzzle of wild sensuality. One more thing that is pushing me toward the edge.

"Do you like it?"

I hesitate, my eyes closed. "God, yes."

He doesn't reply, but rewards me with another spank, but as this one lands, he thrusts his fingers in deeper. I gasp at the unexpected sensation and at the hard and fast way my cunt tightens, clenching around his fingers as if in a silent demand to be fucked— and fucked hard.

He does it again and again and again, and I am so wet that I am dripping, so desperate to be fucked I am almost crying. The pain from the spanking has transformed completely. It is pleasure and need and demand, and when Jackson takes my hips and yanks me toward him so that I slide along the bed, it is all I can do not to burst into tears of joy.

Behind me, I hear Jackson strip. He is out of his clothes in a heartbeat, and inside me just as fast. Soon he is thrusting hard, and with each slap of his pelvis against my red and sensitive ass, another wave of pain-like pleasure crashes over me. It is all so much, and I feel like I am spinning from the cacophony of sensations that are assaulting me. I need an anchor, and as always Jackson knows what I need, and even as he pistons hard against me, he slides his hand around my body until his fingers find my clit.

He strokes and teases me, building me up higher and higher until I can't take it any longer and all this pleasure and pain and wild writhing ribbons of electricity come together in an explosion so violent and wild that I am certain I will not survive.

My body convulses, my muscles tightening around his cock, my back arching up as I try to contain the pleasure. I am still on my knees, my wrists still bound, but I fist my hands in the sheets, then cry out again as Jackson thrusts once more into me, then groans from his own wild release, his body shaking as he bends over me, hot and hard and satisfied.

"Oh my god," I finally say. "That was—"

"Amazing."

I make a soft noise of agreement, but say nothing else. I am so wiped that even those few words exhausted me. We stay like that for a bit, but soon Jackson moves to my side. He helps me turn onto my back, then reaches for the belt that binds my wrists.

I tug them away. "Not yet. Jackson, I want—"

"More?"

I lick my lips, not certain I should say this thought that has come unbidden into my mind. It's too wild, probably too stupid, and if it all went wrong I would be mortified. But it is also a symbol that I've not only survived Reed, but thrived. That I'm strong now. And that it is Jackson—not Reed—to whom I have surrendered.

He watches my debate play out on my face. Now he says, "Tell me what you need."

"I want you to take my picture." I speak quickly, the words spilling out before I can change my mind. "Like this. Bound. Only for you," I add quickly. "But I need—"

"To know that it exists," he finishes, and my relief that he understands is a palpable thing. "To know that you're mine and that you've given this to me."

"Yes." I lick my lips. "Will you?"

"I only have my phone."

I nod.

"And I want to capture you when you come."

"I—oh."

His smile is a little wicked. "If we're doing it, we're doing it right." He walks to me and takes the necklace from around my neck. He turns it on, then puts it in my hand. "Spread your legs, baby, and tease your clit."

I think I should protest, but I am already wet again from the thought that Jackson will watch me. Will photograph me.

I do not know what it means, but I know that it excites me.

He puts a pillow under my head and I do as he asks. I close my eyes, spread my legs, and with my wrists bound, I tease myself with the small pendant. I can't touch my clit directly—I'm way too sensitive for that—but as I move the vibrator in small circles—as I think about Jackson at the foot of the bed watching me, the camera photographing me—my body rises up again, getting wet again, tightening again.

The metal pendant turns warm and that change in temperature

makes me gasp even as the controlled vibrations push me up. Higher and higher, and then higher still.

I come fast and hard and quick, and as I do, I open my eyes. Jackson holds the phone in one hand and he's stroking his cock with the other, and I think it's the sexiest damn thing I have ever seen. "Fuck me," I whisper, and he tosses the phone onto the dresser behind him and takes me once again, wild and fast, because we both need it that way.

And when we explode together, and I lay in his arms and wonder how a day that had started so horribly could become so incredible.

I know the answer, of course. The answer is Jackson.

Soon, when we can move again, he unbinds my hands. I turn and prop myself on my side so that I can face him.

"Thank you," I say. "I feel whole again. Like I'm not going to shatter."

"I'm very glad to hear that."

"But it's all still out there. Reed, I mean. He still has us in a horrible position. The pictures or the movie. We're between a rock and a hard place, and in the end, one of us will get screwed."

"No." He says the word so quickly and firmly that I almost believe him.

"How?" I ask. "How do we fix this? How do we untangle ourselves from this hell?"

"I don't know," he admits. "But we'll figure it out. I love you, Sylvia. I love you, and I will make this right for you."

Love. The word washes over me, warm and sweet and wonderful.

"Jackson . . ." His name is a caress upon my lips. "That's the first time you've said that."

"No," he says. "It's not."

I'm about to argue the point when he continues.

"I've said it every day since I saw you. I say it in the way I look at you. The way I touch you. The way I never stop thinking about you. I've said that I love you a million times, Sylvia. This is just the first time I've said it out loud."

I tremble from the force of his words, and from the emotion with which he said them. They are like a blanket, keeping me safe and warm, and I wrap them tight around me.

"We'll figure this out together," he says, telling me what I said to myself earlier when I was lost in tears and anger.

But now the world is clear and I'm staring into the crisp, cold light of reality.

And even with Jackson's love to bolster me, I cannot help but be afraid.

twenty-four

"Good morning, beautiful."

I open my eyes to the warm comfort of Jackson's voice washing over me, followed by the brush of his lips against my temple.

"Good morning yourself." I smile and stretch, and despite the worry that still hangs over me, I feel as bright and shiny as the California sun seeping in through the window. "Any brilliant ideas in the light of day?"

"None yet," he says. "But the morning is young." He moves toward the bathroom and I slide out of bed to follow him. "Don't worry. He won't do anything too quickly, that would be foolish."

"Foolish?" I repeat as I lean into the shower to turn on the spray. "So far, he hasn't exactly proven to be a brain trust." Then again, he was managing to very efficiently fuck with both of us, so maybe he wasn't an idiot, after all.

The thought doesn't make me happy.

I move my towel closer to the shower and then reach in to check the water temperature. Jackson eyes me, his head slanted to one side. "Are you going in today?" he finally asks. "You have to pick up Ethan."

"Well, yes." The thought of staying in the suite or going home hadn't actually occurred to me. "But that's not until later. I can leave a bit early, but I have a ton to catch up on."

"Syl . . ."

He doesn't say anything else, but I know what he is thinking. I slide toward him and enfold myself in his arms. We're both naked, and though this moment isn't sexual, I can't help but notice the hard press of his body against mine. He feels safe and solid and perfect, and I tilt my head back so that I can look at his face. And at the concern in his eyes.

"Yes," I say again. "I'm going in. And I'm strong enough to do it because I know you've got my back. And that somehow we're going to figure a way out of this mess."

He is silent for a moment, just holding me. Then he kisses the top of my head. "We damn sure will."

I take his hand as I step back, then smile, wanting to lighten the moment. "Come on. I want to enjoy the feel of you in the shower."

He doesn't protest, and soon the water is sluicing over our bodies, and as I stand in the spray wrapped in his arms, I can't help but think how perfect this feels. "I like this," I tell him, though that is about as much of an understatement as an understatement can be. "Intimacy. It feels good. It feels right."

"That's because it is."

"Tell me again." My voice is soft, but it holds a plea, and though I do not tell him, Jackson understands exactly what I need to hear.

"I love you," he says, and I hold him close and sigh with contentment.

"I had a thought," he says when we're in the Porsche and heading to the office after a late morning. And not a late morning in bed. No, Jackson bought me some sweats and a T-shirt from the gift store, and then we'd walked to the Century City mall, where he'd bought me a fabulous new outfit from Michael Kors to replace the dress he'd so deliciously destroyed. I've left my car at the hotel, but I figure we can pick it up anytime.

"A sexy thought?" I tease.

He chuckles. "I have those every moment I'm with you, so there's really no need to remark on them. No, I think I may know a way out."

I shift in the seat, turning serious. "A way out? You mean from Reed's threat?"

"We've been thinking about this as if it's a straight line. Like tug-of-war. You pull your side over, and my side loses. I pull my side over—"

"And mine loses. I get it. So?"

"What if the game isn't tug-of-war?" He takes his eyes off the road for just a second to look at me. "What if it's something else entirely? A triangle and not a straight line."

"I don't know what you mean."

"I mean that Reed is playing you and me against each other. But he's discounting your father."

I stiffen. "My father?"

"Hear me out. Your dad set the whole thing up originally, right? So if your dad confronts him—"

"Are you insane?" I want to stand up. To pace. And the fact that I'm trapped in a moving car only adds to my irritation. "That would mean me confronting my dad first. You know I don't want to do that."

"Maybe it's time," he says gently.

"The hell it is."

"Maybe he needs to understand the full impact of what he did to you," he continues softly, as if I hadn't protested at all.

"No. *No.* Absolutely not." Just the thought makes me want to throw up, and I clutch my knees, desperate to escape this claustrophobic box.

Just the idea—just the thought that my father might know about those horrible photos—makes me both terrified and furious.

"Do you think I would suggest this if I saw another way? This is all I've been thinking about. How the hell do we get out of this mess? And the truth of it is that it all goes back to your dad. To the choices he made and what he did to you."

"To *me*," I say. "And I've dealt with it. And I don't want to open those wounds."

"Sweetheart, we both know you haven't really dealt with it."

"*Goddammit.*" I slam my palm against the dashboard, because trapped in this car there's no other way to lash out.

He winces, but doesn't miss a beat. "And the truth is, it wasn't just you. Your son of a bitch of a father was playing fast and loose with my life, too."

I cross my arms over my chest and say nothing.

"He's responsible for those photographs," Jackson says. "He sold you, Sylvia. He hurt you. He's your father and he didn't protect you, and he's as much to blame for all of this as Reed is."

I keep my lips pressed together, but I don't deny it. I know the role I played—it was my choice not to walk away because at the end of the day it was about Ethan—but none of that changes what my father did. None of that erases the fact that he set the wheels in motion and that he essentially did exactly what Jackson has said: he used me to protect Ethan. Balanced the well-being of one child against the well-being of another.

So, yes, I understand that. And I understand the rest, too. "Reed's threatening me in order to get to you. I get that, Jackson. I do." I lick my lips. "But I can't confront my dad. I'm not ready to talk to him about it." I draw in a breath. "I don't know if I'll ever be ready. Please tell me you understand that. Because I need you beside me tonight. And I need you to not be mad at me."

"Oh, baby." He reaches over and takes my hand. "I'm not mad. Not at you, anyway. As for your father—well, that's a different story altogether."

"A secret story," I say firmly.

"Yes," he says, though I can tell the words eat at him. "A secret."

"Oh my god, look at you!" I throw my arms around Ethan's neck, then laugh as he picks me up and spins me around. My brother is tall and athletic, and he maneuvers me through the air as easily as if I weigh no more than a feather.

That wasn't always the way. When he was sick in his tweens and early teens he'd faded away to almost nothing, and the robust little boy all but disappeared. When he got healthy, he started working out. And though he never told me so specifically, I always figured that he did it as a way to say "fuck you" to the disease.

Now, he's pretty damn hot, even if he is my brother. He's got the cut, athletic body, which is impressive all on its own. But couple that with his dreamy, deep-set eyes and thick brown hair, and he's the kind of guy who never wants for a date.

Speaking of, I slide my arm around Jackson's waist and lean my head against his upper arm. "This is Jackson," I say. "Jackson, this is my brother, Ethan."

"I thought as much," Jackson says with a grin as he reaches out to shake Ethan's hand, but ends up doing one of those mutual shake-and-shoulder-clap things that men do. "Your sister can't stop talking about you."

"Yeah? I thought it was you she couldn't stop talking about."

I roll my eyes and wave a hand at the limo. It's not exactly proper office procedure, but I want to impress my baby brother, and Edward assured me that the car would otherwise sit idle tonight. "Go," I say firmly, and we all climb in and get settled as Edward shuts the door behind us.

"Okay," Ethan says. "Now I'm impressed."

"That was the idea," I admit as Jackson takes care of getting us each a drink.

"Are you still seeing Samantha?" I ask.

He shakes his head. "No. That ended pretty abruptly." He shrugs. "It was for the best."

"I'm sorry," I say. "Why?"

He looks at me like I'm crazy. "Because I was moving five thousand miles away."

I decide not to mention that sometimes people do have long-distance relationships. I know my brother too well, and if he's back in California, he's going to want to test the local waters. And since there are plenty of California girls who will find my brother very appealing, I guess that's okay.

He eyes Jackson. "I would ask you for advice on where to meet girls, but I'm kind of hoping that you don't have a clue. At least not as far as Los Angeles is concerned."

"I don't," Jackson says, shooting a glance my way. "As far as local pickup spots, I'm not even close to a fount of knowledge. Not even a trickle or a drip."

"So, you two are really serious, then?"

"Ethan!"

"What? I mean, I would apologize for being all nosy, but you're my sister and we're trapped in the back of a limo together for the next hour, so I figure now's the time to do my brotherly duty."

Jackson's lip twitch. "Yes," he says. "We're really serious."

"'Cause I had wifi on the leg of the flight from New York to here, and four hours is a long time to surf the internet. Saw a lot of interesting things about the two of you." He turns to me. "You're dating a downright celebrity. You know that, right?"

"Ethan . . ." This time, my voice holds a warning.

He raises his hands. "I'm just saying." He shifts so that he's facing Jackson. "And I'm also saying that if you're screwing around on my sister with that hot little redhead, I will have your balls for breakfast."

Jackson's brows rise. "Fortunately for you, I'm not seeing the hot little redhead. Megan's a friend, as Sylvia knows."

"Fortunately for me?" Ethan repeats. "What? You don't think I could take you?"

Jackson sizes my brother up. To be honest, my money's on Jackson, but Ethan would definitely give him a go. "I think it would be a hell of a fight," Jackson says diplomatically. "But what I meant was that it's fortunate that you won't have to eat such a truly unappetizing meal. And I don't have to sacrifice my balls."

For a moment, Ethan looks shocked. Then he raises his drink in a salute, before tossing the whole thing back. "Oh, yeah," he says to me. "I like him."

"Good," I say, then plant a quick, hard kiss on Jackson's mouth. "So do I."

Ethan fixes himself another drink, then asks me if I want one. I hold up the scotch that Jackson poured for me, still untouched. "I'm good for now. You ought to slow down."

"I'm in a limo," he says. "Slowing down isn't an option."

I meet Jackson's eyes, and he finishes the rest of his. "I'll take another," he says, then shrugs when I lift my brows. "What? Your brother has a point."

"I had no idea you two would turn into a comedy act." I speak sternly, but inside I'm gleeful, thrilled that my boyfriend and my brother are getting along.

"I'm surprised you aren't having another." Ethan's voice has turned serious. "I mean, what with going to see Mom and Dad. I know it upsets you, and I really do appreciate you coming down with me. Honest. It means a lot."

"I'm not upset," I lie.

"Bullshit. I know you, remember? Grew up together. Shared the same house. Built forts out of boxes and blankets." He sticks his hand out. "Ethan Brooks. Nice to meet you."

"When did you turn so sarcastic?"

"Last Thursday. And don't change the subject."

I take a long sip of scotch, and tell myself it's not because I need it. "It's just Mom and Dad," I say. "You know I don't love all the family drama."

"I know you don't love it. I don't know why." He turns narrowed eyes on Jackson. "Do you know why?"

He shakes his head, lying so easily for me. "Lots of people have issues with their parents."

"You got that right. Do you?"

"You have no idea," Jackson says.

"You know she helped out when I was sick, right? I mean, did she tell you that?"

"Modeling," Jackson says. "Yes, I know about that. And I'm sorry you were so bad off when you were a kid. Children shouldn't have to suffer like that."

"They sure as hell shouldn't," Ethan agrees. He looks at me. "But I'm fine now, and you're a big reason why. You and Mom and Dad. And it just bugs the crap out of me that the people in the world who mean the most to me don't get along at all."

"Ethan . . ."

"Come on, Silly. You know you can talk to me about anything."

"I know." The truth is, it's been a very long time since we've really talked. But when we were kids, we had no secrets. And I liked that. I miss that.

"Parents fuck up their kids, Syl. It's what they do. And I know it must have been worse for you. You had to deal with all the shit that went along with me being sick. And you did the modeling thing and that's cool and all, but it's got to have been hard work, right?"

I can only nod. He really doesn't know the half of it. And as I sit there and try to keep my shit together, Jackson reaches over and takes my hand.

Just casually holding hands with his girlfriend. And yet the strength in his touch keeps me sane and steady. *My white knight*, I think. Always ready to rescue me.

"So you're working your ass off, and Mom and Dad are getting the money. For me. Did you even get to keep any of it? I mean, like in a college fund or something?"

I shake my head. "I didn't want the money." My voice is soft, but earnest. "I did it for you."

My voice hitches, and I hope that he doesn't notice.

"Yeah, well." He shrugs, and there is a weirdly awkward silence. "Look, if you don't want to tell me, that's cool. The bottom line is that I love you. I mean, you're my sister, so there's that. But you're also my hero." He glances at Jackson. "Sorry for the syrupy sweetness, but I've been away for a long time."

"I think that kind of sweetness is very appropriate," he says, then kisses the top of my head even as fat tears spill out of my eyes.

"You're not allowed to make me cry."

"Sure I am. That's what annoying little brothers are for."

I laugh—and I cry a little more, too. But it's a good kind of crying and I wipe the tears away. And as I do, I realize I'm smiling. Despite the fact that we are heading to my parents, I'm actually smiling.

And that's the crux of it, just like I told Jackson. Maybe I could have walked away. Maybe I could have said no to Reed. But I didn't.

So yes, I whored myself out.

But I don't hate myself. Because sitting across from me is the reason I did it.

And I love him desperately.

So I'll hate Reed for what he did to me.

And I'll hate my father for not protecting me.

My brother, though, is innocent. And he never needs to know.

twenty-five

The house in Irvine is picture-perfect.

The lawn is manicured. The trees just tall enough.

The cars are tasteful and expensive, but not too showy.

The pool guy comes every Thursday. The cleaning lady every Tuesday.

My mother volunteers at the library. My dad is enjoying early retirement after several long-shot real estate investments paid off spectacularly.

All in all, they're an upper-middle-class couple with a Norman Rockwell home on one of the prettiest streets in one of the prettiest towns in the country.

Too bad what's inside these walls isn't as pretty as the outside. Because even though Vivaldi is playing over the wireless speakers and the dining table has meat loaf and potatoes, I feel as though I'm trapped in that house in Amityville, and any minute now, blood is going to pour out of the walls.

Frankly, that couldn't be any worse than the horror I'm currently experiencing.

My mother has moved from asking me when Jackson and I are getting married to asking me what I do at Stark International. Which would be a reasonable question if this weren't the third time she has asked me that in the last ninety minutes. Everything I say to her seems to go to some other place, and it has been that way since Ethan got sick. As if once he got ill, she had no energy to devote to the other child, and so she tossed platitudes my way and hoped that I wouldn't notice.

And that strange disconnect continued even after Ethan recovered. By that time, I was on my way out the door, but even when I would come home from boarding school, she never asked about my schoolwork or my friends or anything. And if I volunteered information, she would listen, but she wouldn't really hear.

It's something I realized early on, and I used to test her on it. I'd tell her something specific. Once, we were sitting down for lunch and I told her, "Donna bought a horse, and then she fell off and broke her leg."

She told me that was just terrible and she hoped Donna was doing better.

"Did I tell you what happened to Donna?" I asked later that evening. "About the horse?" And she assured me that she'd never heard the story before.

She doesn't have a memory deficiency. She doesn't have Alzheimer's. What she has is a son, and only a son.

The daughter doesn't count.

I don't know why.

I don't know if she was complicit in the sessions with Reed. I don't know if Ethan's illness just made her snap a little bit. I don't know if she is mad at me for something I did so very long ago.

I don't know, and I no longer care. As far as I'm concerned, family is what you make of it, and the only reason I'm in this house of horrors tonight is that Ethan is still my family.

I make a valiant effort to describe my assistant duties to my mom, and then give her a rundown on what I'm doing for the resort.

"She's doing an amazing job," Jackson says, directing his words at both my mother and my father.

He's been the perfect boyfriend so far. Staying by my side, squeezing my hand in support when my parents get weird. And, thank god, not saying anything that even hints at my past or those damn photos that he thinks we should show my dad.

Jackson starts to go into more detail about my job—about how I'm juggling my assistant and project manager responsibilities, about the quality of my work and the excellence of my ideas.

My mom's eyes glaze over, but from the far end of the table, my dad says, "That's what I'm talking about."

I turn toward him, not sure if he's talking to me and Jackson or to Ethan, whose ear he's been bending all evening.

"Talking about what?"

"What Jackson was just saying to your mother," he says. "About your job, and the extra time and work to essentially perform two jobs." He turns back to Ethan. "That's the way to get ahead. Hard work. Sacrifice." He meets my eyes. "I'm proud of you, Elle."

I feel cold. Both from his use of a name I abandoned long ago and from his statement of pride. I want nothing from this man, least of all his validation. And when Jackson squeezes my hand in solidarity beneath the table, I think that I have never been more grateful to have someone in my life who understands me so well.

It's his support that gives me strength to respond. "But sacrifice isn't always about work, is it?" I say, even though I know I should just keep quiet. Because silence is the only guaranteed way to keep my emotions in tight.

Except I don't take my own advice. And I keep talking, the words sort of spewing out as if they have a life of their own. "I mean, some people sacrifice a kidney to save someone they love."

I keep my eyes on my father and my hand tight in Jackson's. I don't want to see Ethan. Not right now. Not when I feel so hollow and raw. "Abraham was supposed to sacrifice his son to God. And in that movie, *Sophie's Choice,* Meryl Streep has to sacrifice one child to save the other." I deliberately take a sip of water, never breaking eye contact. "Must be hard."

It may be my imagination, but I think I see his upper lip start to sweat. I lean back, feeling just a little bit smug.

"I think I'm going to open another bottle of wine," my dad says. He's speaking very slowly and very deliberately, and he is moving in an equally careful manner as he pushes away from the table and heads for the kitchen. "Come with me, Sylvia? Working for Stark, you must have developed at least a bit of a head for fine wine."

If he'd called me Elle, I think I would have said no. But I surprise myself by pushing my chair back.

Jackson doesn't release my hand right away, and when I look at him, he tilts his head in a silent question. *Should I come, too?*

I almost say yes, but then I shake my head. I can do this. I can make it through the night as the dutiful daughter.

And then I can get the hell out of here.

I follow my dad through the butler's pantry, then into the kitchen. Right between the kitchen and the living area is an archway with an iron gate instead of a door. I follow my father past the gate, then down the stairs to a small wine cellar with just enough room for the two of us and the hundred or so bottles of wine stacked neatly in the sturdy wooden racks.

I start to pull out a bottle, wanting something bold and red if I'm going to be staying for any length of time. But before I have a chance to really start looking, my father speaks. "You've been mad at me since you were fourteen," he says, and I jolt upright. "Don't you think it's time to stop?"

I stand there like an idiot as his words register with me. We have never talked about this—*never*—and this new reality has completely flummoxed me.

"Time to stop?" I repeat. "What? Are we baking cookies and now they're done? Has the clock finally run down in the final quarter of the game? Honestly, Dad, what the hell are you talking about?"

"I'm trying to talk with you. I'm trying to get past this."

"Now? We're really going to talk about this now?" My voice is so full of bile and vitriol it doesn't even sound like my own.

"Those years were hard on all of us, Elle—"

"*Sylvia.*"

He pauses, takes a breath, and begins again. "Ethan was sick. Your mother and I were frantic with worry. We all sacrificed, Sylvia. We all did everything we could to help."

"Oh, you sacrificed, all right." I want to shout the words. Instead, they come out low. Powerful. And remarkably steady. "You fucking sacrificed me."

His face turns bright red and he opens his mouth, sputtering as if trying to form words. He says nothing, though, and after a moment, I fear that he is actually having a heart attack.

"Dad? *Dad?*" I'm not even aware that I have moved, but somehow I have ended up at his side. I reach for his shoulder to steady him, trying to decide if I should scream for my mother or get him off his feet or what.

I'm about to do both when he violently jerks his arm away from my touch. "It. Is. Over." Each word is pronounced slowly, carefully, and with the utmost precision. "That chapter in our lives is over. Done. The door is closed, Sylvia. And it is closed tight." He takes a deep breath, his shoulders rising, then falling.

"Over?" My temper has been rising with every word. How dare he. How *fucking* dare he. And though I know that it is a mistake to get into this now, I cannot stop the words that spew out. "Are you insane? It's not over. It's never over, Dad. It will never, ever be over."

I suck in a breath, afraid that it might be me who has the heart attack. "It haunts me every goddamn day. Do you have any idea of what I went through? The hell I've gone through since then? Of what you let me go through—no, of what you *demanded* I go through? So don't you dare tell me that the door is closed. I wish to hell it were. But it's not. And it's never going to be. That son of a bitch used me, Daddy. He *used me.* And even after all this time it hasn't ended. He's still fucking using me. I still can't get away. And I still—*shit.*"

I cut myself off, then turn around and pound my fist into the nearest thing I find, which happens to be a wine rack. It rattles, but thankfully doesn't fall. I don't even try to steady it. I'm bent over, my hands on my knees, and I'm breathing hard.

"What? What are you talking about?"

Just tell him.

Like Jackson said, tell him, and then let him dig you out from this mess. That's what fathers do, right? Protect their daughters?

Except I know better. Because my father had a thousand chances and then some to protect me before. He didn't. I was a child, and he didn't lift a finger.

So why the hell would I believe that he would do anything to help me now?

"Sylvia?" His voice is soft, and his hand on my shoulder is even softer. It doesn't matter; to me the contact burns, and I flinch away. He takes a step back, his hands up. "Tell me."

I stand there, my mind churning and my heart hurting. I want to run, but I feel bolted to the floor. I want to scream, but I have no power inside me to push the sound out.

I am simply frozen in time, at least until Ethan calls down, cheerful and loud and asking what the hell is taking so long.

It feels as though he has broken a spell. I race up the stairs to my brother. "Sorry. Distracted. Sorry." I follow him back to the dining room, needing to see Jackson, but Jackson isn't there.

"I think he went to the restroom," my mother says when I ask. "Coffee?"

She starts to stand, but I shake my head. "I'll get it."

I leave her with Ethan and then head back to the kitchen. I consider going back down to the wine cellar and telling my dad every-thing. Just getting it all out. Just having it *done*.

But I can't do it. I can't stand the thought of him seeing those photos. Of actually talking to him about the fact that I came sec-ond. That he was willing to toss me to the wolves because he had to save his son even at the expense of his daughter.

My hand stalls over the canister of coffee and I squeeze back tears—and as I do, I hear my father's sharp curse rise up from the wine cellar.

I frown, afraid he's dropped a bottle or managed to hurt him-self, and I hurry in that direction, running down the stairs and then stopping short when the room comes into view.

Because there is Jackson with my father.

And there is the envelope that Reed sent.

And there in my father's hands is a photograph, and I don't need to see the front of it to know what it shows. And I don't need to have heard the conversation to know what Jackson has said.

My chest is tight. My heart pounding so hard I think it is going to explode.

Both men are standing stock-still and they are staring at me. Time has stopped. The world has stopped.

And then it all clicks again, and Jackson calls out for me as he takes a step toward me.

"*No.*" The word is ripped so hard from me that it hurts my throat.

I turn back and race up the stairs. Ethan is in the kitchen. "I have to go. Work. A project. I forgot. I'm sorry."

The words tumble out, spilling onto each other in a tangled pile of lies.

I hug him, but I don't wait for either protest or consent. I simply bolt.

I climb into the limo and slam the door shut. I push the button to roll down the privacy screen and meet Edward's eyes in the rearview as he pushes the button on the stereo to turn off his audio-book.

"Go," I say. "Please, just go."

I see him glance out the passenger side window, and I turn that way, too. Jackson is there, standing in the doorway, his back straight, his expression unreadable.

"*Go.*" My voice is shaking, on the verge of hysteria. "Goddammit, just go."

He does, and I fall back against the leather, breathing hard.

"Thank you," I whisper, though I doubt Edward hears.

I push the button to lift the screen again as we drive away, leaving the house, my brother, my parents, and Jackson behind.

The memories, however, come with me.

I don't remember telling Edward where to go, but when he pulls up in front of Cass's house in Venice Beach, I know that I must have.

I haven't called. I haven't done anything except sit in the back of the limo feeling sorry for myself and fighting tears. Which, of course, is why I've ended up at my best friend's door. Because right now, I can't bear to go home. I can't bear to be alone.

I can't stand the thought of this being the end, but I'm so afraid that it might be.

He told my secret. He broke our trust.

And in doing that, I think he broke my heart, too.

It's almost midnight, and as I approach the door, I realize that maybe calling would have been a good idea. She could be out. She could be in the middle of a hot date. She could just be asleep.

But she's none of those things. In fact, she's right there, pulling the door open and hurrying down her front walk with her arms held out to me, a cell phone in her hand. "God, I've been calling and calling."

"Calling?" I'd turned my phone to silent.

"He called." She waves Edward off, and as the limo disappears down the street, she leads me inside. I take off my shoes because Cass is a neat freak even in best-friend emergencies, and then let her get me settled on her couch.

She plops down on the coffee table in front of me. "He told me he fucked up. He wants to talk to you, Syl. But mostly, I think he wants to make sure you're okay."

She leans forward and peers at me, her elbows on her knees. "Are you?"

I draw in a breath and shake my head. "I don't know," I say, and the tears start flowing.

"Oh, sweetie, no." She's off the table and at my side immediately, and I curl against her, snuggling close as she holds me and rocks me. She doesn't say anything, and I'm glad. Right now, I don't want to talk. I don't want advice. I don't want to relive every horrible minute.

I just want to be held. I just want to be comforted.

After a while, though, I just want to sleep, and I stretch out on the couch and pull the warm, soft afghan that Cass found last year at her favorite Goodwill up around my shoulders.

"At least let me pull out the couch for you."

But I just shake my head. I'm too tired to even move, and as sleep starts to pull me under, I hear her calling someone on the phone. "I don't know if she'll be in tomorrow or not. But if she is, it'll be late. Okay, thanks, Jamie. Just ask Ryan to tell Rachel or whoever needs to know. Sounds good. See you Friday, and let me know if you need any help getting ready for the party."

I start to tell her that I'm definitely going in to work. I'm not letting my personal life interfere with my job. But somehow, I can't manage to make the words come. And the next thing I know, there's a bright light in my eyes and the room smells like coffee.

The bright light, I realize, is from the sun streaming in through the wide-open curtains. And it's not the entire house that smells like coffee. It's the mug that is wedged in under my nose.

"Welcome back," Cass says.

I stretch and yawn. Then I sit up and take the coffee. I sip it slowly and feel my body start to come back to life.

I hear a rattling in the next room and glance across the tiny house to see the louvered doors to the kitchen open and Siobhan emerge, her long legs revealed by running shorts and her wild mass of bright red curls partially hidden under a baseball cap.

"Oh," I say. "Wow. I'm sorry. Last night. I didn't mean to—"

"You didn't," Siobhan says. "Don't worry. We were just hanging out and talking. Besides," she adds with a bright smile. "I owe you one."

"We both do," Cass agrees. She turns back to Siobhan. "You out of here?"

"I thought I'd go for a jog and let you two talk. I'll call you in an hour or so and see if you're free for breakfast. If not, maybe we can grab a coffee this evening?"

"Sure. Sounds good."

Siobhan leans in and kisses her cheek, then heads out.

I sit back against the couch feeling smug. "Well, guess I did do good telling you to unblock her number."

Cass actually blushes a bit.

I laugh. "I really didn't interrupt?"

"You seriously didn't. We were really just watching television and talking. But one of the things we talked about was that we're going to take it slow."

"So there's an *it* to be taken?"

"Maybe." Now Cass is bright red, and I couldn't be happier. I've always liked Siobhan, even though she was a total bitch for breaking up with Cass. Because, of course, anyone who breaks up with my best friend is a total bitch by definition.

"Siobhan will keep." Cass parks herself on the coffee table again, and I watch as she visibly pulls herself together. "Right now, the focus is on you. Do you want to talk about it?"

"I don't even want to think about it," I admit. "But yeah, I suppose I should tell you." And not just because I want her advice and comfort. The truth is that although I told Cass how Reed had abused me, I never told her all of it. She doesn't know about Ethan's treatment or my dad's manipulations. She doesn't know how it made me feel.

She's my best friend and I've never told her any of that. And though I know those secrets haven't come between us, I'm tired of hiding behind secrets and shadows, keeping parts of me hidden from the people I love.

And so I tell her. I tell her the past, and then I tell her the present. I start with, "Ethan was sick and my parents needed money for an experimental treatment in Central America." And then, once she's heard all of that—once she's held my hands and hugged me close and battled back tears—I tell her the rest. I tell her about the photographs. And Reed's threat to release them if Jackson doesn't stop trying to block the movie.

I tell her how Jackson exploded once I told him about my dad's role in the horror with Reed, and about how Jackson showed the photos to my dad and what fresh hell he'd set in motion.

"I told him I didn't want to do that. I specifically told him I couldn't deal with it. And then he went and did it anyway."

Tears leak from my eyes and I brusquely wipe them away.

"I ran out," I say. "And then I came here." I shrug, because that's the end of the story.

Cass is just looking at me, and she's completely silent. Still and silent.

And since Cass is very rarely silent or still, I know that this isn't just one of those relationship speed bumps. No, this is a giant wall. And if we're going to get past it, Jackson and I will have to figure out a way to go over it, go under it, or knock that fucker down.

"So what should I do?" I ask when the silence has become unbearable.

She takes my hands. "I don't know. He screwed up with your dad, I'll give you that. But maybe he screwed up for the right reasons."

"I trusted him with my secrets," I say. "And to do that . . ." I trail off with a shudder.

"I know, sweetie. And I get that he violated the trust. But he didn't violate the secret."

I look up sharply to meet her eyes.

She lifts a shoulder. "You may have never talked to your dad about it, but he knew. And just because he'd never seen those photos before doesn't mean that he shouldn't have been able to imagine every horrible thing that pervert did to you."

Maybe. I don't know. I push myself off the couch and cross the short distance to the window that looks out over her postage stamp–size backyard. "I almost told my dad myself," I admit. "I kept hearing Jackson's voice in my head, and I almost told him."

"So maybe that means it was the right thing to do."

"For *me* to do. It wasn't Jackson's place. He—he took a choice away from me." I close my eyes, suddenly getting it. He grabbed control. Just like Reed had done—Jackson took control from me. Not control I'd surrendered, but control that he'd stolen.

He'd thought that he was doing the best thing for me, and I understand that. I really do, because didn't I come close to thinking that same thing, too?

But stealing trust—how the hell do we get past that?

"Hey?" Cass moves up behind me and puts a hand on my shoulder. "You okay?"

I shrug, because I really don't know how to answer that. I feel betrayed. Violated. And profoundly sad. "Are you going to work today?" I ask softly.

"Why?"

"I don't know," I lie. I turn around so that I'm facing her. "Maybe I was thinking we should play hooky and walk along the beach."

"You are such a liar."

I make an effort to look indignant.

She narrows her eyes. "Not that I don't love to practice my art, but you don't need a new tat."

"Excuse me?"

"You heard me," she said. "Every tat I've given you is because you either didn't think you could handle something or because you fought and won. You *can* handle this thing with Jackson, so you don't need the ink for that. And so far you haven't fought, much less won. You haven't even decided what you're going to do."

"Dammit, Cass." She's right, of course, but I don't want to admit it. Because the truth is that this time I want the ink just for strength. And my best friend is basically telling me to suck it up, buttercup, and find the strength inside myself. No crutches. Just me, my emotions, and Jackson.

She crosses her arms over her chest and stares me down. "This battle hasn't even started. You come to me when it's over, and if you need the ink then, it's yours. Until then, you can have me. But not my needles."

I exhale. Loudly. "Fine. Okay. Whatever." I grimace. "I guess you'll have to do."

She laughs. "Guess so." The laughter dies soon enough, though, and she looks at me with serious eyes. "So have you decided what you're going to do? Are you going to talk to him today?"

"I don't know." The admission makes me feel slightly ill. This is Jackson, dammit. The man I love. The man I trusted.

The one person in the whole world with whom I feel the most myself, even more so than Cass who is so, so dear to me.

"I don't know," I repeat, and that one simple truism scares me to death.

"I get that," Cass says, but as she speaks, she looks toward the door through which Siobhan left only a few minutes before. "But doesn't everyone deserve a second chance?"

Do they?

I think about Jackson and the way Cass's words eerily echo his from a few nights ago. Then I hug myself, because I don't know the answer.

And I can't help but wonder how we got to this point. And how the hell we can ever come back.

He'd blown it.

And, dammit, he knew that he'd blown it and wanted to tell her as much.

Not that she was giving him the chance.

She wasn't answering his calls, texts, or emails.

She hadn't come in to work on Thursday at all.

Now it was Friday and he knew she was in the building, but he couldn't find her at any of her usual locations on twenty-seven, thirty-five, or Damien's penthouse.

"She's not working from her desk today," Karen had said on twenty-seven.

"She's in the building," Rachel had said on thirty-five. "But I think she may be camped out in the library."

She wasn't, of course.

"I recommend groveling," Damien had said when he passed Rachel's desk on his way to a lunch meeting. "Of course you have to find her to do that."

Jackson stiffened, remembering all too well that it had been Damien who'd told Sylvia about his paternity action. But that had been public record, and Damien had only been trying to help.

What Jackson had done—insinuating himself between Sylvia and her dad—well, he'd been trying to help, too. He'd just fucked the helping up royally.

Now it was Jackson who was the asshole. And Damien looked genuinely sympathetic.

"Any ideas?" Jackson asked.

"You could try the gym." He grabbed the folio that Rachel handed him. "And if all else fails, you can catch her at Jamie's tonight."

Jackson winced. He'd completely forgotten about the Halloween party. "You think she's still coming?"

"Sylvia's not one to disappoint a friend." Damien pressed a supportive hand to Jackson's shoulder as he passed. "She'll be there. Whether or not she'll talk to you—well, that's a different story."

And it would be a very public one. If that was his last resort, so be it. But first he was going to search every nook and cranny of this office. And when he found her, he'd let her know that hiding from him was counterproductive to getting anything done on the resort. Because right now, he couldn't concentrate on design if his life depended on it.

He needed Sylvia.

And he was determined.

He headed to the gym next, following up Damien's suggestion, and although the girl at the check-in desk told him that Sylvia was running on the treadmill, by the time he got back there, she was gone.

He couldn't prove it, but he had a feeling she'd seen him coming. *Fuck.*

He debated whether continuing to play chase all over the building was worth it, and decided it wasn't.

No, time for a new strategy.

Time to call in the big guns. And as far as Jackson was concerned, that meant Cass.

He headed back to twenty-six, told Lauren he was gone for the day, and beat a path to Venice Beach.

He hadn't yet been to Totally Tattoo, but he found it easily enough. He parked on the street, then went inside, and was greeted by a woman with short, spiky hair, at least a dozen piercings, and a wide, bright smile. "Hey, I'm Joy. Is this your first time to Totally Tattoo?"

"It is."

"Are you looking for a tat? Piercing? You'd look hot with an eyebrow piercing, you know. It would totally rock that scar."

"I actually want to see Cass. Is she around?"

"Oh, sure." She sucked in a breath, then bellowed, "Cass! You've got a walk-in!"

Jackson kept his lips pressed tightly together, trying to hold back a grin. As soon as Cass appeared, however, he lost it. "Like your front desk girl," he said as he followed her back to her table. "I think she'll give me a break on a piercing."

"Are you trying to be funny?"

"Trying," he admitted. "Apparently I'm not succeeding."

"Dude, you screwed up so bad you're going to need Black & Decker to fix the damage."

"Shit." He dragged his fingers through his hair. "Do you think I don't know that? Do you think I haven't been kicking myself every single minute since I laid into her dad?"

"Honestly, Jackson, I don't know what the fuck you were thinking."

He drew in a breath, and in that moment he felt as broken as he'd ever felt. "I can't not be with her, Cass."

She cocked her head and studied his face. "Then you need to get your act together. Because you're going to lose her if you don't give it a rest."

"Have I lost her?" Just asking the question burned a hole in his gut. "Can I fix this?"

"I don't know." She sighed. "Look, she loves you. I know that. But you know that song? Love is all you need?" He nodded. "Well, it's bullshit. Love isn't all you need. You need love and respect and communication and—"

Jackson couldn't help it. He pulled her close and kissed her cheek. "Christ, Cassidy. She is so damn lucky to have you."

"Hell, yeah, she is." She plunked herself down on her stool and studied him. "So what are you going to do?"

"Whatever I have to. I fucked up, and I'm going to make it right. I can't lose her, Cass. I love her."

Cass's smile spread wide. "Good answer. But I'm not the one you need to be saying that to."

"No," he said, "you're not." He checked his watch. "Jamie's party's in a few hours. She's still going, right?"

"Yup. Siobhan and I are picking her up at eight."

"Good. That leaves us just enough time."

"For what?" she asked.

He met her eyes. "There's something I need you to do for me."

twenty-six

I'm not wearing the biker jacket—I tried, but all it did was make me long for Jackson. All it did was confuse me, because I want him beside me—I'm craving his touch. I miss talking with him. I miss being with him.

And despite the way he fucked up, I miss the way that he understands me.

But at the same time I want to push him away. To scream and yell and demand that he tell me how he could have done this. How he could have taken everything good between us and turned it so horribly, terribly around.

How he could have screwed me over like he did.

Him. The man who knows me so well. Or, at least, who I thought knew me so well.

"Did you come to the party as you?"

I look up to see Nikki smiling at me, looking fabulous in a Native American princess outfit. We're in the kitchen of Jamie's condo.

I'd come here to hide from the crowd that fills this small apartment and has overflowed to the pool area downstairs.

"What?" I say stupidly.

"Your costume. Or lack thereof."

"Oh. No, I'm an alien." I grin, then indicate my pink T-shirt and pleated white skirt. "I'm from a planet far, far away and I'm blending in seamlessly with the local population." After I abandoned the biker idea, I didn't have the heart to wear anything else. So I just wore my regular clothes. So far, everyone who asks likes my answer.

Nikki doesn't look fooled, though. "I saw Cass. I'm sorry."

"What did she tell you?"

"Nasty fight. Possible pending reconciliation, but the jury is still out."

I grimace. "Yeah, that's pretty much the sum of it."

"It's nice you came. Jamie would have understood if you skipped out."

I lift a shoulder. "I didn't want to blow her off. But I am feeling a little . . . I don't know . . . unfestive."

"Like I said, I think you have license to leave. But if you just need time to get a grip, you can use my old bedroom." She points to the two steps that lead up to the condo's two bedrooms. "Jamie uses it as an office now. So there's a couch. I'm pretty sure it's unlocked, but if you want I'll ask and grab you the key."

I shake my head. "Thanks, but I'll be fine."

"Men fuck up, you know. Except for Damien," she adds with a completely straight face. "He's perfectly perfect."

She manages to hold it together for a minute, and then we both laugh.

"You're telling me I should forgive him?"

She lifts a shoulder. "I don't know what he did, so I can't really say. But I do know how the two of you are together, and I hate to see you both hurting. That's all."

Behind us, Cass and Siobhan and Jamie step into the kitchen. It's galley style, and with the five of us, it's a little crowded.

"Are we gossiping?" Jamie asks.

"Always," Nikki says.

"Cool," Jamie says. "What about?"

"Boyfriend drama," Cass says. "See, this is why I'm a lesbian."

"I thought you were a lesbian because I'm so good in bed," Siobhan snaps back, making us all laugh.

"This is the Jackson thing, right?" Jamie asks. She points at me before I can answer. "See, your problem is that you guys have been in bliss. So it's confusing."

"Um, what is?" She's right. I'm very confused.

"Fighting. You have a fight and you think it's the end of the world."

"It wasn't exactly a fight," I say. "He did something—"

"Boneheaded," Cass says.

"And that's breaking news?" Jamie asks. "He's a guy, right? He's got a dick and all the parts?"

"Last I checked," I say wryly.

"And this is your first big fight?"

I think about that. And realize that it is. We've butted heads about secrets before—Damien, Ronnie—but this is different. This isn't a secret, this is a fuckup. And I don't do well with fuckups.

"Yeah," I admit. "I guess it is." I frown, thinking about what they've said. About being used to bliss and not knowing how to handle a fuckup.

And the truth is, as mad as Jackson made me, at the end of the day, I have two choices. I can walk away. Or we can move forward.

I ended it once before, and it just about killed me. I can't do that again. Not if I can put this relationship back together.

At the very least, I have to try.

I take a step toward the living room.

"Where are you going?"

"The marina," I say. "I need to go see about a guy."

"You don't have to," Jamie says.

"No. I really do."

"I mean he just got here. He was walking toward the pool as I was coming up the stairs."

"Oh." My stomach turns over a few times. I want to see him, yes. But I thought I'd have a long drive to get myself ready. "Right. Here goes."

With my friends wishing me luck, I head toward the open front door, then through the crush of people lingering near the threshold. I turn left, intending to take the stairs that go directly down to the pool, and end up walking right into him.

"Jackson!"

"How did you know?" he says. He's wearing jeans and a T-shirt and a black mask, much like the Lone Ranger.

I can't help but smile. "I'd know you anywhere."

He reaches out as if to touch me, then pulls his hand away, and his tentativeness twists my heart. *Yes,* I think, *it's time to get past this.*

"You didn't wear the biker jacket," I say.

"My heart wasn't in it without my old lady."

I swallow. "Yeah. Well."

He points to the mask. "But I thought if it wasn't actually me, then maybe we could talk. We need to talk, Syl."

"You screwed up, Jackson," I say, which is not what I was planning to say at all. But it popped out, and behind the black mask, I see his eyes go wide.

In for a penny and all that. I press ahead. "You screwed up, and you hurt me. A lot. You were so concerned about protecting me that you forgot to see me."

"You're right. You are." He takes my arm and tugs me to the side, out of the flow of traffic. The touch is simple and innocent, and yet it is electric. It's a connection. And god help me, I have missed it.

"I screwed up on a massive scale. And I'm goddamn terrified that I screwed up beyond all repair. I should never have gotten between you and your dad. I should never have taken that decision—that choice—out of your hands. I was so full up with my own shit about what a father should do to protect his child that I lost sight of the fact that the decision was yours. The choice was yours. I stole it, and I'm sorry."

"Oh."

I feel weirdly anticlimactic. He's saying everything that I wanted to force him to admit.

"I love you, Syl. I love you, and I fucked up, and I will do whatever it takes for you to forgive me."

I draw in a breath, then take a step back. "Come with me."

I turn and head for Jamie's condo, and I don't look back to make sure he's following. I pass through the crowd in the door, then glance toward the kitchen as I head for the two steps that lead up to the bedrooms. Nikki and Cass and the gang are gone, and that's okay. I don't need moral support anymore.

Right now, I know exactly what I need.

I try the door on the right, and breathe a sigh of relief to find it unlocked. I open it, and step inside.

Jackson enters right behind me, and I close the door, then lock it.

"You hurt me," I say.

"I know."

I press my lips together to fight back tears.

His back is against the door and he's looking at me warily. "Are we okay? Syl, I need to know if we're going to be okay."

I hesitate. And then, very slowly, I nod. "Yes."

For a moment, his face is simply blank. Then I see the relief flood it, so profound and powerful that it seems to propel him across the room. And then he is there, his arms around me and his mouth on mine.

The kiss is wild, hard. With teeth and tongues, as if we are trying to devour each other.

I pull away, gasping, then grab the hem of his T-shirt and pull it out of his jeans, then struggle with the button of his jeans.

"Here? Are you sure?"

"God, yes," I say. "Please, Jackson. I need you inside me." I need to feel his hands. His touch. I need that physical connection that is so rare and special between us.

I need to know that I am his and that he is mine, and that despite losing our bliss for a little bit, everything is back to normal.

"Now," I say as I tug his shirt over his head, pulling the mask off with it. I pause for only a moment, looking at the man I've revealed. The man that I love. Then I turn my attention back to his jeans, unzipping them, tugging them down, and then gasping at the mark on his pelvic bone, nestled into the triangle formed by his thigh and pubic hair.

SB—right there, and freshly tattooed.

I look up at him, my breath catching in my throat.

"Cass did it earlier today. I needed to be close to you."

I make a small noise that does nothing to reflect how much that simple act has moved me. I try again. "Jackson," I say, and that is all that I manage before the heat that has been flaring in his eyes seems to explode out.

"Baby, I can't wait."

I start to tell him not to, but before I can say a word, he's spun me around and pushed my skirt up. We're by a bookshelf, and I grab hold for balance as he tugs his briefs down, then pushes my panties aside. He strokes me, then slides his fingers inside me as I moan with pleasure. "Now," I demand. "Please, Jackson, now."

I need it hard and fast. I need to feel him.

And, thankfully, he doesn't disappoint. He takes me from behind, his fingers finding my clit as his other hand clasps my breast and he pounds relentlessly in me, as if he knows that for both of us this fuck is a way to work it out. To pound the past out of our systems. To move forward together, and find each other once again.

I close my eyes, letting the sensations take me. Letting his touch tease me higher and higher, as pleasure builds and his body claims mine, making me his. Making me whole.

And then, right when I'm at the edge, his voice washes over me, low and hard and commanding. "Come for me," he says. "Dammit, Sylvia, you come for me now."

I do—exploding into a thousand sparks that scatter and hum and sizzle before coming back to earth and restoring me to life.

"Wow," I say as he uses a tissue to clean us both up and then adjusts my clothes. "Wow."

His expression looks pretty wow, too, and I snuggle close as he carries me to the couch. I curl up next to him, exhausted, and yet energized all at the same time.

"I love you," he says, and I sigh with contentment.

"That's convenient," I say. "Because I love you, too."

I lean against him, simply breathing, until I get my head back. I know we should get out of here, but I really don't want to move. This room is safety and fantasy and reconciliation.

Out there is the real world, where bad things can happen. And though we've gotten past our hurdle, the bigger problem still looms. "What are we going to do?" I ask. "The photos. Either I'm screwed or you are."

"I'm going to let them make the movie." His voice is flat. The words completely unexpected.

"What?" I shift on the couch, sitting up so that I'm facing him directly. "You can't. Ronnie's completely innocent, and no matter how we look at it, I bear some of the responsibility for those horrible photos. We can get the police involved. Extortion."

"You'll be dragged through the muck," he says.

"I don't care."

"I do."

"Fine. I care, too. But it's the best thing. That little girl. *Your* little girl."

For a moment, he just sits there. Then he scrubs his face with his hands and stands. "I want to do right by her," he says. "I don't want to be the father I had, and I don't want her lost in scandal. But the truth is I don't think I can stop that movie no matter what I do. I wish I could, and god knows I've tried, but I can't even file a defamation action. The things they want to say are true."

"It will be horrible."

He nods, looking miserable. "But if you have people around you who love you, it's bearable."

"Is it?"

"Look at Nikki and Damien."

I frown, but have to concede the point. They've survived all sorts of shit. I rise, then go to him. "So what do you want to do now?" I lean in close, my body thrumming with the beat of his heart.

"I'm going to see Ronnie. I want my attorney to set a court date. I want my daughter, Sylvia. And I want to bring her home."

He bends his head and kisses the top of my head. "I'm hiring Evelyn and however many PR people she thinks I need. If the movie gets made, we'll deal with it. But as soon as there's even the slightest hint that it's been green-lit, I want to get in front of it. Minimal focus on Ronnie. And whatever we have to do to keep the sensationalism down. This is her life, not a circus. And I'll pay whatever it takes to keep it from spinning out of control."

I nod my head, my eyes closed. I know that he wants all those things, and I understand now how deeply he feels about Ronnie—about being a dad—and I'm just a little bit in awe about how much he's put her first. About how he's preparing for the worst, essentially building a little citadel of paternal protection around the child.

"When are you going?"

"Tomorrow," he says. "I talked to Damien. He's letting me have the use of one of the jets."

"Oh." I feel guilty for feeling sad, but we've only just gotten back together, and already he's leaving. "Well, I think that's great," I say brightly. "How long will you be gone?"

"Just a few days. I'll have to go back once the hearing is set, but in the meantime, Ronnie can come here with me. I should probably see about renting a house. I don't suppose the boat is particularly childproofed."

"I can look for you," I say. "I don't mind."

He frowns at me, and my stomach twists. I want to be involved, and if he's uncomfortable with me helping him look for a rental, how comfortable will he be with me in Ronnie's life?

"Won't that be hard?" he says.

I cock my head. "Um, why?"

"Long distance, I mean. From Santa Fe." His brow furrows. "You're going with me, aren't you? For the weekend at least. And Monday if you can work from the road."

The relief that sweeps over me is warm and sweet.

"Sylvia?" He brushes my cheek. "Why are you crying?"

"Sorry." I wipe away a tear. "I'm just—I guess I hadn't thought that you'd want me there."

He pulls me close and holds me tight. "Sweetheart, I will always want you. More than that, I need you."

twenty-seven

Jackson stood in the jet's open doorway before descending the stairs. Above them, the sky burned as blue and bright as a sapphire, contrasting the browns and greens and reds of the mountains that rose in peaks and crags around them.

On the ground, the black tarmac spread out around the plane, like a smooth blanket covering this valley. He glanced around, but didn't see a car, and both fear and disappointment cut into him.

"Are they here?" Behind him, Sylvia put her hand gently on his shoulder.

He shook his head. "No. Nobody."

"Maybe the timing didn't work out." Sylvia moved into the doorway with him, her hand finding his and their fingers twining together. "Herding kids can be tricky, and Betty's older. She could have easily gotten waylaid."

He'd called Betty, Ronnie's great-grandmother, before they left LA and suggested that she come meet the plane at the Santa Fe airport. Jackson had always flown into Santa Fe on commercial planes before, and he thought Ronnie might get a kick out of touring the private jet and maybe even sitting in the copilot's seat.

He hoped Sylvia was right and they were just running late. He'd thought that Betty supported his effort to become a true dad to Ronnie. And he damn sure hoped he wasn't wrong about that.

It was bad enough that Megan was putting up barriers. He loved her like a sister, and he hated the fact that she was opposed to his decision, especially when she was in no condition to care for Ronnie anymore.

Bottom line, he wanted his daughter. And he hoped to hell that getting her wasn't going to land them both in the middle of a family feud.

Surely it wouldn't come to that? Would it?

He'd done so much to get Ronnie back. Taken so many personal risks. But he was all-in now, and he would do what it took. Whatever it took.

He only hoped the price wouldn't be too high.

"It's going to be fine," Sylvia said, as if reading his mind. "You're doing the right thing, and it's all going to work out."

He turned and saw her looking up at him, her expression so ferocious in its sincerity that it twisted him up inside. Without even planning to, he pulled her close, one arm around her waist and the other cupping the back of her head. He heard her surprised gasp, then took that opportunity to kiss her.

She melted against him, as if right then, he was the only thing that existed in her world. And that moment—that reaction—gave him strength.

He held her longer, not wanting the kiss to end, not wanting to feel that sense of loss when he let her go. So he let his lips linger on hers until he finally had the strength to pull away.

"Thank you," he said.

Her smile was bright and pleased. "You're very welcome, but what exactly are you thanking me for?"

"For believing in me. For coming with me. For watching my

back." He paused for no more than the length of a heartbeat. "For loving me."

"Mmm." She slid her arms around him again. "In that case, you really are welcome."

They stood like that for a moment longer in the open doorway of the Stark International jet. When they broke apart, her eyes were dancing. "The crew probably wants to disembark. Maybe it's time to brave the stairs?"

"It probably is." He took one step, then another, with Sylvia right behind him. When he was on the third step, two cars pulled up and parked on the tarmac a few yards from the plane. The first, a dark blue Mercedes that he knew belonged to Betty. The second, a four-door Oldsmobile sedan that he didn't recall seeing before.

"Is that them?" Sylvia asked.

But he didn't need to answer because by the time Sylvia finished the question, the driver of the Mercedes had stepped out and gone to open the back door. He leaned in, and a moment later a small burst of sunshine leaped from the car and raced toward the jet stairs, all the way calling, "Uncle Jackson! Uncle Jackson!"

He hurried the rest of the way down, then scooped her up, enveloping her in a big hug before turning her upside down, to the child's total delight.

"Sylvie!" Ronnie squealed when Syl joined him on the tarmac. Syl bent over to face the little girl, still locked upside down in Jackson's embrace.

"Hey, Ronnie," she said. "What are you doing down there?"

"Swinging! Up, Uncle Jackson! Up, up!"

He obliged her, swinging her out, then catching her and balancing her on his hip. He gave her a big kiss on the cheek and received a sloppy wet kiss of his own in return. And when she held out her arms and demanded kisses from Sylvia, too, a wash of emotion so clean and crisp that it had to be joy swept over him.

In front of them, Betty was now standing by the Mercedes, having emerged from the car while Jackson was scooping up his little girl. She was a tall woman in her early seventies with silver hair and the manner and bearing of royalty.

Now, she met Jackson's eyes and nodded. Just the slightest tilt of her head, but it told Jackson everything he needed to know. As far as the paternity action went, Betty was on his side.

With one last dramatic swoop, he swung Ronnie down to her feet.

"Let's go see Grammy," he said as he took her little hand in his left. At the same time, he reached out for Sylvia with his right. She squeezed his hand, her smile bright, her eyes glistening with tears. Not of pain, but of joy.

He wanted to hold her close and tell her everything she already knew. That he loved her. That she was the only woman for him. That she made him desperately, passionately happy. That he wouldn't be able to get through everything that was to come if she wasn't at his side.

"Ready?" he asked instead, and when she nodded, he stepped forward toward the future.

They were almost to the Mercedes when the passenger's and driver's doors of the Oldsmobile opened and two men in suits stepped out. They headed toward him, walking in long, confident strides. And when they reached him, one held out a Santa Fe police badge.

"Jackson Steele?"

Fear, as ice-cold as a knife, cut through Jackson. He pushed it back. Kept his expression flat.

"How can I help you, officer?"

"Detective," the taller man corrected. "I'm Detective Parker. This is my partner, Detective Jamison. We're going to have to ask you to come with us."

Sylvia's hand tightened in his. "Why? What's going on?"

"We're working in cooperation with the Beverly Hills police department." Parker kept his eyes on Jackson. "And you're wanted for questioning in the murder of Robert Cabot Reed."

.....

The murder of Robert Cabot Reed.

Though the words ring through my head, I have to work to understand what they mean. I'm too numb. Too shell-shocked.

Reed is dead.

The man who abused me, raped me. The man who starred in my nightmares, who made me afraid.

The man who would have made a movie that exposed a little girl's life to the worst kind of scandal.

The man I hated.

He is dead. He is gone.

And though I want to dance for joy, I can't.

Because Jackson is about to be ripped from me, and I don't know how I will survive without this man beside me.

This man who maybe, just maybe, killed the man who tormented me. Who tormented us both.

I think about his temper. About how far he would go to protect me. To protect his daughter.

I think about what I know he fears, and what I know he is capable of.

I could lose him, I think, this man that I love.

Only two things are certain now:

That everything is going to change.

And that I am very, very afraid.

Jackson Steele and Sylvia Brooks are back
in the powerful finale of J. Kenner's
provocative, sizzling-hot new trilogy

under my skin

Coming soon from Bantam Books.

Read on for a sneak peek.

one

There is peace in these moments between sleep and wakefulness. In the soft minutes that seem to stretch into hours, warm and comforting like a gift bestowed by a benevolent universe.

This is a world of dreams, and right now it is safe. It is right. And I want to stay here, wrapped tight in the comfort of his arms.

But dreams often turn into nightmares, and as I move through the corridors of sleep, dark fingers of fear reach out to me. My pulse pounds and my breath comes too shallow. I curl toward him, craving his touch, but he is not there, and I sit bolt upright, my skin clammy from a sheen of sweat. My heart pounding so hard I will surely crack a rib.

Jackson.

I am awake now, alone and disoriented as a wild panic cuts through me—I am afraid, but I don't remember why.

Too quickly though, it all rushes back, and as the memories return with wakefulness, I long to slide back into oblivion. Because whatever horror my mind would fabricate in dreams can't be any worse than the reality that now surrounds me, cold and stark.

A reality in which the world is crumbling down around my ears.

A reality in which the man I love desperately is suspected of murder.

With a sigh, I press a hand to my cheek. I have a vague memory of a soft kiss and a murmured "I love you."

I close my eyes, the memory sharpening as I shake off the haze of slumber. He'd brushed a kiss over my cheek before slipping out of our warm cocoon and into the chilly morning air. At the time I'd been content to stay behind, snuggled tight in the blankets that still held his scent and radiated the lingering heat from his body.

Now I wish I had roused myself when he did, because I don't want to be alone. Alone is when panic creeps closer.

Alone is when I'm certain that I will lose him.

Alone is what I fear.

And yet even as the thought enters my mind, the solitude is shattered. The bedroom door bursts open, and a dark-haired, blue-eyed bundle of sunshine races toward me, then leaps onto the bed and starts bouncing, her energy so vibrant I laugh despite myself. "Sylvie! Sylvie! I made toast with Uncle Jackson!"

"Toast? Really?" I manage to keep my voice perky and upbeat despite the fact that fear still clings to me like cobwebs. I give Ronnie a quick, tight hug, but my attention isn't on her anymore. Instead, I am focused entirely on the man in the doorway.

He stands casually on the threshold, a wooden tray in his hands. His coal-black hair is untidy from sleep, and he sports two days of beard stubble. He wears flannel pajama bottoms and a pale gray T-shirt. By every indication, he is a man who has just awakened. A man with nothing on his mind but the morning and breakfast and the bits of news that fill the headlines of the paper tucked under his arm.

But, dear god, he is so much more. He is power and tenderness, strength and control. He is the man who has colored my days and illuminated my nights.

Jackson Steele. The man I love. The man I once foolishly tried to leave. The man who grabbed hold and pulled me back, then slayed my demons, and in doing so claimed my heart.

But it is those very demons that have brought us to this moment.

Because Robert Cabot Reed was one of those demons. And now Reed is dead.

Just thinking about him makes me tremble, and I hide the reaction by shifting my position on the bed as I watch Jackson stride into the room and then set the tray on the small table tucked in beneath the still-curtained window.

He comes over to sit on the edge of the bed and is immediately assaulted by a three-year-old cyclone demanding to be tickled. He smiles and complies, then looks at me. But the smile doesn't quite warm his ice blue eyes. Instead, I see sadness. More than that, I see my own fears and worries reflected right back at me.

We arrived in Santa Fe late yesterday afternoon, both of us feeling light and happy and eager. Jackson had intended to spend the weekend with Ronnie and then go to court on Monday in order to set a hearing on his petition to formally claim paternity and establish that he is Ronnie's legal father. That plan, however, was sideswiped when local detectives met our plane, then informed Jackson that he was wanted back in Beverly Hills for questioning in Reed's murder.

The afternoon shifted from a happy, laid-back reunion to a frantic flurry of activity, with calls between New Mexico and California, lawyers squabbling, deals churning.

At the end of it all, Jackson was permitted to stay the weekend, on condition that he go straight to the Beverly Hills Police Department Monday morning. In truth, Jackson could have garnered much more time—unless the police wanted to actually arrest him, their leverage was limited—but his attorney wisely advised against it. After all, playing games isn't the way to win either police cooperation or public opinion. And while we don't yet know what physical evidence the police have collected, we do know that the cops can point to plenty of motive for Jackson to have killed Reed.

Motive.

The word sounds so clean compared to Reed, who was a dirty, horrible man.

Not only had he abused and tormented me when I was a teen, but he'd recently threatened to release some of the vile photographs that he'd taken of me back then if I didn't convince Jackson to stop trying to block a movie that Reed was trying to greenlight. A movie that would expose secrets and deceptions—and that would thrust Ronnie, an innocent child, into the middle of a very public, very messy scandal.

Did Jackson want the movie stopped? Hell, yes.

Did he want to protect me from the horror of seeing those pictures flashed across the internet? Damn right.

Did he want to punish Reed for the things he'd done to me so many years ago? Absolutely.

Did Jackson kill Reed?

As for that one—I truly don't know. For that matter, I don't care. My only fear is that Jackson will be taken away from me. That if he did kill Reed, the system will make him pay, even for the death of a monster. And that if he didn't kill Reed, it won't matter. He will be an innocent man falsely convicted, punished for the potency of his hate rather than the reality of his actions.

I can't bear the thought of losing him, and yet that fear now colors my world. It is Jackson's fear, too, I know. Only, his is even more potent. Because he would lose not only me, but Ronnie. Not to mention the life and career that he has worked so hard to build.

I reach for him and take his hand in mine. How many times in the hours since we arrived have I searched for the perfect words to soothe him? But there are no perfect words. I can only do my best. I can only just be here.

I squeeze his hand and he smiles, just a little, then wraps his free arm around Ronnie and pulls her close, the action so full of wild, heart-breaking emotion that it almost shatters me.

"You should go outside," Jackson tells the little girl. "Fred's probably wondering where you are."

At the mention of the new puppy, her blue eyes, so like Jackson's, go wide. "You'll come, too?"

"Absolutely," he promises. "Let me talk to Syl while she drinks her coffee, and then I'll come find you."

"And eat your toast?" she asks, her earnest question aimed at me.

"I can't wait for the toast," I say. "I bet it's the best toast ever."

"Yup," she confirms, then shoots like a rocket out of the room.

Jackson watches her go, and I watch Jackson. When he turns back, he catches me eyeing him, then smiles sheepishly. "It's hard to believe sometimes," he says. "That she's really mine, I mean."

I think about the little girl's dark hair and blue eyes. Her cleverness coupled with a vibrant personality and fierce determination. "Not hard to believe at all."

I had hoped to coax a smile, but still he just looks sad.

"Are you okay?" It's a stupid question, of course, and it hangs there, as awkward and inadequate as I feel.

He shakes his head, just a little. "No," he admits. He brushes his fingers lightly over my cheek, his attention on my face, his eyes searching mine. At first, he looks lost, but that soon changes as heat and need build in his eyes. Both are directed at me, and neither are a question. There is no permission to be granted, no request to be made. He simply slides his hand around to cup the back of my neck and pulls me toward him, then captures my mouth with his.

I open to him without hesitation, not just my lips, but my whole body. I am his, wholly and completely, and however he needs me.

He deepens the kiss, his tongue teasing and tasting. His mouth hot and desperate against mine.

I expect more. The crush of his hands upon my breasts. An explosion of breath as he pushes me back on the mattress, then rises to slam the door shut and flip the latch. The shift of the mattress as he returns, and the sound of ripping cotton as he strips me of my panties.

I anticipate the feel of his body over mine. Of my wrists bound tight by his T-shirt that I wear in lieu of pajamas as he yanks it over my head and then uses it to bind me.

I imagine the tightness in my inner thighs as he roughly spreads my legs, and the quick burn of friction as he enters me hard in one thrust and then loses himself to this wild passion that he needs. That he craves.

I expect all this because I know him. Because his world has spun out of control, and Jackson is a man who not only needs control, but who takes it. He is not a man to be swept up in the tide, battered by the rise and fall of circumstance. He fights back. He wins. He *takes.*

I channelled control into sex.

He'd told me that once. And he's shown me as much many, many times.

And yet he doesn't come. He doesn't take. He doesn't claim.

Instead, he stands and crosses from the bed to the window, then drags his fingers through his hair. His back is to me, and the table is in front of him. My coffee and toast are still there, untouched. He pushes the tray aside and opens the curtains, letting in the morning light.

We are in Betty Wiseman's house, Ronnie's maternal great-grandmother. The family is well-to-do, but this New Mexico home is a small getaway, a "mere" five thousand square feet. Jackson and I are in one of the guest rooms that overlook the back of the property. The view I'd seen yesterday evening is magnificent—the rocky, rising terrain of the mountains, dressed up in their fall colors. The verdant grasses and evergreens. The browns and reds of stones and foliage. And, of course, the vivid blue sky, so wide and resplendent that it seems to slide into and fill your soul.

But from where I still sit, stiff and awkward on the bed, I see only a small section of our covered patio and a view of the side of the house. I'm not at the proper angle to see the beautiful panorama that Jackson is looking at right now. Instead, our perspectives are entirely different, and that small reality eats at me, making me feel distant from him. Disconnected.

I lick my lips, feeling impotent and lost. And, yes, a little bit angry, too. Because, dammit, I don't want to see him in pain, not if I can soothe him.

But that's the heart of it, isn't it? That's really my greatest fear.

Not that I'm unable to soothe Jackson, but that he would rather bear this burden alone.

No.

I toss the covers aside and walk to him, then slide my arms around his waist from behind so that I am pressed against him, my cheek against his back. I breathe in the scent of him, male and musk and just the tiniest bit of fabric softener. It's clean, maybe even a little bit domestic. But on Jackson, it's also very, very sexy.

My hands are at his waist, and it would be so easy to ease them down. To stroke him and make him hard. To tease and coax. To seduce and please.

To make him so hot and so hard that he wants nothing but me, can think of nothing but me. To tease and seduce until he picks me up and throws me onto the bed in a violent explosion that not only consumes us both but destroys the shadows that have crept in between us, banishing them with fire and heat and light.

But even that's not what I want. Not really. What I want—what I need—is for Jackson to come to me. To use me as he has in the past to soothe his wounds and make himself whole.

So instead of sliding my hand down to close around his cock, I simply hold still, clinging to this man whom I love and need. And hoping against hope that he is not slipping away from me.

A moment passes, and then another. I hear the dog barking on the back lawn and the high-pitched squeal of Ronnie's laughter followed by the lower tones of her great-grandmother and Stella, the housekeeper-turned-nanny.

Jackson is perfectly still, but then his hands rise to his waist to close over mine, so that as I hug him from behind, he is holding me in place. I close my eyes, relishing the strength of his touch. And when he turns me in his arms and his hands slide down to cup my rear—modestly covered by a pair of bikini-style panties along with the cotton of his shirt—I almost weep with relief.

He kisses the top of my head, and I tilt my face up to him. His mouth closes over mine, and he groans softly as his pelvis presses hard against me, his hands tight on my ass. "Christ," he finally says. "Christ, Syl, I'm a fucking mess."

"You'll get through this," I say. "We'll get through it."

"All I wanted was to take my daughter home."

His words seem to twist inside me, as if they are just slightly off-kilter. It takes me a moment to realize why. "'Wanted'?" I repeat.

He releases me, then steps back so that he's leaning against the edge of the table. His face is hard, and when he speaks, his voice is flat and emotionless, as if he is working very hard to keep it that way. "I called Amy this morning."

"Oh." I take a few steps back and sit on the bed. Amy Brantley is his family law attorney in Santa Fe. She's the one who filed his petition to establish paternity and parental rights. And although I have yet to meet her in person, I know that she's the one who will be setting the hearing on that petition as soon as possible. "So what did she say? When are you setting a court date?"

I see a shadow in his eyes. "We're not. We're going to wait."

"Wait? But—" I draw in a breath, trying to gather my thoughts even as I realize that I should have expected this. Because I know what this means. This means he doesn't think he'll be around to take care of her.

"Oh, god, Jackson." I don't mean for it to, but my voice is full of dread and fear.

"No," he says, then repeats it more firmly. "*No.* I'm not giving in. I'm not folding. Not even close. But I'm also not taking risks with my little girl. What if the worst were to happen and I end up in a jail cell? Megan may be her legal guardian right now, but she won't be once my rights are established. Would a California court send Ronnie back to New Mexico? To a former custodian with bi-polar issues and an elderly great-grandmother? Maybe. But more likely she'll end up in foster care. I can't risk that. I won't risk that."

I want to protest. To point out how much this means to him. To beg him to believe that he'll get through this. But I fear that saying those words will only highlight the extent of his loss. So all I say is "I'm sorry."

"Me, too."

He pulls me to my feet, and I slide into his embrace. He holds me tight, as if he needs something solid to hold onto, and I am happy for it to be me that he clings to. I return the embrace fiercely, holding him close, pressing my face against his chest. Breathing him in. I want to lose myself in him. I want to wish away all the bad things.

I want to not worry about where we go next.

"You haven't asked," he says, after an eternity has passed in his arms. "It's been over twelve hours since the detectives said I'm a person of interest, and yet you haven't asked if I killed him."

I close my eyes and take one quick breath. "I haven't asked be-cause it doesn't matter. I love you," I say. "I'll always love you."

"Sylvia." His voice is firm. Maybe a little sad.

I shake my head, but now I lean back so that I can look at his face. He's looking back at me, and I cannot read his expression. Is he about to confess to me? Deny his involvement? I don't know, and it frustrates me that I also cannot guess.

I know only one thing for certain, and that is that I meant what

I said. *It doesn't matter.* I reach up and press my finger to his lips, then shake my head to silence him. "No matter what, we're getting through this. Now tell me what the plan is. You have to be in Beverly Hills in the morning. What time are we leaving here?"

"This afternoon," he says. "I want some face time with Charles before I walk into the lion's den tomorrow," he adds, referring to Charles Maynard, his attorney back home.

"Then this room isn't where you need to be." I ease out of his embrace and nod toward the window. "Go spend some time with your daughter, Jackson Steele." I reach up and stroke his cheek, his beard stubble scratchy against my hand. "Just a bit today, but that's okay. You'll be spending a lot more time with her later."

For a moment, I think he's going to argue. Then he nods. "Are you coming?"

"I'm going to shower first, and get dressed. And," I add, picking up the now-cold toast, "I can't go out there until I've eaten the best toast ever."

He actually laughs a bit, and I'm proud of myself for my rather lame joke.

He tugs me to him, then kisses me softly.

"I'm not okay," he says, once again answering my question from earlier. "But thanks to you I'm a little bit better."

I watch him go, then shut the door behind him before returning to the window and waiting for him to appear on the lawn. It takes a few minutes, but he finally shows, and as I watch, he calls to Ronnie. Both she and the puppy lope toward him, and he scoops her up and swings her around, his expression glowing.

My heart twists. Because I know that his happiness is fleeting. And I fear it will get worse before it gets better.

More than that, I fear that it won't get better at all.

PHOTO: KATHY WHITTAKER PHOTOGRAPHY

J. KENNER loves wine, dark chocolate, and books. She lives in Texas with her husband and daughters. Visit her online to learn more about her and her other pen names, to get a peek at what she's working on, and to connect through social media.

juliekenner.com

Facebook.com/JKennerBooks

@juliekenner